PENGUIN BOOKS

ORANGE WEDNESDAY

Leslie Thomas is one of Britain's most popular writers: a bestselling novelist, a travel writer and a television and radio personality.

He was born in 1931 of a South Wales seafaring family. At the age of twelve he found himself in an orphanage following his father's drowning in the South Atlantic during a U-boat attack on a wartime convoy and his mother's subsequent death within six months. His experiences were recorded years later in his first book, *This Time Next Week*, quickly followed by his first bestselling novel *The Virgin Soldiers*, which became a highly successful film.

Leslie Thomas has written nineteen novels, including his bestsellers *The Magic Army*, *The Dearest and the Best*, *The Adventures of Goodnight and Loving* and *Orders for New York*, all published by Penguin. His travel books about the lesser-known parts of the British Isles, *The Hidden Places of Britain* and *Some Lovely Islands*, in which he explores islands off the British coast, have also been published by Penguin. *A World of Islands* is another of Leslie Thomas's lyrical travel books. He also wrote and presented a television series *Great British Isles*. There have been television adaptations of his novels *Tropic of Ruislip* and *Dangerous Davies*, *The Last Detective*. His autobiography, *In My Wildest Dreams*, was published in 1984 by Penguin.

Leslie Thomas lives in London and Salisbury, Wiltshire, with his wife Diana and son Matthew. He has three children from a previous marriage. His hobbies include cricket, photography, philately, music and antiques.

LESLIE THOMAS

ORANGE WEDNESDAY

PENGUIN BOOKS

PENGUIN BOOKS

Published by the Penguin Group
Penguin Books Ltd, 27 Wrights Lane, London w8 5tz, England
Viking Penguin, a division of Penguin Books USA Inc.
375 Hudson Street, New York, New York 10014, USA
Penguin Books Australia Ltd, Ringwood, Victoria, Australia
Penguin Books Canada Ltd, 2801 John Street, Markham, Ontario, Canada l3r 1b4
Penguin Books (NZ) Ltd, 182–190 Wairau Road, Auckland 10, New Zealand

Penguin Books Ltd, Registered Offices: Harmondsworth, Middlesex, England

First published by Constable 1967
Published in Penguin Books 1991
10 9 8 7 6 5 4 3 2 1

Copyright © Leslie Thomas, 1967
All rights reserved

Printed in England by Clays Ltd, St Ives plc

He says, *my reign is peace*, so slays
A thousand in the dead of night.

Walter Savage Landor

I

When the first snow of the winter was down and settled, the forest keepers used to go and start counting the deer. With the trees standing thin, and the snow clean, it was easier for them to pick out the loitering deer and add them up.

It seemed to Brunel that these keepers always gave him a strange, squinted look when he descended from the forest carrying a gun or two. It was as though their sums were not working out well and they thought he and his guns might have some bearing on it. Sometimes, in those late days of the year, he passed them on the golf course side of the trees as he was returning to the town, and they were going up for an afternoon's adding. They would trudge along in a rough file, lumpy with furs of various sorts, looking, Brunel fancied, like trolls or teddy bears.

But that was at a distance. When he passed them Brunel would pleasantly recite 'Guten Tag', to the first keeper, then to one about the middle of the expedition, and eventually to the man at the rear. They would groan or nod, or blow the fur away from their mouths, but he never heard a single frozen syllable of German come from any of them.

He concluded that they were a miserable load of bastards.

Not one ever looked into Brunel's face. Each stared

accusingly at the rifle; or the backside of the pistol sticking out of his holster as though the suspect weapon had dived in there to take cover.

It would have been satisfying to stop them and get them gathered around him like a propounding uncle assembling nephews and then to explain in his staggering German that he had never shot so much as a hedgehog in the forest. He visited there for target practice only, shooting at bus tickets which he fixed to trees. Even then he was particular to choose the trees which were stout enough to take a few bullets without notice. There was not even incidental danger to the deer because Brunel was a dead shot with pistol or rifle. Only the bark and the bus tickets suffered.

Far from ever having shot at any *living* thing, Brunel could never recall ever pulling a trigger on any *moving* thing. His work with firearms was completely still-life. Sometimes, when considering this, a handicap for a British infantry officer, he realised that the only military circumstance where he might be of decisive use was in a firing squad, and so far this had not arisen.

Actually Brunel had left the army about a year after he had joined it. Looking about him he knew he was part of a buffoon's paradise, a pantomime played for all of every day from the bugle at morning to the last sergeant to sick up at night. The drill and the shouting, the killing and the memorials, he looked at with a wise man's pity. He thought it was all quite unnecessary. The army did not know he had left it. On the other hand it had never been more than distantly aware that Brunel was one of its soldiers. He preferred to think of himself as not so much on its strength, as the manifest reports put it, but rather on its weakness.

Brunel had, in effect, opted out. Not only from the army but from a great mass of life anyway. Lacking understanding of either, and being unwilling to learn, he had quit both.

Had the army wished, at any otherwise vacant moment, when there was no fighting anywhere, to count its full complement, like the keepers usefully totalling all those deer in the snow-sheeted forest, it might eventually have discovered Brunel under some such file or title as: 'Lieutenant Kingdom Brunel Hopkins. Royal Welsh Border Regiment. Attached Moribund Documents Section, The Medicinal Baths, Fulsbad, West Germany.'

There was certainly a catalogue of this kind somewhere because Brunel's pay arrived every month without worry, and he occasionally got Roneoed notices about N.A.T.O. exercises at North Rhine Westphalia, reminders about the importance of such institutions as the Post Office Savings Bank, the Army Christian Council, optional transfers to the Veterinary Corps, and about not going with dirty women in Stuttgart. But he imagined, rightly, that these had been piped through one of those interminable army channels which, like tendrils, search out a soldier anywhere. Even him.

No one in military circles remembered him individually now. Not the wet nosed civil servant in whose presence he had imprisoned himself for seven years in the Regular Army; not the red, bull-roaring sergeant major at the training battalion who had tried to touch him up at the night of the camp concert; not the others in the platoon; nor those shades who suffered, though not so much as he did, at the officers' training course. No one recalled him at all, only some inky clerk in an army pay office somewhere, and some Adrema plate in an addressing file in yet another maggoty wooden hut.

Because of this his uniform had deteriorated from the famous bull and badges of the Royal Welch Border Regiment to merely garments. There was, Brunel felt, even some delicate distinction, something to give him confidence in isolation, in that fact. Not every serving officer in the British army could turn out at noon every day in summer wearing a Waikiki shirt and unpressed battle-dress trousers. Few, no matter how callow, could get away with three days' growth of fair beard, and a straight, long fringe across the forehead giving him the appearance of a military monk. Not many reported for duty at a steam baths either, or slept with a tabby cat. Brunel did.

True the vapour from the various goings-on in the baths underneath sometimes sidled into his office like infant ghosts, and over the years they had infected many of the Moribund Documents with chronic damp and with occasional growths of mildew. The cat could not be relied upon as far as its homecoming habits were concerned, but it had a purr like a heating pump to compensate. The sound was enough to give warmth in winter to the barren room.

Brunel's life had, in fact, attained a simplicity, a kindliness, that Bede might have recognised. At thirty-two he had evolved the personal calm of a hoary mystic. He wallowed in a little pool of military peace above a steam baths, and, sweeter still, was guardian of the moulding paper records of a war he had only witnessed from a nursery window.

The sameness of his days at Fulsbad had squashed him into an indolent, almost happy, man. He was billeted in a small hotel, a place sitting contentedly as a child on the banks of the little River Agoos, not far from the Fulsbad Kurhaus from which the sounds of a string quintet came painful and sweet on summer afternoons. His various predecessors in office, right back to the genius who had in 1945 first established the Moribund Docs. Section, had been billeted there in the care of a gummy old German couple, Herr Snellhort and his Frau, who chewed the inside of their own mouths with four yellowed excavating teeth between them. Sometimes when Brunel was eating his breakfast and they were waiting on him, each chewing away, he wondered how huge the inward caverns had grown over the years, and horribly, if the teeth would ever succeed in breaking out.

The little river was full of careless fish and when he felt like it and the weather was reasonable Brunel would fish from his window which hung over the bank, the line tied to his big toe while he lay on his bed reading. When he caught a blue trout he would put it on his dressing table until the afternoon peace was finished and would then take it to Frau Snellhort who treated him to a smile with her brace of cheese-coloured teeth, and indicated that he had wrought at least a small miracle. You were not really permitted to fish in the river.

Brunel imagined that the army through one of its unconscious reflexes paid his bill at the Snellhort's hotel. The accommodation had been requisitioned at the end of the war and he had never questioned that the arrangement was still valid even though he was the only vestige of military occupation for many miles.

Fulsbad is an old tinkling town, purposefully Edwardian, and Brunel was at times conscious that he may have cut an unusual dash in his Waikiki shirt and battledress trousers as he slouched in spring or summer through its preserved streets on his daily way to his office. He went to the Moribund Docs. Section every day, even if he did not stay long. He liked to know that whatever history those files contained was still intact after the night, although he could not imagine anyone stealing them, and they were damp enough to survive anything but a fierce outbreak of fire.

But he liked to go in. On his way he habitually

bought a pastry, erupting with cream from a sticky-smelling shop, and bore it, couched in greaseproof paper up the impressive steps of the medical baths. In the entrance hall, marble like solidified ice-cream, you could hear the padded echoes of the therapeutic activities of the building. There was a hot water fountain near the door. The baths' authorities called it a mineral cocktail and a cupful was free to each visitor to drink. Every day Brunel filled his army issue mug with the hot water and bore it gravely up to his office. The white-aproned assistants nodded with approval and whispered among themselves on what an improvement the cocktail had made to Brunel's vitality. Nevertheless, after tasting the cocktail once only, and finding it to be merely unexciting hot water, Brunel took his daily mug to his office and there used it for shaving.

Every day he took a slow walk around the shelves of Moribund Documents, at a steady pace like some ceremony of keys or similar idiot ritual. But his expression, far from the sternly-acted regimental, was one of placid satisfaction.

It was good for him to see a war reduced to this; row and shelf and pile and gallery of soggy records, chronicles of mistakes and stupidity, gallantry and lethal adventure. This was all that was left; these mouldy files here, the mouldy bodies in the world's graves.

When the fighting was done, and all those that remained on their feet were in a hurry to get back and start the juicy, good life they had each promised to themselves, all the defunct papers of the huge allied army in the south of Germany were bundled together and brought there to remain and rot. The composing of generals, colonels, and scampering orderly room clerks, was all there, in serrated racks—decomposing. It was like looking at a dead dragon.

As Brunel had long discovered, there was no order to the museum. Everything had been unloaded from lorries, humped on to the shelves, and abandoned in the mad rush for peace. True the first officer in charge had been visited by some conscience and had tried to bring a kind of sense to the mess. He had written out twenty-six cards, lettered 'A' to 'Z', and pinned them to the topmost tier of shelves. Brunel had detected a pinhole where the letter 'Z' was apparently supposed to have been. But the originator of the system, having spaced out his index found that the 'Z' became positioned over the door of the small toilet, so it was dispensed with.

Not that the alphabet signified anything. On the day of his arrival, following the suicide through madness of the previous incumbent, Brunel had opened the first file in the 'A' Section, and discovered it was full of private letters from soldiers which, for various reasons, had never been sent to their loved ones.

In some cases when the military secrets, or imagined secrets, had been censored from them there remained nothing else to send. In others the letters had been so festered with foul thoughts, desires, and language that a right-minded postal officer had refused to forward them. There was one sad bundle apparently unsent because the writers had been killed before addressing the envelopes, and no one knew who 'Darling Lil' might be. To take a guess might have been dangerous and distressing. One soldier had left four letters, identical in every endearing word and sugared phrase, except in the Christian name of the loved one.

In the next section, lettered 'B', Brunel had found illogically, a detailed plan for the encirclement and capture of the town of Minden, marked in red as Top Secret and leaning against that the dinner menus from the officers' mess of the 10th Hussars, encompassing the entire period September 3rd 1939 to May 8th 1945. Leave applications, stores requisitions, sick reports, and all the waste paper of an army filled the files. Browsing through the records of an infantry company Brunel found a neatly selected cricket team, and stuffed near it a casualty list, dated a week later, and containing eight of the eleven names and both umpires.

It took only a little time, however, for exploring the files to pall as an amusement. It was like panning for sparse gold. There were hundreds of dreary everyday pieces of paper to every letter admitting that the Colonel had indeed mistakenly ordered an attack on the American positions, or confessing that the wrong man had got the Victoria Cross. But, Brunel appreciated, war was like that.

Before lunch each day, all the year, Brunel would stroll into town for an aperitif with Otto Furter, the local Nazi. Otto had been very slim once in his uniform but with the years, and the lack of opportunity for wearing the outfit, he had stored a lot of fat. He owned a small cafe-bar, dusty within and rusty without, and one day, when he had been talking to Brunel over their drinks, and they had known each other some time, he tip-toed into the dim room behind his cafe and beckoned for Brunel to follow. He showed Brunel his S.S. uniform hanging up in a secret cupboard, and then went discreetly into the bedroom and put it on. He reappeared with all the pride of a successful conjuror or male model, showing off the black apparel and looking eagerly for Brunel's reaction. The uniform bulged a lot because of Otto's physical deterioration, but the boots were very shiny and Brunel imagined that Otto must have been an impressive Nazi. He did however notice a small flash on one sleeve which said 'Post' and indicated that Otto had been in the S.S. postal section, although he angrily refused to admit the existence of such a department. Sometime, Brunel thought, he would show Otto, merely out of interest, the file of unposted British army letters back in the Moribund Docs. section.

Otto liked to talk about the war, and Brunel was isolated, unbiased and uncaring enough to listen well.

'When your armies were advancing on Fulsbad,' he said one spring day when they sat outside at a rusty iron table, 'there was great excitement in the town. All the girls got themselves prettied up to be raped. But there was very little. They were very disappointed. Not even a nun was touched, which was disheartening for them too because that is about the only time a nun really gets any experience of outside life, you understand.'

'What did you do when the town was taken?' asked Brunel. He could feel the sun warm on his neck for the first time that year. He was wearing a thick fisherman's jersey with his battledress trousers, but he knew now that he would soon be able to wear his Waikiki shirt.

'I was disgusted that it was so easy,' grunted Otto. 'No resistance. Not a shell, not a bomb, not a tile from a roof. They didn't want their precious steam baths damaged.'

'But *you* resisted?'

'Of course.'

'I thought you might.'

'Yes, I put on my uniform and marched out into the street.'

'Swastika and all?'

'Well, no.'

'But you went out.'

'Yes. Into the street, and I challenged a British officer. But he, like you, misunderstood the badge on my arm, and gave me a bundle of letters to post.'

'And that was the end of your resistance.'

Otto nodded his tubby head. 'Yes. I saw no point in resisting such fools. But I threw the letters in the river.'

The lieutenant who had been in charge of the Moribund Documents Section immediately before Brunel, two years before, had killed himself by leaping from the lip of a saucer-shaped chasm on to the sixth green of the Fulsbad Golf Course. It is a famous golfing hole, cupped minutely like a jewel in the bottom of the funnelled chasm, with brutal grey rocks walling it in on three sides. It is difficult to strike a golf ball so that it falls vertically and unchecked into the mouth of the chasm and then far down on to the green. But the lieutenant had been extremely accurate, had jumped and hit the green near the flag. It was summer and the green was dry and hard and the officer had made a splintered dent in the surface which altered the contour and made it even more difficult for putting than before.

Brunel had never really understood why he did it. Otto said: 'It was, I believe, through loneliness, too much schnapps, and reading those terrible files on the misconduct of the war against the Third Reich. It is very depressing to anyone who knows the truth.'

Although he was disinclined to argue with Otto, who, after all had known a war which he himself had escaped, Brunel privately thought that the schnapps and loneliness had more to do with it than the Moribund Docs. To a minor extent the same thing had happened to him. With the hunting instinct peculiar to the rich or the under-employed he had foraged about until he discovered something about which he could worry. With the great painful relief, known only to the born hypochondriac, he discovered he was anaemic.

In the early summer of his second year above the medicinal baths at Fulsbad he had gone through the repertoire of personal tests, as put forward in *Every Man His Own Doctor*, and having deduced that the anaemia was far advanced he went to see a doctor.

'The balls of my eyes are all yellow,' Brunel told him.

'*Jawohl*,' agreed the doctor. 'All yellow and sick.'

'And my finger tips and toes get all cold in the winter.'

'*Jawohl*, just as I thought.'

'I've got anaemia, haven't I? I'm thoroughly anaemic.'

'*Jawohl*, it is no use trying to deceive you. You have anaemia.'

The doctor, whose opinion he greatly respected, suggested an old remedy of soaking calves' liver for an hour in port wine, and then drinking the port wine. The treatment was to be twice a day.

Each morning, as soon as he reached his desk, Brunel placed a quarter of a pound of fresh, raw liver in a glass bowl he had lifted from Herr Snellhort's hotel, he splashed a generous wave of port across it, stirred it and then let the two red components soak together. A large glass of the reddy liquid before lunch, then two afterwards, combined with his normal aperitif with Otto, and the wine with his meal at Otto's cafe, made him very fatigued by the early afternoons. He fell into the habit of stretching his relaxed body across his desk and letting himself fall steeply asleep. The tabby cat, which he called Jackson, which belonged downstairs but didn't care for the steam, made a point of coming up and eating the soaked liver. Thoroughly drunk it would throw itself blindly up at the desk on which Brunel lay. Several times it would flop sadly back, but then a final clawing attempt would get it up there and it would collapse bemused, across his chest and they would sleep breathing port into each other's face.

It was in this bland, innocent situation that Lieutenant-Colonel Frederick Burleigh, a retired British army officer, discovered them at three o'clock one afternoon.

Colonel Burleigh had with him his wife, a big curly woman, a wan son, a good looking daughter-in-law, and three American friends. Brunel and the cat, both deep in port, were tight asleep on the desk.

In July 1945 it was the Colonel who had thought up the answer to the question that everyone in the zone was asking: what a suddenly peaceful army should do with its old papers.

He had commandeered the room at the Fulsbad medicinal baths, breathing fiery authority, and had then sent a lorry to all the resting units to collect their unwanted documents. The Colonel liked to tell how some maniac at headquarters had suggested that the papers should be burned, or even pulped to provide some sort of winter fuel for the German population, and how he was firmly chopped down by the force of military opinion.

Burleigh's idea had relieved the undecided situation like a laxative and he had been hoisted from Major to Lieutenant-Colonel, a rank he had been attempting to reach, without success, throughout a murderously fine war career.

Finding Brunel and the cat both snoring on the desk was made worse by the fact that on the drive to Fulsbad, the Lieutenant-Colonel had told his holidaying friends of the enterprise and acumen which had established this important section of the British Army.

'Only British unit remaining in this part of Germany,' he grunted proudly as they came from the forest road and drove down the angle to the town. 'Montgomery himself, or so I heard, said that the idea would be of value for years. And so it has proved.'

He lectured them on the importance of foresight as a military quality and they agreed dumbly.

They left the car at the steps of the baths and Burleigh led them with the sure stride of the commander of a raiding party through the damp corridors to the far door marked 'British Fourth Corps. Moribund Documents Section.'

They trooped in and came upon the solitary soldier flat on his back on the desk, harmonising his edgy snores with those of the tabby cat gracing his stomach.

'God in Heaven,' said the Colonel.

'Moribund,' commented his wan son, suddenly happy.

The Colonel rushed at the desk and howled into Brunel's sagging face, 'Hey you!'

Brunel made no perceptible extra movement. At the second 'Hey you!', however, the cat raised its chin a sixteenth of an inch from Brunel's chest and looked slant-eyed at the shouter. Having taken him in it returned to sleep. The port was a heavy one.

The Colonel felt his self-control fly. He grasped Brunel brutally and shook him by the shoulder and the left arm. Eventually Brunel opened his eyes and without getting up from the desk asked the retired officer what the hell he was doing.

'What are *you* doing?' returned the Colonel in a subdued shout. 'Where is the officer in charge?'

'I am, more or less,' answered Brunel sitting up. The action caused the cat to roll like a detachable beard from his chest. 'That's Jackson,' he added informatively.

'What ... What's happened to this section?' moaned the Colonel staring around like a traveller returned home to find his family all mad or poxed.

21

Brunel looked about him for some recent calamity. He said: 'Nothing's happened to it.'

'It has since I started it! I demand to know.'

The revelation that here was the inspired mind behind Moribund Documents had no effect on Brunel. He turned his legs over the side of the desk, smiled a brief greeting at the remainder of the visitors, and faced the Colonel again. 'I'm afraid dead documents are like dead people, sir,' he said. 'They don't improve over the years.'

He dropped the couple of inches to the floor. 'As a matter of fact they are not much more than a load of old pulp now,' he added.

Brunel took in the rest of the visiting group. The son was grinning only just below the surface of his white face, the nice daughter-in-law glanced at her husband uncertainly. The Colonel's wife regarded Brunel with loathing and the trio of Americans, two women and a man, stared as though an exhibit at a museum had come alive.

The Colonel performed a little mad dash around the shelves. He looked at the burst files, the ragged envelopes, the sagging shelves. 'Ruined,' he kept muttering 'Ruined all ruined.' He was like a king returned to find his kingdom demolished. He straightened his back and returned to Brunel, suddenly sharp and military. He looked at Brunel, the hybrid in his Waikiki shirt and khaki trousers.

'Are you,' he demanded patiently, 'a civilian or a soldier?'

'Officially a soldier,' admitted Brunel. 'Lieutenant Brunel Hopkins. Royal Welsh Border Regiment. Er ... detached.'

'Officially,' returned the Colonel, 'I am a civilian. My God, it's a good job I am or I'd have you inside, sir.'

'I was thinking you might,' said Brunel, blinking as though against strong light. 'But instead you are going to report me to the British Army. You're going to tell on me, aren't you.'

'Exactly,' said Burleigh. 'And very soon.' He turned to his party. 'I apologise for this shambles,' he said solemnly. 'We will go.' He turned sharply as the others followed. Brunel gave a small salute, using only two fingers. 'Please mind the cat,' he called after them. 'He's gone to sleep at the door.'

That evening Brunel went by the bus into Stuttgart, where he had visited only once before, and got filthy drunk. It was not a familiar sensation to him and he ranged the lighted town, quiet outwardly and not stumbling or staggering, but conscious of a violent frothy storm within himself.

He went into the first bar he saw with a U.S. Army 'Off Limits' sign outside. There was an old lady crouching like a beggar in an alcove by the door and Brunel drunkenly but civilly wished her 'Good evening' whereupon she rose and followed him with a rabbit hopping movement, sitting down at a table one second after he had settled himself there. A waiter came to Brunel's elbow and Brunel steadily ordered a beer. When he turned the old lady had her face thrust close to him. It was a face rampant with age; chewed, twisted, alcoholic. Brunel found himself replaying a childhood book game with her wrinkles, the game where you followed a drawn line and whirled about with it, not crossing any other lines, until you reached the Pixie's Treasure at the centre of the maze.

'You like me?' she said mistaking his inspection.

'I think you're great,' said Brunel.

She then removed her teeth and sat a foot away from

him rolling and champing her gums like a mechanical mixer. Then she opened her mouth like a nasty red hole and pointed her finger towards it, grunting.

'You want a drink?' guessed Brunel.

She seemed deflated but nodded at the offer of the drink and Brunel got her schnapps. The waiter looked at him with disgust. Suddenly, convulsively, she began to cough and choke, bending forward with the force of it. Brunel, immediately concerned, gave her a series of bangs on the back. As he thudded her he could feel the bones of her old frame shuddering.

When she had recovered she thanked him and then said: *'Der kabaret.'* She began clapping her thin hands together as though she were a dowager applauding a chamber ensemble. 'First kabaret goot,' she said clutching his forearm. 'Big woman strip. *Grosser* tit.'

'Super,' breathed Brunel. A volcanic woman, all trembling fat, appeared on the small stage, splashed by a spotlight and heralded with watery ballet music from a gramophone. Her blonde hair was tight in baby curls and she wore a giant ballet dress with satin boots. She began to thud around the stage.

'Good heavens,' said Brunel.

'Goot hah?' said his old lady.

The woman, her fat rolling like tripe, continued her dance, a kindergarten grin on her big face. Satisfied murmurs began to seep from the shadows of the club from the alcoved customers. Brunel had hardly been aware of them before. The monstrous dancer performed a pirouette, revolving like a fair ground roundabout, and as she did so splendidly whipped off the top of her satin dress, and Brunel ducked instinctively as she whirled to the front. The customers howled in a low key and began to applaud. Brunel laughed so much that the old lady at his table punched him in the face with her boney fist. There was an indistinct crisis after that, shouting, hands grabbing, and the stripper weeping obese tears. Several angry Germans caught Brunel, bore him to the door, and threw him out into the street.

He went next to a club where they showed Charlie Chaplin films to the customers, and there, during the screening of *The Gold Rush*, he met a young hostess. They left after Brunel had seen the sequence where Charlie ate his boots, and went to her flat. With her clothes off, he saw that she was patterned with teeth marks, which gave him second thoughts, but he had already paid so he stretched himself on the bed with her. It was not too bad, he thought, except that at the crucial, and wrong, moment he had made some sort of a grimace and she burst into laughter. Brunel asked her what was so funny and she pointed to his face and guffawed again.

He became very annoyed at this and decided she was ugly. After all, it was he who was supposed to be entertained.

A week after Lt. Col. Burleigh had found him Brunel walked up to the steps of the Baths, carrying his daily pastry, and saw a military motor cycle parked outside.

The dispatch rider, despite the summer, heavy in waterproofs that gave him the mean hunch of a toad, sat in Brunel's office waiting for him. He stood up when Brunel entered, but did not salute because he clearly could not make up his mind whether Brunel merited it or not.

'Sir,' he began, 'I've got a message for Lieutenant Brunel Hopkins, sir, Royal Welch Border Regiment, sir.'

'Me,' said Brunel taking the envelope. The dispatch rider stared at his beach shirt, then flung a belated salute to his forehead, which Brunel acknowledged by lifting his little finger, curled at the end. He opened the message which told him to report at once to Colonel James Wilsher, commanding third infantry battalion, B.A.O.R., Hanover.

'It's taken you three days to get this here,' pointed out Brunel looking at the date.

The soldiers looked uncomfortable. 'Yes, sir. I wasn't sure of the way, sir, so I stopped last night in Stuttgart, me knowing the place a bit from being posted there once, sir.'

'Hmm,' said Brunel. 'Have you been in the club where the big fat woman does a strip?'

'No . . . no, sir,' said the dispatch rider.

'You should,' said Brunel. 'It's quite novel.'

'Yes sir. I s'pose it is. But I'm Plymouth Brethren, sir, and I stay with some people who run a little Christian hostel there, sir.'

Brunel flushed. Only he could be sent a Plymouth Brethren dispatch rider. 'Well,' he mumbled, 'she's not all that novel. You didn't miss much at all really.'

'That's all then,' he said folding the message. 'Thanks very much.' This time he acknowledged the man's salute with a decent one of his own. The soldier turned and went to the door. 'Give my love to the Brothers,' said Brunel. 'Yes, sir, I will,' said the man.

Brunel sat down at his desk and re-read the instruction. He could already feel the hard hand of militarism on his shoulder again. He could almost smell the army. He realised that in the past ten minutes he had been called 'sir' more times than in the entire previous two years. He did not like it.

2

Otto was out in the town delivering leaflets advertising a protest meeting to demand the return of Germany's Lost Territories. Brunel sat at the sloping table outside the cafe and watched the angle of the coffee in his cup skimming the lower rim. He drank a mouthful to make it safer. One day, he thought, Otto would do something about the junk-yard of tables outside his cafe.

The trees standing along the short street were at their fattest, pregnant with green, and beneath them the street itself had become a quiet cavern of summer dust. Hilde, Otto's daughter, was wiping an unenthusiastic cloth over the cafe's speckled window.

'An old fool,' she said referring to her father. 'all this playing games. Nazis and all such foolishness.'

He had never really looked at her before. He did not look closely at many people. He needed to know them some time before he had digested their shape, their age or their voices. After two years in Fulsbad he was still only sure about five or six people. Hilde, he now saw, was very lean and when she stretched without effort to wipe the upper part of the window her short skirt climbed the backs of her legs which were brown and with just enough flesh behind them to give them form. Her jumper rode up with the same elongating movement, leaving her midriff bare and that was brown too. Brunel thought she must spend a lot of time sunbathing.

He tried to recall how old she was. She must be getting on, he concluded, to have definite legs like that and she had breasts too.

'At school yesterday,' she said looking down from the face of the window, 'we saw some films about Hitler. We laughed until we fell out of our desks. Some of us. What a funny man.'

'Hilarious,' said Brunel. 'One of the greats.'

She said: 'And then, in the afternoon ...' She climbed down and scraped a metal chair from the table and sat down, her face in her small fists. 'In the afternoon I heard three of the schoolmasters arguing. About the battles of the war. Who had fought well and who had not, and how cowardly the Italians were. I like the Italians, don't you? They become very angry with each other and I couldn't understand why. They are very old battles now.'

Brunel drank his coffee in three uncouth mouthfuls. He put the cup back on its slant.

'You should get your father to straighten out these tables,' he said. 'Look, nothing's on the level.'

'I always tell him this,' she said. Her English was good but hesitant. She liked to take her time and select what she considered the right word, like a printer choosing the correct fount.

'Some people don't think the battles are old,' said Brunel. 'They were before you were born, so-for you-they couldn't be any older. They might as well argue about Waterloo.'

'I know about *that*,' she said. 'I have a very clear view of that battle from my books. The newer wars are the confused things.'

'A lot of people,' said Brunel, 'think that the war was marvellous. Nothing happened to them before, nor since. They put out fires and walked across deserts and did lots of terrific things. In my country they still care, and argue, and write to the papers about it. There's nobody as proud as the private who writes up to say he was in Burma, or in Africa, and *he* never saw a Yank. So there!'

'You are very strange for a soldier,' she said agreeably. She got up and went into the half light of the cafe.

Brunel truly wished that he could make up his mind about just one thing in the world. Any one thing. Whether it was how to judge the age of a girl or whether Hitler was amusing. He had, he realised quite miserably, reached the ultimate in non-involvement. But this is how he had always wanted to be. Not caring. Not caring about wars, nor sex, nor inflation, nor politics, nor deaths on the road, nor colour prejudice, nor starving peoples, nor religion.

He had precisely brainwashed himself into this non-involvement, alone and without becoming involved with any other non-involvers. All his protests were inside himself. All were passive. He had done so because he believed that whoever thinks about anything in the world is quite wrong from the start. Other people thought opposite and they thought they were right too. But they were wrong. Heroes are villains, the giving of love is deep down the most selfish of all acts, charity just an insurance with God against hard times. Wars were not to end wars, but to start other wars. Allies were the next to want your blood, friends plotted, success, achievement in anything was a font of jealousy, vanity, greed, and the top of the slide to failure. The whole world was bloody awful which was why he didn't want any part of it. He preferred to live and later to die. Probably of anaemia.

He had been a strong practising Christian up to the age of eight. He had been born late in his father's life and his father, a failed missionary, had told him all about the Goodness of Christ and His church. Brunel had believed gladly and was actually looking forward to Eternity. Then one late spring evening he had walked to the back of the church to have a look at the tombstones, to ascertain who was already enjoying Heaven, when the cassocked choirboys grabbed him. Their pink, hymned faces full of the peculiar brightness of sadism they laid him across a grey grave—Thomas Aldridge, Esq., a Merchant of Earlham, At Rest—and punched him, kicked his shins and his balls with huge joy until he had no sympathy left with organised religion.

'Don't you think he is an old fool?' said Hilde breaking into Brunel's memories. 'Putting on that crazy uniform.'

'Well,' said Brunel regarding her from beneath his monkish fringe, 'it gives him something to do.' He almost said 'something to believe'.

She gave up wiping the window, leaving a scollop of dirt near the top, and sat down on the chair opposite him. They were the only two in the small dusty street under the trees. Brunel was bulky and quite tall. Slow in his movements because there was never anything to make him hurry. She regarded his round face, set in bewilderment under its hedge of fair fringe.

Brunel said: 'How old are you anyway?'

'Fifteen,' she said.

'I'm going. Tell your father when he returns from reclaiming the Lost Territories, that I think I am going to be moved from Fulsbad.'

'Moved? How? Who will move you Brunel?'

'The Powers. The British Army will come and remove me soon, I think. They know now that I am here.'

'Didn't they know before?'

'They'd forgotten—I got lost. Will you tell Otto?'

'He will be sad, Brunel. He will need to find someone else so he can display his Nazi uniform. That's not easy in a democratic country like this.'

'There's no freedom anywhere,' agreed Brunel. He got up to go and looked at the girl. She had a small bright face, like a coin, and very delicate eyes. When she grew old her eyes would probably remain the same, as the face faded. He thought that when she reached sixty or so she would really be worth looking at.

Leaving Fulsbad, even for a short time, was like leaving the world. Frau Snellhort had packed him some sausage sandwiches, and cried a little over them, making the solid bread wet, although he assured her and Herr Snellhort that he would be back in a couple of days. Otto and Hilde went on their bicycles to the station to see him off. Before he went aboard the train Hilde walked the length of the nearest carriage, looking in each window, and then returned and instructed him not to travel in the second compartment.

'Why not?' asked Brunel.

'There is an attractive woman sitting in there,' said the girl seriously. 'She would disturb your journey.'

He shook hands with Otto who clicked his heels. Hilde put her arms around him and he was shocked to feel the small pads of her breasts flattened against his chest, her thin hands clutching the back of his neck and her lips dabbing his cheek. '*Auf wiedersehen*, Brunel,' she said. 'Do not let them punish you.'

Brunel laughed. 'They can't punish me,' he said unsurely. He climbed aboard the train, dutifully avoided the second compartment, and sat down.

So he was going away. The sadness was puffed inside

him. Going away from Otto and Hilde, the Snellhorts, the helpers in the pastry shop, the nodding assistants in the baths' foyer, Jackson, his drunken cat, his friends, the forest rangers, and all the decaying documents he had guarded so well for so long. He had told them confidently that it would only be for a few days and he had not packed his kit, but privately he did not doubt that Colonel James Wilsher had plans for him.

He stood up and regarded himself in the wall mirror. He was alone in the compartment. The train, in fact, was almost empty, except for the second compartment in which the attractive woman was sitting. There, Brunel had noticed, every other seat was occupied by a man.

Brunel was wearing his full uncomfortable uniform. He had spent some time trying to rub the green discolouration from his cap badge and had partially succeeded. Under his cap was piled and pushed his rick of fair hair, with several ends of it hanging down his neck. He practised a quick salute into the mirror, as a sort of military refresher course, then sat down quietly and ate his sausage sandwiches.

Fancy that dispatch rider being a Plymouth Brethren, or Brother, or whatever it was, Brunel thought. How did you get *involved* like that. Was he riding his motor bike one day when the vision came to him to become one, like it had come to Paul on the road to Damascus? Strange how people hung on to these little religions. Assemblies of God, Seventh Day this and Eighth Day that. High, low, middle, bead-tellers and story-tellers, shouters, yellers, singers, and some who were vowed to silence. If there was an Eternal Life they would be at each others celestial throats before the end of the first week.

His father, the missionary, had taken the Love of

Jesus to people in far swampy countries. and had converted them and made them truly happy. He was best known as the Father of Road Safety in Africa. It was he who had taught the black man to raise his white palm to the headlights of on-coming motor cars in the areas around the cities of Rhodesia. In this way the drivers saw the white area and did not kill nearly so many natives.

When he became an old man, very old, about ninety, he lost Jesus himself. And he couldn't find Him again. His faith slid away from under him like a rug and he stumbled and staggered to Death in the most awful heathen terror. That was his reward, thought Brunel, for getting involved.

Brunel went to sleep. He woke up at a station where the attractive woman got off the train. She walked proudly down the platform on her excellent legs. She carried a small case and as she walked it collided regularly with her hip and part of her backside. Then he heard the sound of the men who had got involved, fighting in the compartment up the corridor. He went back to sleep.

Colonel James Wilsher was behind his British Army desk in Hanover when Brunel was announced, marched in, and saluted. The Colonel was one of those diminutive men who look even smaller in uniform. He had a rough, bright face, with single long hairs growing from it at wide points. When he spoke his right hand, then his left, wandered over his face, his fingers gently tugging each hair, then passing on to the next, like an owner inspecting a plantation.

'Ah,' he said as though he had known Brunel in some

previous life and had just remembered him. 'Lieutenant Hopkins.'

'Yes, sir,' confirmed Brunel.

'From Fulsbad,' said the Colonel glancing at some papers on his desk. His tone was not hostile.

'Now just where *is* that?' said the Colonel. He got up and moved towards a map on the wall. 'Had a glance this morning and couldn't find the damned place.'

He began moving his nose over the map, which was hung low, as though he thought he might smell the location. The scent he was pursuing stretched across Northern Germany, back and forward from the Ardennes to the Baltic, disregarding even the border with the East. Brunel felt embarrassed, eventually putting his finger on the far south of the country and bringing the Colonel's nose in a long, downward arc until it hovered over Fulsbad.

'Of course,' nodded the Colonel indicating he had really known all the time. 'Fulsbad. Yes, Fulsbad.' He wandered back to his desk, thinking about it, tugging the hairs about mid-field on his cheek. He motioned to Brunel to sit down.

'What an interesting name you've got,' he remarked suddenly pushing his eyes at the papers in front of him. 'Kingdom Brunel Hopkins.'

'I was named after the famous bridge builder, sir.'

'Oh, Telford.'

'No sir. The other one. Isambard Kingdom Brunel.'

'Oh, him. Naturally.' The Colonel looked through the papers again. 'Hopkins, I might as well be frank with you. It seems that the army lost you for a couple of years.'

'*Lost* me, sir?' whispered Brunel. He blinked under his fringe. The Colonel had said nothing about his hair, which surprised him.

'Lost you,' repeated Colonel Wilsher. 'Presumed missing, I suppose you could say. But the fact is that nobody in this command, under which you are supposed to come, knew anything about you being in that place, or in Germany, or in the army, or in the bloody world for that matter.'

'But they sent me my pay, sir.'

'That's something I suppose. I had begun to wonder if we owed you a lot of back-pay. This occupation army, or whatever they call it nowadays, is costing enough as it is, without dishing out lump sums.'

He laughed a bit but then tugged at one of his hairs too violently and looked hurt. 'The pay was one of those things which came through automatically, I suppose,' he continued. 'It's nice to know something in the command works as it's meant to work, anyway.'

Brunel said: 'Yes sir, it was most satisfactory. But I'm owed sixty-four days leave.'

'Hmm,' commented Colonel Wilsher. 'That will come, no doubt. But tell me ... er ... what exactly were you doing in Fulsbad? A former officer turned up here very annoyed, and bawled something about soggy documents. Couldn't make out what it was all about.'

'Moribund Documents, sir,' said Brunel.

'Oh, I see. Moribund Documents. Yes.' He paused and looked up from his papers. 'What's Moribund Documents?'

'Records, sir,' replied Brunel. 'Papers, orders, messages, and that sort of stuff. From the war, sir.'

Serious-faced the Colonel looked up. 'The 1939 one,' he muttered, and added skillfully, 'I imagine.'

'Yes, sir, that's the war. They got all the records and documents and put them in this one big room, over the steam baths at Fulsbad.'

'Over the steam baths?'

'Yes, sir. They must have requisitioned a room just after the war, and that's where they put the Moribund Documents Section, and that's where it stayed.'

'The steam couldn't have done the documents much good,' said the Colonel. 'I suppose that's why they became soggy.'

'Exactly,' agreed Brunel.

'And you've been in charge there for two years,' said the Colonel patiently. 'What happened to your predecessor?'

'He committed suicide, sir. On the golf course.'

The Colonel looked as though nothing could surprise him now. 'Was he playing? Golf, I mean, not suicide.'

'No, sir. I don't think he did play. He jumped on to the sixth green from the tee, sir.'

'The tee is a long way above the green?'

'Yes, sir, it's very high. It's a short tap with a six iron from the tee and the ball drops vertically on to the green.'

'How interesting. Do you play?'

'I'm scratch, sir.'

'Plenty of practice, eh?'

'Yes, sir,' said Brunel. Then thoughtfully added: 'But I've always been good, sir. Even at school.'

The Colonel added nothing more for an entire minute. It was obvious to Brunel, who began to accumulate a feeling of unease, that Wilsher wanted to say something but found it difficult to begin. Eventually he did begin. Still with his eyes pinned down to the desk, the Colonel said measuredly: 'I know it's against the rules and all that Hopkins, but I'm old enough and I know enough for you to trust me.'

He's queer, thought Brunel in a fluttering panic. He fancies me.

'Sometimes it's necessary to go around the back way,'

continued the Colonel. 'And I must know. I've got to know what the score is.'

Brunel was thoroughly frightened. 'Know about what?' he said.

The Colonel kept his eyes down. 'You're Intelligence, aren't you?' he said in a hushed voice. 'Just tell me. Confirm it, that's all. You don't have to elaborate on it.'

'How did you know?' asked Brunel, unable to credit the words of his own voice. The thought opened up in his head that if they ever asked him why he had lied, he could always say he thought the Colonel had said: 'You're intelligent, aren't you?'

'Oh, I added things up,' said Wilsher, looking up and smiling a thin, pleased smile. 'We're not just dumb soldiers, you know.'

'What things,' asked Brunel, 'did you add up?' He had dropped the 'sir' now, not for rudeness but for authenticity.

'Your haircut,' remarked the Colonel. 'It's fantastic. No serving soldier ever went around with a mop like that. And you obviously aren't used to wearing uniform. Your cap badge is upside down.'

'That's very shrewd,' said Brunel squinting at his cap on the next chair. He remembered thinking there was something different about it.

'And that ex-officer who came here after seeing you at Fulsbad said you were wearing your pyjama top with battledress trousers,' added the Colonel emphatically.

'He's not as observant as you,' muttered Brunel. 'It was a special shirt, not my pyjamas.'

'Truthfully,' confided the Colonel, 'I thought he was a bit of an old fool.' His hand flew around his face, giving quick tugs here and there to some of the lonely hairs. He got up and went to the door, opened it dramatically and seemed shaken not to find anyone crouching there.

Eventually he strode back across the carpet and, hands behind back, looked out of the big window in a classic cinema pose. Without turning around he told Brunel in a fierce monotone: 'I have orders for you. You have to go to 39 Dankestrasse, Hamburg, tomorrow. Be there at noon. Whoever answers the door to you will say "What colour day is it?". And you must say "Orange Wednesday".'

The colour sank from Brunel's face. He sat there shivering and the Colonel turned and saw what had happened to him.

'It's one of *those* assignments is it?' he said grimly. He thrust up a childlike hand as Brunel stood up, much taller. 'Goodbye, Hopkins,' he muttered. There was a pause and he still held Brunel's palm. Then he dropped his eyes and said: 'And good luck.'

3

Bending between the children and dustbins of Danke-strasse, Hamburg, Brunel rehearsed the secret words that Wilsher had told him. 'What colour is the day?' 'Orange Wednesday,' he answered himself to the surprise of a small German playing at a corner. He checked the numbers off and found No. 39, at the side of a butcher's shop. Everyone in the shop hung backwards and peered around at Brunel as he rang the doorbell. He stood trying to look like an intelligence agent not noticing a shop full of staring people.

He knew it was the right door because it was painted the khaki shade the army used for latrines, corridors and ammunition boxes. He wondered why they extended themselves to passwords and secret phrases when they painted the door khaki like that. The door opened. A man in a dressing gown stood there, a coffee cup sagging in his hand. 'Yes?' he said.

Brunel blinked at the unexpected word. 'What do you mean "Yes"? he inquired huffiily. 'You're not supposed to say that are you?'

The man seemed to appreciate immediately what he meant. 'Oh wait a moment,' he said tiredly. 'We're all at sixes and sevens this morning.' He went away, leaving the door mildly ajar and returned in a couple of minutes looking at a letter he had opened. 'This is it,' he informed Brunel. 'What colour day is it?'

'Orange Wednesday,' replied Brunel hugely relieved.

'Come in, old chap,' said the man. He led the way down a khaki corridor, his cup and saucer champing together like a china drum as he marched. He knocked at a door at the end and they stood waiting.

'Sorry about that,' he said. 'They're always changing these passwords and we hadn't opened the mail this morning so we weren't really up to date on this one. Suppose we've got to have the damn things, simply because if you're in Intelligence you've got to have them. But it's easy enough to get in here. Next time you come just lean on the door. The catch doesn't work. It opens quite easily.'

From inside the room a thin voice said, 'Enter', and they walked into a huge untidy area, in the far corner of which a British army major was sitting on a divan. He was shaving. 'Orange Wednesday chap, sir,' said Brunel's guide. He turned and left. Brunel tried to look beyond the lather at the man's face, but it was like trying to see through Santa Claus.

'You'll be the chap from Fulsbad,' said the shaver. 'Sit down, will you. Won't be long. We had a bleeding terrible night with the Yanks last night, old man. That vodka muck they mix doesn't hit you until the next morning. Delayed action bomb. But they love it. Just like the Russians. If we could get them all pissed at the same time we might get peace in the world for one morning at least.'

He had taken great folds of lather from his face now, dropping them on to a newspaper spread on the bed. A sardonic expression emerged as the suds were removed; and a thin face pared down to the cheekbones.

The major wiped his chin and cheeks on a towel and threw that on the bed when he had finished. He unrolled rather than stood, a man like a fishing rod, thin, tall and bending towards the top. 'I'm Findlayson,' he said. 'J. H.—John Henry. You're Kingdom Brunel Hopkins, I know. Bridge-building family eh?'

'Not really, sir,' said Brunel. 'My father was merely an admirer.'

'Why didn't he go the whole thing and call you Isambard, as well?'

'I understand that my mother thought it sounded immoral, sir,' replied Brunel.

Findlayson thought. 'Hmm, she might have had a point. It would have been hell at school, and later on, I'd say, a definite disadvantage in getting hold of women.'

He paused as though trying to recall something. 'Now where were we?' he muttered, moving the newspaperful of lather over and sitting on the bed. 'Oh yes, this Orange Wednesday rubbish.'

'Yes, sir,' confirmed Brunel. 'Can you tell me what it's all about?'

'Can't, old boy. Not yet, anyway. But you're involved in it anyway.'

'Thank you, sir,' said Brunel.

Findlayson said: 'It's just that the Yanks say nobody must know about it as yet. Only those of us at the top. They're a nuisance, I know, but they're more or less running the show, although it's supposed to be a partnership. But they've got more of everything than we have, so they're running it. And *they* say you can't be told yet.'

Brunel had a revealing, terrifying thought. 'It's nothing to do with the space programme is it, sir? I've missed all the wars and that sort of thing since I was born, *just* missed some of them, and I wouldn't like to think I'd been through all that to be shot at the bloody moon.'

Findlayson grimaced. Brunel didn't know whether

to like him or not. 'Nothing like that, son,' he said. 'This is very much on earth.'

Brunel said: 'Can I be told how I came into it at all sir? One minute I'm lost by the army and most of the world, and now ... well, now I'm in this, whatever it is.'

'Purest accident,' said Findlayson. 'Chance put her finger on you. Old Wilsher, who's a daft old twit, had some retired officer complaining to him that you were down at Fulsbad sleeping with a cat, or some such story.'

'That was Jackson, sir,' said Brunel. 'The cat, I mean. He was drunk.'

Findlayson said: 'There's nothing worse than a drunken cat. Unless it's a plastered goldfish. Have you ever seen them when somebody's poured whisky in their tank at a party?'

'No, sir,' said Brunel truthfully.

'Christ, you've missed something. They bristle. They really do. They skid around pretending they're killer whales. Terrific. How did Jackson get drunk?'

Brunel was glad he had asked for a logical reason. His estimation of Findlayson ascended. 'He'd eaten some liver which I'd soaked in port, sir. It's an old-fashioned cure for anaemia.'

'That cat was anaemic?'

'No, me, sir. I still am. I had to drink the port, and he finished off the liver.'

'I see. Well anyway old Wilsher thinks that if anyone is reported to him doing something which more or less qualifies them for a psychiatric discharge, then they must be in Intelligence. He asked us if you were one of us, and, of course, we knew nothing about you. But the next day all this Orange Wednesday business was suddenly sprung on us, and we were told to find immediately a British officer who was completely familiar with the Fulsbad area.'

'I see,' said Brunel.

Findlayson never smiled, but bared his teeth almost cutting his face in half with the habit. 'Frankly, hardly anybody knew where Fulsbad was. It's not the centre of the universe, I think you'll agree.'

'No, it certainly isn't,' nodded Brunel.

'And the only chap we could unearth who knew much about it from some previous posting, couldn't be got at. He's the wicket keeper for his regiment in the command cricket championships which start in Cologne next week, and they just couldn't let him go. Then, out of the blue, Wilsher comes up with this query on you, and here you are—the complete expert on Fulsbad!'

Findlayson went on quickly. 'It's a quiet place, isn't it?'

'Deadly silent,' said Brunel.

'Forest, golf course, casino, very elegant too I hear, medicinal baths, old ladies with rheumatics and that sort of picture.'

'That's about it,' agreed Brunel. 'But more old men with rheumatics.'

'There's a hotel up by the golf course, isn't there, Brunel, what's it called?'

'The Golf Hotel, sir,' said Brunel apologetically.

'Yes, it would be, wouldn't it. It has a terrace and a swimming pool, yes?'

'Yes,' confirmed Brunel.

'Good enough. We got that lot from the guide books. We want you to show us the back alleys, so to speak. Anyway you and I have got another call to make. We're going to see the Yanks, because we'll be more or less working for them, although we're not allowed to admit it. Now we'll fix you up with an Intelligence Dossier, but don't, for Christ's sake, let on that you've never been in this mob before.'

He dressed quickly, discreetly going over to one corner to get into his trousers. As they left the room he said: 'You can say that you've been detached—working for S.I.B. for a time. We'll fix the background for you, so don't worry. We like them to think we've got our fingers on all the keys.'

They drove to a new looking building, the only clean one in a morose street of the St. Pauli district, and as they were going in, Brunel decided to ask the question.

'Sir,' he said defensively, 'what's the S.I.B.?'

Findlayson glanced quickly at Brunel but kept his step and replied: 'The Army's Special Investigation Branch. But if they ask you say "S.I.B.". It sounds better.'

The American behind the steel desk was a civilian and he had a disconcerting way of using a polite 'sir' with his questions, especially the more difficult and unpleasant ones. His name was Keenor. He wore thin tinny spectacles, and his black hair was brushed squarely from a middle parting to half an inch above each ear. He was squat with a growing jowl. He had the disconcerting habit of nervously backing his head away while asking a question as though he expected a heavy punch.

'You've got a fancy name, sir,' he said looking at the papers before him. 'When Major Findlayson read it over the phone I had difficulty in getting it down right. Look.'

He held up his pad and Brunel saw there were three crossings out before his name was finally achieved. 'Kingdom Brunel Hopkins,' said Keenor rolling out the words. 'What kind of a name is that?'

Brunel sighed inwardly. 'My father was an admirer of

the famous engineer and bridge builder, Isambard Kingdom Brunel,' he said.

Keenor looked annoyed. 'My old man was crazy about baseball,' he claimed. 'But he didn't call me Babe Ruth.'

'He might have done had you been a girl,' said Brunel genuinely.

This time Keenor jerked away and stayed back, looking over Brunel from apparently a safe distance. He decided not to pursue the point. He changed his attack. 'That's a kinda strange haircut for the British Army,' he said.

Brunel jumped in. 'S.I.B.,' he muttered as though it explained everything.

'Sure,' said Keenor without blinking. 'And they let you have hair like that?'

'At Moribund Docs,' said Brunel, 'things were different.'

Keenor had to throw that one away. 'Can you shoot?' he said lunging back as though he expected Brunel to demonstrate immediately.

'I'm a good marksman, to a point,' said Brunel.

'What's the point?'

Brunel leaned forward as though glad to get something off his mind. 'I've only shot at targets,' he admitted.

'You've never killed anybody?'

'No. Certainly not.'

'You don't know what it's like to shoot at people, then?'

'No.'

Keenor laughed unpleasantly. 'We'll get some people for you. Have them running about a bit. Then you can have some practice.'

Brunel displayed a little grin to show he realised it was a joke.

'What else can you do?' asked Keenor scribbling on his pad.

'I'm off scratch at golf,' said Brunel pleasantly.

'You don't say! That's great! We could use more men like you.' His tone changed. 'Let's stop farting about, Lieutenant. The important thing is that you know this Fulsbad place.'

'Yes,' admitted Brunel wishing he could deny it.

'That's good,' said Keenor. 'Because you're going to be the errand boy of this outfit, the fetch and carry man, the one who knows where the john is, who's got the keys, and who's shacking up with who. That's your job.'

'I suppose,' ventured Brunel, 'it's impossible for me to know why I'm doing this job, what it's in connection with, and whether it is possible for me to back out or not?'

'Sure it's impossible,' said Keenor.

4

They had put him in a small hotel which he immediately established was used more as a brothel. It was near the Reeperbahn and the traffic both inside and out was busy. In the early evening Brunel lay on his bed, sad as a refugee, thinking of the sun, chest high in the mountains now at Fulsbad, filling the gentle town with late light. There would be little traffic in the streets, people would be walking by the miniature river, Otto would be polishing his S.S. boots and young Hilde wiping down the cafe tables. Frau Snellhort would have cleaned and tidied his room and opened the small window over the river. The last customers would be on the pummelling tables at the baths, the velvet curtains would be drawn at the casino, and the string quintet at the Kurhaus would be playing a Mahler minuet. Old gentlemen would be telling their friends how their rheumatism had improved, and old ladies would be eating fresh cream cakes. All would be right in Fulsbad.

But for how long? What were they planning and scheming with their idiot men behind steel desks? He didn't like the way Keenor had suggested getting people for target practice, even if it were a joke. He liked Findlayson a little better but he knew that because of what they were, the type of soldier men they were, Findlayson would, if it were necessary, also order people for target practice. But he would tell them they were going to enjoy it.

Of all people they had to find him. Him, Brunel, the reluctant denizen of the world, the soldier rebelling for peace—his own peace. Now he was picked and destined to be the dogsbody of the operation, whatever it was, to show them where the john was, and who had the keys. How did the Americans ever come to call it the john? It was enough to prevent anyone being christened with the good name of John ever again. He bounced it about in his mind. The Gospel According to St. Bog.

The ceiling above his head was ribbed and wrinkled, as though debauched by all the things it had witnessed in that room. The side mirrors on the depressing dressing table were turned to the wall indicating that they, at least, had the decency not to look. Noises were filtering from the rooms on either side.

Two customers had apparently arrived simultaneously, for identical low tones could be heard through the thin walls to his left and to his right. The business discussion was first. A slightly raised voice at a raised price, but then mumbling again. Two wardrobe doors creaked, and then he heard the bedsprings going. They were not quite perfectly co-ordinated so that Brunel, in the middle, received the impression of stereophonic sex, the sounds crowding on him at the centre.

The left-hand lover left off peacefully enough and Brunel heard nothing more from there until the door opened and closed after some minutes. But on the right the bedsprings began to multiply their noise like a revving engine. Shocked, Brunel turned his face to that wall. Two feet away *that* was going on. Then he jerked his head back in sheer fright as the customer began banging the wall with his fist, sending snowflakes of plaster on to Brunel's cheeks and nose. Brunel lost his temper then and swung his fist at the partition, catching it a tremendous blow. 'Shut up, you bloody pig!' he shouted.

The springs gave a huge sound like an orchestra in sudden discord. Then some scufflings, the door creaking, and silence. Brunel felt pleased with the effect. Then he wondered if they planned to drop a small atomic bomb on Fulsbad, or squirt it with nerve gas.

Although the bedsprings on both sides had begun to operate like pistons again – it was a warm sticky evening in Hamburg – Brunel drifted to sleep and woke with a jump when a large German woman entered the room.

'Not here,' he shouted at her. 'Do it somewhere else, madam.'

After her frightened look her voice was flat and uninterested. 'Herr Hopkins,' she said. 'Telephone.' Then she went.

Brunel scrambled up and put his shoes on. He wandered around the wooden passages for some time before finding a hole that led him to the front reception area of the hotel. A whore and her customer were waiting at the bottom of the stairs, holding hands, and even on his hurried way to the phone Brunel thought how quaint it was that they had to observe the charming formalities of real love.

'Hopkins here,' he said into the phone. There was an earwig asleep in the hollow of the mouthpiece and he awoke, terrorised by the typhoon of Brunel's voice. He ran about in the cup, two inches from Brunel's lip, and Brunel squinted wildly down to see what was rushing about. He had a nasty feeling that the animal had dropped from his nose.

It was Keenor at the other end. 'Say, Brunel,' he called familiarly, 'how's the pad?'

'Terrible,' said Brunel.

'Too bad,' Keenor said so quickly that Brunel knew he had the answer ready to fire. 'We'd like you to start a little boy-scouting for us, Brunel. As you're the local expert.'

'The local expert for Fulsbad,' Brunel pointed out. 'This is Hamburg.'

'I'm sure you'll get by, Brunel,' said Keenor happily. 'Now listen, we've been having a get-together today with some of the communications and security people involved in Orange Wednesday, and they've all had a hard day ...'

Brunel said: 'Do *they* know what it's all about?' The earwig suddenly leapt on to his lower lip and he blew it off again.

'Some of them do and some of them don't,' said Keenor, not changing his tone. 'That's why it's been a hard day. Now what we want you to do ... Are you blowing raspberries at me?'

'I'm blowing,' admitted Brunel. 'But not raspberries. There's an earwig taking jumps on to my lip and I keep blowing him off.'

'Sure there is,' said Keenor. 'But never mind him now. We want you to round up some women for the fellas.'

'*Women!*' Brunel said the first syllable in a whisper and the second at a scream. The earwig, in hell, turned over and over in the mouthpiece.

'Check,' said Keenor. 'We're having a little party and we want some nice pliable women. Not too rough. A little touch of class.'

Brunel levelled himself. 'How many?' he asked. 'Any particular colour?'

'Aw now don't get sore, son. We'll be asking you

small favours from time to time. That's what your job will be. They won't be big things, but they'll be important. You can count on that.'

'How many women would you require?' asked Brunel through straining teeth.

'Half a dozen will do,' said Keenor.

'Are you sure?'

'Brunel,' said Keenor suddenly cold. 'Don't let's have any more negative thinking. Bring them to 12a Herrickstrasse, about midnight. And, there's one more thing, if you can get a couple of dark fat ones so much the better. The Russians like that sort.'

The Russians? Brunel kept thinking as he went out into the streets to look for women. What did the Russians have to do with it? The Russians? The Americans? The British? *Who* were they going to fight? They could hardly be massing at Fulsbad to attack the Chinese? Perhaps they were going to turn on the French. That was the trouble, as soon as you became involved, whether or not it was your own doing, you never knew who you were supposed to like or hate.

He was wearing, for the first time in three years, a doubtful brown suit, a cream shirt and a tie curled like a short rope.

At that moment he hated the Americans as solidified in Keenor. Get them some women! How did you go shopping for women? If he turned up with any old ragbags, Keenor would throw them, and him, out. And then they would eat him. No, Keenor wanted a touch of class. He had put the matter as delicately as he could to the concierge at the hotel who seemed surprised that such a mild young Englishman should require six women, two of them dark and fat. With his eye on his own business he had suggested that having got the women perhaps Brunel would like to move to a bigger room. Brunel had become abusive at that and the concierge had cooled him by suggesting he went to the Kafe Klinker down the road where only ladies were allowed to ask for dances.

With no great hope Brunel went there. It was a voluminous place with a noisy Yugoslav orchestra. It was crowded with patiently standing men and predatory females who cruised the floor seeking and pinning their prey. Brunel sat down at a shady side table, his face in the dark, to survey the scene. A great number of the women looked as though they had come straight from an ugly convention, but some of the others were not too bad. He had mentally and, he admitted to himself, quite academically, picked out half a dozen for Keenor, including the two outsizes, when there was a thin tap on his shoulder. It was like the peck of a bird. He turned and shrank down in his chair. She was like thin steel and concrete, like some hard fancy of a bitter modern sculptor. She was tall, gutted more than gaunt, and her general dreadfulness was heightened by the close blonde curls and the red ribbon that topped her skull.

'No,' snivelled Brunel wriggling away from her hand. 'Not tonight, thanks.'

'Tanse,' she insisted. 'You tanse.' She was obviously accustomed to rejection.

Brunel rose to his feet and looked up at her miserably. 'Tanse,' he agreed in surrender. She was half a head taller than he was, and she led him to the floor like a pet. Men scurried out of her way and hid themselves. At the edge of the dance area the woman seized him with iron hands and began to drag him in time with the music.

'American?' she said in her metal voice.

'English,' he muttered trying to work his fingers in her grip.

'*Ja, ja,*' she sighed. 'I say English good. I love you. You have apple face and big hair.'

'That's very sweet of you,' agreed Brunel, trying to keep up with her marching paces. If he could only get Keenor into this thing's clutches.

'After tanse,' she said. 'I take you home.'

'Thank you for asking,' said Brunel desperately. 'But I'm going home with my friend.'

Then the woman stopped; stonily she crunched around. There was a girl tapping her on the arm. A nice girl, a wonderful, beautiful, angelic girl.

'Excuse me, Princess,' said the girl. She spoke in an American voice with German edges. Brunel nodded shameless encouragement to her.

'Vot excuse me?' said Brunel's partner.

'That's right,' said the other girl moving in. The horror at first looked as though she would fight, but then released Brunel and he grabbed the new partner and whirled her away in a frantic circular waltz.

'It's a tango,' said the girl.

'It's anything,' said Brunel. 'Thank you for saving me.

She looked less than completely beautiful now that he was released from his crisis. In fact she had a small shiny pimple on the left side of her nose, embedded like a boulder in the sharp valley made by nose and cheek. She had another, better disguised, on the apex of one eyebrow arch. But her overall effect was synthetically pleasing. She was like a chorus girl, tall and in the right dimensions, with an anonymously pleasant face and big white teeth. Her hands, Brunel had already decided, were by a long way the best part of her. The one that held his was so slender and fine in texture that he might have been supporting an empty velvet glove. The other did not rest on his shoulder so much as pause there like a bird.

'It's very difficult dancing with a lady like that,' he observed politely, slightly regretting his first remarks after rescue. 'She wanted to lead me all the time.'

'She wanted to eat you,' said the girl. 'I could see her gnashing her tooth. My name is Prudence.'

'It's a good name,' shouted Brunel. He had to shout because their course was orbiting them dangerously near the band and more particularly the Yugoslav female singer who was letting go a huge noise. He pulled Prudence quickly back into the dancers, there was a noticeable vacuum on the floor around the singer, and said: 'You are an American, I suppose?'

'Father was American, mother was a Hun,' she said simply. 'He was the first Allied soldier to penetrate the no-fraternisation rules after the war.'

'That's why they called you Prudence,' guessed Brunel pompously. 'You were the first tangible being of the new relationship between Germany and the Western allies. After you, and only after you, came the tanks, and the Bundeswehr, the miniature submarines, and N.A.T.O., and the H-bomb.'

'I was the first of the line,' she agreed. 'But listen, Brunel, this is not going to find you six naughty women, two of them dark and fat.'

Brunel was shattered. 'Shut up,' he spluttered. 'It's all top secret. Classified. No one must know.' He was astonished to find himself speaking in the garble of Keenor. A tremendous lump had swollen in his throat. He swallowed it like a bun, and took her gentle hand, leading back to his seat in the corner.

'*How* did you know?' he demanded. 'You knew my name too.'

'Yes, Brunel,' she said sweetly. When she only half

54

smiled it was better because only fifty per-cent of her big teeth showed and they looked white and sweet. Now they were sitting down and he was not so close and did not have to look directly into her face, he could see down the open neck of her dress, where a long speared shadow pointed. She must have a big bust, he thought, surprising himself again, to have a spear like that. His eyes went back to her face. Almost everything was big about Prudence. Her eyes too, round and blue, like a nineteen-forties film star.

'Well *how*?' he said.

'I'm Mr. Keenor's confidential secretary.'

'I'm sorry for you,' observed Brunel.

'Aw, he's not that bad. Pretty bad, but not that bad. He has people breathing fire at him all the time. People worse than he is. I'm pretty sorry for him at times.'

'And you're his right hand maiden,' said Brunel. He caught a waiter's glance and ordered drinks for both of them. She just had a tomato juice, and he had a small port, although when he drank it he had to admit that it lost much without the liver taste.

'I'm more than a secretary,' she admitted. 'This job tonight is not exactly taking dictation, is it? More of an assistant.'

'And he's sent you to check on me,' grunted Brunel. He really did not like port without liver. He pushed the glass away wondering if they had any liver.

'Can't stand port without liver,' he said.

'I noticed that in your dossier,' she said. Brunel went cold. He remembered telling Findlayson about the liver.

'My dossier?' he asked. 'I've got a dossier?'

Prudence looked at him as though he were questioning his possession of a right leg. 'Of course you've got one,' she said. 'Everyone has.'

'It didn't stop Keenor asking me damn stupid questions.'

'He likes to do that. To assess character, he says. But they've got a file on you.'

'He thought I was a strong enough character to go and lasso half a dozen birds for him then?'

'He was slightly doubtful. That's why he sent me. To see if you were operating the right way and to help you if you weren't.'

'I'm not doing very well,' admitted Brunel relieved at the revelation. 'Fancy sending someone like me on this sort of jaunt. Anyway, what's all this about? All this Orange Wednesday rubbish.'

Immediately she looked genuinely frightened. 'For God's sake,' she said. 'Don't shout. It's secret.'

'I thought it was a code name to cover up something secret,' said Brunel reasonably. 'Now we're making the cover-up secret too.'

'Nobody calls it Orange Wednesday in public,' she said. 'It might get to the wrong ears and into the wrong hands.'

'And there's no knowing what they would do with it,' said Brunel bitterly. 'How the bloody hell they'll be able to understand it beats me. I can't. Anyway, if we can't use the code name, what is the code name for the code name?'

Prudence dropped her voice. The spear down inside her dress grew longer, more tapered, and darker at the tip, as she bent forward. 'I still can't tell you what it's all about. There's a lot I don't know myself yet.'

'There's a lot more I don't know,' grumbled Brunel. 'But if we're getting pally with the Russians again to clobber China, I'm having nothing to do with it. Nor nerve gas either.

She didn't answer. She bent down to her watch. The spear ran deeper towards her navel. 'Time's running on,' she said. 'We'd better round up these women. You came to the wrong place here, for a start. *You* need to be able to take the initiative. This is the one place in Hamburg, possibly in the world, where a man can't.'

'How did you find me here?' he said miserably.

'The guy at your hotel. I think he fancied me because he asked me if I was going back there for your orgy.'

Brunel shrugged. 'The man's a screaming sex maniac,' he said. 'It's a wonder the place is still on its foundations, what with the way they hammer the walls.'

Prudence stood up. She was about his height, a fact which seemed to reach them simultaneously. He looked at her. 'I've got stilts on,' she said, lifting one foot to show her shoes.

'I'll get you a job in a circus,' he said.

They walked up the hill of the Reeperbahn and Brunel felt like a child on a day trip to Hell. Prudence was apparently undisturbed by it all, but the sights and noises and sausage smell of it hung on Brunel.

Peach and yellow neon lights staggered in the upper dark. Erotica, Kinky, Sexy, Crazy Sexy, Kuntabunt, and other words in full hideous colour. The pavement was wide, expansive enough for the buyers and those ready to be bought, wide enough for the touts in their comically official-looking peaked caps beckoning people from the darkness into the darkness. Two candy-floss blondes wearing identical cheap black suits and heavy, high, boots, paraded under the trees, their wrists chained together with a silver chain. Once, as Prudence and Brunel passed, the double doors of a den opened like a mouth in a wall, and were held for a few moments by some customers being ejected. Brunel looked and saw within, held in a drum of yellow light, two fat women, naked as putty, and pulling each other's hair. Strange how the Germans, in their basic moments, were excited by big females. He remembered the admiration the fat stripper had evoked in Stuttgart the night he was thrown out for laughing. He thought they liked large women with large breasts, perhaps, in the same way as they liked large armies. There was constantly joy in strength.

'Up here,' said Prudence and turned across the road. They went around a magazine kiosk, threaded their way through a pimps' meeting, and entered a gap in some armoured doors stretched across the entrance to a minor street.

'Perhaps here,' said Prudence sniffing around. 'I don't know this town, but this is Herbertstrasse.'

If Brunel had been suddenly introduced into a zoo, with humans in every cage, and animals laughing at them, he could not have been more staggered. Prudence took his hand and led him firmly along the street. The shop windows were dainty bays, like Victorian sweet shops, each with its light burning, each with its harlot sitting, like goods awaiting purchase.

Women in every variation of shape, age and size. Women in every degree of poor condition. They sat on chairs or small couches, some dressed, some in their underclothes, reading books and papers, picking at little samplers with an embroidery needle, drinking coffee and munching cream cakes. Each window had its own capsule life, and the women never looked out into the gloating, thronged street, at the monstrous people. They only paid attention when a customer tapped on their window. Then they opened a small hinged pane and the proposal was discussed. Sometimes the customer went around through a side door and the woman put a bookmark in her book, tidied away her embroidery, or left her coffee and cakes, to attend to the business of love.

Prudence saw the white expression on Brunel's face. 'You feel okay?' she said. They were being pushed and jostled by the thick crowd in the street, men and women, most of them merely window shopping.

'Fine,' said Brunel. 'I always find it stimulating to see something truly horrific.'

'You knew about Herbertstrasse, surely?' she said.

'No,' he admitted truculently. 'No, I didn't bloody well know about it. I'm the world's greatest innocent. Didn't you realise? But I'm glad I didn't know. I only wish I didn't know about it now.'

They had wandered into an off-shoot of the market, but Brunel quickly turned and pulled Prudence away from there when he saw a young man in petalled pyjamas sitting in another picturesque window.

'Let's clear off,' he said. 'This is making me sick.'

'You're a prude,' she answered without heat. Then she laughed. 'I wonder if they'll take them out of the window for us?'

'Shut up,' grunted Brunel. 'Anyway I can't imagine even Kennor wanting anything from here. It looks like remnant week.'

Eventually they went out. To Brunel even the Reeperbahn smelt like a sweet-watered meadow after that little street.

'You're too sensitive,' reprimanded Prudence. 'That's a lump of life, whether you take to it or not. It's the Germany nature to put the meat in the window.'

Brunel did not answer. He was thinking of young Hilde wiping the tables in the cafe, riding her bicycle through the quiet town.

Eventually he said to her, quietly but with suppressed anger: 'How anyone can go into an arse-holing place like that, a human supermarket, and shrug and say "that's life" knocks me flat. That's death, that is! Very serious death.'

Prudence smiled, showing her whole teeth, and took his hand. 'Let's have some coffee,' she said soothingly. They went between the pavement tables of a cafe. There were clean lace curtains inside the door-pane, and the interior sound of a sadly scraped violin. Brunel pushed the door and they went into the cafe.

It was another big place, with tables set out cleanly, a small gypsy orchestra scraping in a corner, and tailed waiters moving about. There was a bar, bare and un-cluttered, with a coffee drum at one end, and a pumpkin-headed woman busying herself with cups.

What made Brunel stop, and made Prudence pull up quickly behind him, was that almost every table was occupied by a stately girl in a brilliant Ascot hat. They sat elegantly, expensively dressed and jewelled, their fine handbags beside them. Some talked, two or three at a table, their voices and gestures mute as ballet movements. The truly beautiful girl nearest to the stationary Brunel crossed a magnificent pair of legs, glanced coldly at him, and gently adjusted the hem of her skirt.

'The chorus from *My Fair Lady*,' said Brunel.

'And not the touring company either,' Prudence said.

They shuffled forward. They sat on stools at the bar and kept half turning around their coffee cups to see the sight again.

'Seeing these makes me think I ought to be a window-dresser in the Herbertstrasse,' said Prudence hopelessly.

'They're very nice women,' observed Brunel. He extended his head towards the woman working the coffee urn. She waddled over. He decided not to risk his German.

'Do you speak English?' he asked.

'Yes,' she replied clearly. 'Waldorf, London, nineteen-thirty to August thirty-nine.'

'Glad you got out in time,' observed Brunel. 'What are these ladies doing here?'

'Soliciting,' she said simply.

Brunel was no less astonished than he had been in the dirty Herbertstrasse. 'But the hats?' he said to Prudence.

'That should have told you,' said Prudence impatiently. 'No moral woman would wear a hat like that at this time of night. I thought you realised what they were.' She looked at him stonily. Then she said: 'No, maybe you wouldn't. Anyway, we'd better get half a dozen. Go out and get a couple of taxis. Make it three, I wouldn't want them to be too squashed and crease up their things. Keenor wouldn't like it.'

Brunel got down from his stool and went out. He felt himself shivering as he walked by the ladies at the tables. It was all he could do to prevent himself bowing to them as he made his exit.

Brunel travelled in the first taxi with two of the ladies. They sat opposite, conversing industriously in German, with their fine, long legs crossed and the slim toes of their shoes pointing at his stomach as though they had chosen only him. He tried to look out of the window.

At 12a Herrickstrasse, Keenor came to the door, and herded them in. He patted each girl on the taut backside as she went through the door as though counting them. He said to Prudence: 'How much?'

'Two hundred marks,' she said.

'Each?'

'Of course, each,' she said. 'They're the top girls.'

'Beautiful,' he agreed. 'But over-expensive.'

'The others didn't look very fresh,' interpolated Brunel.

Keenor had been drinking. He looked at Brunel as though he did not know whether to like him or not.

'Did you get two fat ones for the Reds?' he asked. 'None of them looked fat.'

Brunel said: 'We didn't get the fat ones. We thought perhaps if the Russians really wanted bulk, one could have two girls and then the other jump in afterwards.'

They were in the flat now, Keenor hesitantly leading the way. The main room had plenty of comfortable chairs and two big divans. There was Smirnoff on the cocktail cabinet and Bacharach on the radiogram. The girls were all in the bedroom around the mirror and Keenor, like some public employee, was doing a tour of the main room dousing every other lamp and light.

There were five other men in the flat. They were all in civilian clothes. Prudence handed Brunel a drink and he stood examining the strangers. The two Russians were sitting coyly on the edge of one divan, a space between them into which they obviously intended to insert two girls. The space had been a good deal wider at first, but when no fat girls turned up the Russians closed ranks a little.

One of the Russians had a Josef moustache, a huge, kindly head topped with luxurious silvering hairs, and ridiculously large, soulful eyes. Brunel remembered seeing someone like him in a film with Nelson Eddy. The other Russian was short and brisk, with a clenched face and fair, cropped hair. Brunel wondered who's trousers would be off first.

An American hung across an obese armchair, his clothes creased, his face clouded with cigar smoke, his shirt volcanic with cigar ash. He was swallowing vodka straight and kept referring to the big Russian as 'Red Mac'.

Findlayson was at the other end of the room, vaguely waving his pipe to Brunel and with him was a young, vicious looking British army officer, whose eyes went hard very quickly when the first of the girls came in.

'I'll be going then,' said Brunel turning awkwardly. He wondered whether he ought to risk springing to attention and boldly saluting to all as he went.

'Drink this,' said Keenor appearing from behind him and handing him a glass.

'Thanks, but I don't want any more,' said Brunel.

Keenor looked angry. 'Son,' he said, 'I wasn't *asking* you to have a drink. There's nothing social about it. I just said "Drink This".'

Brunel got a half-impression that Prudence moved forward, but he was two sips through the syrupy drink by then. He remembered thinking that it tasted like glycerine cough mixture, but he did not pursue the comparison because he blacked out immediately. When he woke up one of the girls, wearing only her lovely hat, a girdle and stockings, was bending near him.

The room was very hot and full of heavy, sleepy, breathing. Brunel felt tired but cool in his head. He was on the floor near the radiogram which was playing something anonymous in a low key. He wondered if anyone had made a record called 'Music for Fucking'. The girl, the one who had sat opposite Brunel in the taxi, was arched over a chair trying to reach something, her breasts hanging from her tall frame like inverted bells. She straightened up holding a bra, looked around the room, saw Brunel staring and unworriedly put the bra across her front.

She turned her back on him, then hunched down near where he sprawled, and motioned for him to hook up her bra. He did so with a facility that surprised him.

'You're with us again?' Prudence was there. The girl diplomatically crept away. Brunel looked up and was strangely pleased to see that Prudence was still in her clothes.

'What did he give me, the bastard?' asked Brunel.

'Just one of his drinks,' said Prudence. 'It's his hobby. He cooks them up in all sorts of ways. The people always go out just like you went out. It's very useful in the work, sometimes.'

She said: 'I'll take you home.' She was slightly drunk, looking at him with a sad joy, tender for him, but glad he was so perplexed. It was a sad look usually reserved for a ready woman by a man who has planned well. Brunel didn't notice. He was squinting about the dimmed flat, trying to feel his tongue with his teeth and his teeth with his tongue, and taking in the various forms and shapes lying about. The girl who had stood by him was in one corner carefully replacing her expensive skirt. The two Russians, he noted, had ended up snoring side by side, and Keenor had three girls. Brunel thought it would always work out like that.

'Take me home?' he said miserably to Prudence. 'Thanks.' Then he muttered miserably: 'Home.' He did the final button of his jacket and indicated to Prudence that he was ready. 'A couple of sweet weeks ago,' he grunted, 'home was a little window overlooking a nice cool river. I used to catch trout with my big toe. Well, with a string tied to my big toe. That was home. To-night my home is a knocking shop.'

He felt quite assured, firm within himself, even if his thoughts wandered, but around him solids had a habit of floating and becoming gas or liquid, moving about, out of his way. Prudence helped him down the stairs.

'Tell Mister Keenor I've got a hobby, too,' he muttered as they went. 'It's shooting. If he slips me another of his amateur bleeding mickies, I'll get him between his nasty close eyes with one of my amateur bullets.'

Prudence said she would tell Keenor. Brunel fell the last three stairs, and sat cursing and inwardly whirling, on the final one while she went to get a car from the back of the building. She asked him not to go away and he told her not to worry.

'Shit,' he quoted quietly to himself. 'I feel so terrible. Why me?'

She returned, heard the sentiment, tutted at him, and then gave him a full smile. She helped him to the car.

'Prudence,' he said. 'Perhaps I shouldn't mention this, and I probably wouldn't if I didn't feel so awfully buggered up, but you look *much* better when you do the half smile—you know, so only the ends of your teeth show. They're too big for the full thing.'

Her eyes grew quickly bigger and he thought she was going to give him her fist, but she changed her mind, said nothing and pushed him into the car. He fell asleep as soon as he had the support of the seat, and he did not awake until she and the manager of his hotel, encouraging each other in German, were dragging him up the winding stairs to his room.

The manager got him a cup of black coffee and Prudence carefully emptied a jug of cold water down the open neck of his shirt. At the front. It went down like a double icicle, freezing his chest, running over his belly, and cutting uncomfortably down each groin. That partially woke him up. He began to get out of his wet clothes.

'Let me help,' she said, quite urgently, and began stripping him. He let her do it, like a lad lets his mother undress him for the bath.

'Kick,' she said, as she pulled on the wet ends of his trousers. Dutifully he kicked and felt the legs pulled away from him. She was kneeling in front of him and he was looking down at her with doped eyes. She took her hands and full span just encircled his calf muscle.

'My, my,' she muttered, looking up with full eyes and half smile. 'What have we got here?'

'It's a leg,' he said simply. 'Look. I've got another, just the same. They prevent my bum scraping along the ground.'

Prudence, without a fumble, undid her jacket and then the front of her dress. It fell away from her like curtains.

'I like you,' she said with clear understatement. 'I like you because you're worth looking at, and all sorts of things, and yet you haven't got an idea what's going on around you. You're so innocent, Brunel.'

'Thank you,' he mumbled. Even as he was he could appreciate her magnificence. Under the dress, shapes and shadows, he could see her body. It was like looking into a boiling cauldron.

'What are you going to do?' he said. She did not answer but threw her dress away. He stood up and put his arms about her, his forearms flat against her, his hands a cradle under her backside.

'I had a man friend once,' she said in his ear, 'and he had an arm blown off in the war. Once I said to him "Darling, when I'm in your arm ...!"'

Brunel began to laugh and his body, which had been still, moved against hers with the laughing. He felt as though he was being deluged by a warm waterfall. She took one set of fingers away from his thick thigh and expertly hooked them in the loop of the mattress at their side. She pulled it fiercely, completely away from the bed, moving it around the backs of her knees as a matador moves his cape.

'What's that for?' inquired Brunel. He thought perhaps she preferred the mattress on the floor because she knew the bed would creak.

But she lay instead easily, luxuriously, now naked across the diamond-shaped, wire springs of the bare bed.

She called him with her splendid hands, her eyes and her smile both half closed.

'Come, Brunel,' she said. 'It is better on the hard springs. It is more *urwüchsig*. More primitive, more basic, you understand. *Everything* is felt.'

'Christ,' he muttered. He put his right knee on the iron frame of the bed, brought his other knee up and inched forward like an apprentice fakir. The wire pressed into his flesh and he leaned to take some of the weight on his hands. She watched him, her lashes just touching as though she peeped under a blind. Brunel advanced as he would have progressed through a minefield. Eventually he reached the island that was her. He hesitated.

'I'm thirteen stone,' he informed. 'It will hurt.'

'Hurt on, darling,' she said. 'But come aboard gently.'

Brunel did.

'Happy now?' she asked.

'Very,' admitted Brunel. 'Those springs were hurting my knees.'

Strangely the bed did not creak at all. After a long time, when they were quiet again, she said: 'You don't find many of these iron bedsteads now. The interior-sprung mattress has taken the excitement out of sex.'

'You've taken the excitement out of me,' he said.

'Not yet,' she said. 'Again, Brunel?'

'Oh no,' said Brunel. 'I'm dead. What with the concoctions Keenor dreams up, and the concoctions you dream up . . .'

'Again,' she said. 'Once.'

'Prudence,' he said desperately, 'I can't. I'm stunned, finished, done, kaput.'

'Once,' she promised, 'and I'll tell you something.'

'What?'

'Orange Wednesday,' she said. Her eyes were closed

and her body very still, fixed into the wire springs.

'You'll tell me? What it is?'

'I will,' she said.

'Tell me first,' said Brunel suddenly revived and strong. 'Then I promise.'

'Promise?'

'Yes, Prudence.'

She lifted her head a little. It was dark, with just the putty light of dawn coming through the small window. Her eyes half opened to slivers and he could see how much alive they were and she was. He felt her breathe.

'Orange Wednesday,' she said, 'is the code name ... the code name for the signing of the peace treaty. For the Re-unification of Germany. I'll tell you more some other time.'

Ten minutes later, when Brunel was just precipitating into his deserved oblivion, the bed in the next room began to creak.

'Darling,' said Brunel hardly able to get the word out. 'Do something.'

'What, darling?' Prudence asked.

'Bang on the wall, darling.'

5

The girl in the cake shop smiled at Brunel when she gave him his curly creamed bun. She had missed him and she was glad he was back. Brunel only half-smiled in return. He was not only preoccupied with the things that were happening to him, that unwanted intrigue and undesirable adventure seemed to be sprouting like warts on his hitherto clear face; but he was concerned about Fulsbad, which he liked; about its quiet people, about Otto and Hilde, and the Snellhorts and the girl in the cream cake shop. What was to become of them when the Keenor cohorts moved in? He did not, of course, he told himself, really believe that Keenor would use the inhabitants, even the older folks, nor the most rheumaticky of the visitors, for target practice. Not physically anyway. But he would do so in other ways. Wait until Keenor discovered, and Brunel was most certain that Keenor would discover, that Brunel's best friend and conversational companion was Otto, a Nazi. It would be of no use explaining that Otto's uniform had shrunk to comedy, or that he had only posted the S.S. mail anyway. Anyone thus involved in anything the least bit disturbing would have Security Risk stamped on their forehead and would have to be eliminated from Fulsbad before the peace treaty was signed. There would be a hard rooting out. Keenor would not allow any risks.

As he slowed up the stairs of the Medicinal Baths,

watching a tongue of cream on the cake trying to climb over the edge of the pastry, he wondered why he thought of the whole Orange Wednesday business as though it were completely in the hands of Keenor. After all the treaty wasn't between Keenor and the Rest of the World. It was between politicians and leaders and generals, wasn't it? Keenor was merely there to see that the floor was swept.

From habit he drew his hot water cocktail from the fountain and the neolithic lady attendant smiled at him in a wide mouth manner that stopped just short of a silent scream. It occurred to him, as he went up the stairs towards his Moribund Docs. Department, that something might have happened to the place while he had been away. He opened the door with a small anxiety on him, but apart from the collapse of a shelf at the far end, one that had been sagging for some weeks, there was nothing wrong. Jackson, like a pillow of fur, was limp on the desk, although he opened a splinter of eye for a second when Brunel entered.

'Sleep on, sweet puss,' said Brunel giving the cat's fur a soft tug. 'There won't be much peace around here soon. They're signing a peace treaty.' He went on his habitual brief amble around the shelves. 'We'll have a liver and port session this afternoon,' he promised the cat.

He was wondering whether to eat the cream cake or shave while the medicinal water was still hot, when the telephone sounded. This was an event so unique that the cat jumped from sleep and fled from the room. Brunel could never recall anyone ringing him before and it was some moments before he could remember where the phone was located. He eventually went to the end of the files, raised a pile of mouldy casualty lists, and picked up the receiver. It was old and coated with a cold damp feeling. It was like picking up a long buried femur.

'Yes,' he muttered carefully like someone expecting trouble.

'Brunel,' she said. 'This is Prudence.'

'Oh, Prudence.'

'What's the matter?' she asked.

'Nothing,' he said. 'It's just this phone. It hasn't been used for years and it's rotting.'

'That's what you'll be doing. Keenor's on his way up there now.'

'Keenor?' jumped Brunel. 'Coming here?'

'He's here in Fulsbad,' she said. 'I am also. At the Golf Hotel. He's just left.'

'God. Thanks, Prudence.'

'Not at all. I'll keep you posted. If you keep me posted.'

'On what? . . . Oh, yes. I see.'

'I've had them take the bed out of my room,' she said coyly. 'Box mattress. They've brought in an old, old bed which the manager's mother had. Iron. Very old. Some of the springs are rusty.'

He put the phone down and looked wildly around in some stupid hope of putting things right before Keenor got there. He straightened one shelf of R.A.S.C. transport indents and immediately realised that the neglect of years could not be atoned in minutes.

'Outside,' he ordered himself. 'Get outside.'

Keenor was coming up the steps to the Baths, stamping a little stamp on each one, black hair stuck down, expression unpleasant in the eyes framed by the metal spectacles. Brunel thought what a wonderful Nazi he would have made.

'Let's go and have The Treatment, Brunel boy,' said Keenor, sniffing at the building. 'And we can talk. I want to have a look at this place.'

'The Treatment?' said Brunel. 'The Baths?'

'Sure. Familiarise-wise. I want to know everything that's going on in this town. That's the way I work.'

Brunel had never been into the baths. 'They're brutes in there,' he protested. 'The masseurs. Ex-Auschwitz, I swear. Bang, bang. Thump, thump. They knock hell out of you.'

Keenor spread his nasty personal smile. 'Maybe we'll recruit some of them,' he said. 'We could do with some strong men in this organisation.'

In the entrance hall the lady gave them each a drink of hot water cocktail and this time Brunel had to drink his. It tasted like soup made of nothing, but Keenor downed his as though it were vodka and was already making for the steamy interior by the time Brunel had sipped his away.

Keenor looked less impressive with his clothes off. He had a hanging paunch, oval, and stiff with hairs like the bottom half of a coconut. His white chest, oddly smooth and free from hair, fell away as it ascended towards his stony jowl. His legs were hairless too, but, as he turned towards the initial damp door Brunel could see that the hirsuite band about his lower trunk continued around his backside, as though he were wearing a muff.

They went first into a big bath, a warm, expansive pool, where floated German businessmen, like icebergs, nine-tenths beneath the surface, their large heads close to the side rail. Some talked, some read newspapers, keeping them skillfully half an inch from becoming waterlogged, and some merely stared across the platform of brilliant green water that lapped half an inch from their noses.

At one end there was room for two and Brunel followed Keenor into the blanketing bath, hung his hands over the rail behind his head and let his body off its leash, let it float tranquil as a fish, just below the surface. He thought that Keenor might have chosen this moment to reveal to him the purpose of Orange Wednesday, but then realised that this was the last place, for voices travel well over water.

Every now and then Keenor's hairy lower stomach crawled from the water, like a hog. He said: 'Now I *like* you, Brunel. I really *like* you.'

Brunel waited. 'But,' said Keenor, just as Brunel knew he would. 'But you've got to revolutionise your attitude, your thinking about this concept.' He pursed his lips as though such a statement had to be followed by a long suck of a cigar, and he didn't have a cigar.

Brunel brought his lips above the water. 'It would be easier and better,' he said and then added 'sir' nicely, 'if I knew what the concept is. Then I could er ... you know ... revolutionise my attitude to it.'

Keenor blew some phantom smoke across the surface. The German heads going away from them in straight rows, bobbed easily like buoys. 'Well, son,' he said, 'I'd tell you right how, but I can't because the sound of my voice travels across water too easily and these lousy krauts will hear everything I am saying. But I'll tell you later. You've got to know sometime.'

One of the Germans a few positions away began to leave the water. He did not look towards them, so Brunel thought he might have been going to leave anyway. He was a slim, well-constructed man of middle age, his arms stringy with sinew. He levered himself up on to the rail, threw one leg up on to the tiled side, and followed this with half a leg. It was taken off not very cleanly at the knee. Brunel realised he went to the bath to make his old wound feel easier.

'You *feel* too much,' said Keenor, not noticing. 'For

instance, I get the idea that you *feel* too much about this place, this town.'

'Well, I *do*,' admitted Brunel, wondering how Keenor knew.

'You don't have to worry, son. Nobody's going to hurt it. There won't be any nerve gas.'

Brunel realised this had come from Findlayson. He would remember in future. Two of the floating Germans looked up briefly, one from his newspaper which gained a rim of wet along its edge as he did so. The German looked annoyed as though he had contravened the rules. Keenor saw them at once and seemed equally annoyed. He lowered his tone.

'You mustn't get too much of . . . too much of a stupid feeling about any place, or anybody when you're in this,' he continued. 'Know the location, but don't fall for it. It's like laying a woman.'

He did not seem inclined to pursue the train for a while. Two Germans at the far end climbed out of the bath, the first of them had thick, Nordic hair, hanging low over his eyes with the wet of the water. He turned and helped his neighbour who was struggling, trying to get out of the water with the leverage of one arm and a primitive stump like the place where a branch has been torn roughly from a tree. The second German got from the bath and to his knees on the tiles, then to his feet. He formally shook hands with the first man, and performed a minor bow—a strange action with his infirmity, then went out. The first man returned to the water.

'Aw, I've been in places,' Keenor jolted on again. 'Places and places and places. But I don't *love* them. Any of them. I don't love this crummy country, and I don't love this crummy town, nor this crummy bath. You know, this place to me is just like Vietnam, like

Saigon. It's a place for a job and nothing after that. You must be the same, Brunel boy.'

Brunel reflected quietly on how much he hated Keenor. I could drown this uncouth bastard right now, he thought. Now he's naked and in this big deep bath. One way would be to reach down and grab hold of the American's cock and pull him under with that. That was a commando trick he had read about, although presumably it could only be perpetrated on enemies who were naked or had, at least, their trousers down in the water. But the victim could not escape. Like a barracuda you pulled him under and hung on to him until he was finished.

Instead of doing this Brunel said: 'I've never been in Saigon.'

'Great place,' said Keenor. 'Great place to leave behind. Like your ass.' Brunel watched two Germans, with two left legs only between them, climb and crawl from the bath. The end of their limb stumps were purple and red, gutted by frostbite and shell splinters. This was the morning, Brunel thought, when they all came to get comfort from the aches of non-legs and phantom arms, when old holes and craters in bodies were soothed by the thermal water. He glanced from head to head, wondering what twenty-five year old nightmare each was concealing and ministering to under the silky water. The German nearest to Brunel's left rose to the surface like a spitting whale, and his chest was revealed, a model Stalingrad in itself, pitted and gashed with old wounds, and having something of the cold deadness of the Russian front in its bruised blue and white texture.

'Saigon,' muttered Keenor. 'Jee—se. They have a bar in Saigon, Brunel, where they have a big round stone. Real big and real round. Like that guy's head across the water there.'

Brunel looked sideways at Keenor's crudity. He was blowing the water away from his lips as he smoked his imaginary cigar again.

'That stone,' he went on, 'was just the darnedest thing you could see in Saigon, son. Real round, like a ball. If you could stand on it for three minutes without tipping, then the place was yours. Drinks on the house and any girl in the place.'

'Which one did you have?' asked Brunel. A man with no arms and re-cast legs had just left the bath, and he was wondering whether the German head opposite, the head Keenor had talked about, had any body attached to it at all.

'You *guessed*,' said Keenor without dislike. He was apparently oblivious of the infirmities of his fellow bathers. 'And you guessed *right*. I stood on that lousy stone for three whole minutes. I could have done even more. But that was enough. What a night we had! Nobody had done it before, only a couple of niggers at different times.

'Well the guys went crazy. And they carried me on their shoulders so I could look over the slope-heads in the place and pick out a girl. And there was this one ... this parti-ic-ular one. Sweet as a grape. Little and sweet as a grape. Little tits just like grapes too.'

'Did you try treading?' asked Brunel.

Keenor said: 'Oh she was just sweet, this slope-head kid. And she was mine, because I was the guy who balanced on the stone, see? I went to her place and I had me a night, I can tell you. I had me a night, and after I had me a dose too. Yep, together we chose gonorrhoea.'

Easily Keenor began to paddle himself away from their mooring, and, still on his back, his feet thrust out in front, facing forwards, his eyes cruising just above the water line, he made for the far end of the bath where it was shallow. Brunel followed like a barge in tow.

Keenor had difficulty in getting from the bath even at the thin end. Brunel got out and watched his efforts, but did not attempt to help him. Eventually Keenor landed and flopped about on his stomach like a walrus for a moment, before finding his legs and standing up. He was looking at Brunel keenly, but he said nothing about Brunel standing there and letting him slide on his belly.

They walked towards the deep steam room, and then, when they had broiled, to the other sections, hot and cold.

At one point they came to a still warm pool, which an attendant said was only in use at private sessions during the day, where a wooden chair, like a medieval ducking stool, stood out over the water.

'Gee,' enthused Keenor. 'That's cute. How does it work?'

Brunel put the question to the attendant, who explained the stool.

Brunel said to Keenor: 'People with certain troubles in their arms and legs and suchlike go for treatment there. They're strapped into the chair and it goes down slowly into the warm water and it's supposed to do something for their aches. After a while they haul them out again.'

'Cute,' said Keenor again. They went to the massage room and lay on the tables while the hands there worked them over. Brunel did not enjoy it, but he got some satisfaction from seeing Keenor being thudded. Keenor turned his sweating face towards Brunel and grunted between blows. 'Did you—huh—notice—huh—something kinda odd about those krauts in the floating bath? Huh —did you? Why—huh—those guys can float like that for hours, Brunel—huh—boy, without—huh—moving their arms or legs.'

When Keenor had gone Brunel waited for half an hour then walked down to see Otto. He went sadly, very alone, as one would walk when visiting friends and knowing privately that the world was going to end at midnight.

Somehow the streets seemed all the more charming, the town a pattern of sun and cornered shadows like a fragile mosaic. The little turrets on some of the houses stood out with miniature bravery against the sky and the windows were clean and honest along the uneven pavement. There were nodding people and the children brightly playing with a wooden ball against a new Mercedes parked in the cobbled square. Beautiful, thought Brunel. Beautiful and quietly breathing the breath of seventy years ago. If Queen Victoria and the German Emperor were to appear on the steps of the Kurhaus then, Brunel imagined, the only reaction of the Fulsbad people would be to raise a respectful cheer, with possibly a little clicking of heels.

He felt very unsure and isolated in his knowledge that Fulsbad, this Rheumatics Capital of Europe, would soon be spoiled, hauled brutally into the distasteful boil of world politics, poked at and investigated by Keenor and his band. Versailles had never been the same after 1919. It was as though a chaste old maid had shockingly lost her virginity.

He wondered where Keenor would procure his willing women in Fulsbad. Unless Prudence was willing to expand her activities generally, Brunel could not imagine where the sexual entertainment, apparently an appendix to such affairs, could be obtained. Diversions in the gentle spa traditionally meant the casino, the scraping of the string quintet in the afternoon tea-time, or the modest and modish dancing of waltzes in the municipal night-club. An elderly visitor, it was said, his ear to the quintet and munching cream cake, had once, absently dreaming perhaps of good but olden times, put his hand up the skirt of one of the waitresses, and that she had allowed it to rest at the top of her stockings for some time before moving on to another table.

When Brunel reached Otto's cafe, Hilde was putting glasses of light orange tea in front of an American couple, two fawn piles of middle-aged tourism hunched outside on the thin chairs. Hilde was wearing a red dress that Brunel thought was too short for her. She placed the tea in front of the customers, and then turned to see Brunel. 'Oh, Brunel, you have come back. I am sixteen next month.' She said it quietly but in one long breath.

'Well done,' said Brunel discouragingly. 'Keep it up. Where is your father?'

She squeezed her face from the inside. A tail of pale hair fell down across her small nose and she carefully took it away again. 'He is mad,' she said firmly. 'Gone all mad. Worms in the mind, I tell you.'

At that moment Otto's unmistakable fat white fingers crawled around the door. One of them detached itself from the bunch and curled upwards in an invitation to Brunel. Brunel went into the cafe, and then saw that the finger had retreated to the door of the back room where Otto kept his S.S. uniform. The finger was still alternatively straightening and curling at him. He followed through the door, into the normal dim vision of the back room, and there found his friend dressed in a cowboy suit.

'Very nice,' said Brunel.

'It is good?' Otto beamed.

'A splendid fit,' commented Brunel. 'Better than the S.S. rigout.'

Otto looked at him as at one who has accidentally fallen upon the answer to an ancient mystery. 'Nein,' he croaked, 'you must not say foolish things like this.' He scuttled to the door, pushed his fingers around the side, and followed them with a sole frightened eye. He did not return to Brunel until he was sure that there were no enemies outside.

'It is empty,' said Otto.

'It always is,' Brunel pointed out. 'The day you've got customers inside this place is the day the de-nazification people have caught up with you.'

'God forbid,' muttered Otto as though crossing himself.

Brunel stepped back one pace and surveyed his fat friend. Otto was wearing a bright blue and white check shirt, a neckerchief incorporating a yellow star, low-slung six guns, and fringed breeches. He caught Otto's plaintive look, seeking approval and understanding.

'Well,' said Brunel after his inspection. 'As I said, it is very nice. It really is. Apart from the yellow star. I don't think that's very wise for you. They'll think you are a Jewish cowboy.'

'God forbid,' said Otto a second time. 'I will get another star today. I would not like the others to notice it.'

'There are others?'

'Many others,' confirmed Otto. 'We are the Cowboy Club of Fulsbad.'

'Spendid,' said Brunel. 'That's a real gun?'

Otto struck an offended attitude. 'But of course. We are not *kinder* playing at boom-booms. It is real and loaded, my friend.'

'Good for you,' remarked Brunel. 'What's the object of this Fulsbad Cowboy Club?'

Otto simpered fatly. 'There are Cowboy Clubs in many places, Brunel. In Munich there is a big club, and in Paris. Cowboy Clubs are for studying, you understand, the things of the Wild West. We study the stories and the firearms and the dress, and we ride the horses through the forests.'

'The cowboys rode across the prairies,' Brunel said.

'A difficulty,' admitted Otto. 'We have no prairies, so we take to the forest. We would like to ride across the golf course. It is very open, but they will not allow it.'

'Otto,' said Brunel quietly. 'What's the idea?'

'My friend . . . ?'

'Come on,' said Brunel suddenly angry. 'You and your pals haven't become all Buffalo Bills for nothing. Perhaps the cowboy clothes are more acceptable outside than the old shiny boots, eh?'

Otto looked at the floor and ran his fat fingers over his gun butt. 'We thought perhaps we might even wear the shiny boots. After all cowboys sometimes wore them, not just the S.S. . . . '

Brunel regarded him coldly. 'You silly old German sod,' he said quietly. 'You stupid old, fat kraut. What are you?'

'A stupid old, fat kraut,' repeated Otto. 'I have never seen you so angry like this.'

'Look,' said Brunel sitting the old man down on a kitchen chair and pulling up another chair to face him. 'Get that stuff off and tell your mates to get it off too. This is the wrong time for this sort of caper. Understand? Tell that bunch of retarded old Hitlerites to stop it and stop it now. I can tell you Otto that somebody will clean you up. And it won't be the bloody Sioux either.'

Brunel stood up and went to the door. Otto pouted then got up, twirled his chair around, back to front and sat on it again, defiantly, saddle fashion.

'It is above ground,' he grunted. 'All the town knows about it. They have seen us.'

There was still no one in the inner cafe, although Brunel would not have been surprised to see Keenor sitting there. He returned to his seat, looked coldly at Otto's equestrian posture and said: 'It's above ground, is it? That's more than you will be.' He looked closely into the old man's face. Otto looked as if he were going to cry.

Brunel said: 'Otto, I don't care what happened twenty five years ago. I really don't. I don't care about Adolf Hitler or Goering or any of the other people. I don't even care about Churchill. They're gone. It's gone. It's only words in books now. Anyway, all you did was post the bloody letters, why don't you tell the truth?'

'I was in the S.S.,' affirmed Otto quietly. 'I have the uniform.'

'I've seen it.'

'The only hope for our country,' said Otto, 'is to be one again. East and West. Somebody must care. I am one of the somebody.'

'Somebodies,' corrected Brunel. 'Listen, the young Jews these days don't spend *all* their living hours thinking about a gap six million wide in their lot.'

'An exaggeration,' said Otto.

'All right. So you say they miscounted. But the Jews don't keep crying. Not the young ones anyway. They've got *life* now. There's no time for death. Death's too bloody old.'

'They ruined this country and we ruined them,' said

Otto philosophically. 'But at least they have a complete homeland. We have not.'

'Hard luck,' said Brunel. 'Let's have a look at your gun.'

'You return it?' checked Otto suspiciously.

Brunel assured him: 'You'll get it back. I just want to see.'

Like someone pulling out a stubborn plug Otto hauled the gun from its holster and gave it to Brunel. He then shuffled back from the chair until he was clear of it and turned it around and sat on it the correct way.

'The chair,' he explained, 'was hurting my balls.'

'They don't make saddles like they used to,' commented Brunel. He was looking at the gun, a heavy imitation Colt, poorly made, with bad balance, and a hesitant mechanism. He spun the chamber and it stuck. He handed it back to Otto who looked at him anxiously for a verdict.

'Great little weapon,' said Brunel. 'For shooting your own army. You'd shoot more of the enemy if you joined them.'

Otto clouded with unhappiness. 'How many have you got in this cowboy club?' asked Brunel.

'Seven, sometimes eight, but Herman Golink cannot always attend because of his wife. We hope to get more. Perhaps eleven very soon with the men we have in mind.'

'Get into a football league,' said Brunel. 'There would be more point to it.'

Otto flushed in odd blotches on his big face. 'There *is* point,' he muttered. '*Much* point.'

Brunel leaned towards him. 'Friend,' he said, 'I've told you I don't care. I don't care about wars, past, present or future. All that sort of thing I threw out a long time ago. But I care about you, Otto, and I care about your little girl outside. Now be a good kraut and take that stuff off, and leave it off until I tell you it is safe to wear it. Otherwise something nasty is going to happen.'

He left it at that, turning and walking from the dim inner room. Hilde was coming through the street door with a tray holding the drained tea glasses of the American couple who, Brunel could see, were preparing to shuffle away for some more tourism.

She nodded towards the other room. Her eyes rolled in young disgust. 'You saw him, Brunel? Like Trigger.'

'Trigger's a horse,' Brunel told her.

'It is not important,' she contradicted. 'Is he not crazy? First the Nazi party and the Lost Territories, and now this Wild West. Sometimes I think perhaps we will not make a living from this place.'

Brunel took her arm and she reacted immediately he touched it. Her glance made him release her quickly.

'Put the tray down,' he said. 'We must go somewhere to talk.'

'To talk?'

'Yes, about the Lone Ranger in there. He's going to get himself into trouble.'

'Trouble?' she argued. 'Nonsense. It is crazy, but it is no harm.'

'Let's have our talk,' he said turning her towards the door. They went out into the fine sunlight of the September afternoon. It was a month which suited Fulsbad, a gentle yet regal month that gave a hazy, indistinct beauty to the town, that lent a quieter green to the lawns about its buildings, and the forest all around was crowded and clouded with autumn. The small river ran reflectively and there were very few people about.

'The Cowboy Club and the Nazi thing are one and the same,' began Brunel. They were walking close to the river and she had taken his arm. She had been watching an obese fish among the shadowy stones in the river, following its indolent movements.

'Not good,' she answered without looking at him.

'You don't know how much not good,' muttered Brunel mimicking. He thought now that he had said too much. But she did not pursue the thread, seeming to sense that he could not tell her more. They went under the lindens, orderly and beautiful in German array, left small clear islands with their feet in the leaves on the paths and finally went into the Kurhaus, where it was stuffy and smelled of sweet cream cakes and old ladies. The string quintet were varying Bach with Mahler: four thin men and an especially thin one, long and stringy as string quintet players should be.

'It is nice.' She smiled her pleasure as they found cushioned chairs and a small table. 'I have never been here.'

'Why is that? You are so near.'

'We are in the business too,' she shrugged. 'It would not be good to take trade to other places. We have no music, of course, and the chairs are soft here.'

'But you've got the wild west show,' pointed out Brunel. 'Now listen.' He leaned towards her and put his hard fingers about her wrist. 'You must see that he stops this nonsense now, right away. There is a *special* reason.'

She grinned beautifully at his fingers. 'No passion in here, please,' she admonished. 'I am a young girl and all the old men and old ladies are staring at you. They think you are dirty.'

Brunel screwed a guilty glance about him and saw the pattern of faces. Cobwebbed widows had paused with custard creams and black forests half way to their dying mouths, and there was a strong light like memory in the remaining eye of an old man at the next table. Brunel took his fingers away.

'How was it when you were away, Brunel?' she asked. He thought she was purposely leading the subject off her father.

'Great,' he said. He let his voice drop. 'Went sightseeing down a street where they sell wicked women in the shops, and I went to an orgy. Nothing special.'

'They are playing a slow little waltz now,' she said looking up at the violins. 'Shall we dance?'

Brunel was startled. 'You can't dance in here,' he said.

'There is a dancing floor,' she replied. 'There, see.' She pointed. 'I think they would like to see someone dance. It must be many years.'

'For God's sake, no!' protested Brunel. But she was already on her feet and moving with grace between the tables as though already dancing, trailing her thin hand behind to call him on. Blindly Brunel rose and moved after her. The soft mushing of cakes and the sipping of tea was arrested, even the music faltered. But by this time she was at the edge of the circular dance area, turning and smiling encouragement to him. He arrived next to her, closed his eyes and rubbed his teeth together in exasperation. But when he had completed the demonstration she was still waiting, and had given a lovely smile to the musicians, who were now smiling back like charming old waxworks. They played their very best for the dancers because it is much better to play for two people in each others arms than for a hundred filling their mouths with pastry. They played a light, lilting minuet, so easy to follow. And Brunel danced with Hilde.

'My God,' he stuttered. 'You'll have us both in front of a firing squad.'

'We will dance for them, so they won't shoot us,' she sweetly replied. 'It is better for us to do this, anyway, because out here we are alone. The head waiter is another of my father's cowboys. He was close and listening to us at the table.'

'Oh no,' said Brunel miserably, missing his step. She smiled while he corrected himself, then danced on. 'Be careful,' she warned. 'You will disappoint the musicians.'

'Your father,' he said with force, 'will be in trouble, danger if you like, if he doesn't forget he's a Nazi for the next few weeks. Understand that Hilde. Stop him doing anything to draw attention to himself, and especially stop him wearing those ridiculous togs.'

'I will try,' she promised. 'But it will be difficult to stop him. His new horse is coming today.'

They danced on, one pair on the floor, with the minuet spun out by the happy musicians, and watched by all the other people. An elderly man who returned to Fulsbad each year for renovation, watched them and felt romance welling within himself. He put his hand to the top of a waitress's stocking and she let it remain there for some time before moving on to another table.

6

The Golf Hof, as Keenor insisted on calling it, was built on a stubby plateau just above the first tee of the Fulsbad course. The eighteenth green was on the other side of the hotel, a full, beautiful kidney of fine short grass, and above this was the tabled terrace and swimming pool.

The Duke of Windsor had played there and Eisenhower, and other notables, coming in smiling with their scores because the course was slyly constructed to please people. It looked hard, but it wasn't, only at the famous sixth hole where Brunel's predecessor had done his suicide. The tourist, marvelling at his score, went back the next day and played again. The hazards were still as obvious, but he returned again with another good score, and feeling that his holiday was giving him much benefit.

Around the course the forest grew like a shaggy beard. In the summer it was green and fine, rising in hills, and touched at intervals with white, shapely castles, very small castles, each one childlike and enchanting. Hunting lodges were lodged up in the greenery too, but you would not see them from the course. Golf was played from April until the end of November when the snow arrived. To extend the season they had tried playing with red golf balls against the white sheeted background but it was not the same.

A group of men in gingery tweeds was standing in

the foyer of the Golf Hotel when Brunel went there to meet Keenor. Their thick clothing was unsuited to late summer, even at that cooling altitude. It was new too, not shaggy nor shapeless.

For a moment Brunel, through his glasses, thought they might be newly recruited forest rangers doing their basic training, then one spoke to him roughly and he realised it was Keenor.

Brunel halted and examined the stout ginger figure, then looked at the others and saw they were the same men who had taken part in the Hamburg orgy. There was Findlayson, and the other Britisher, thin and unpleasant, and the two Russians, standing so close they were either in love or were afraid of each other. The second American was missing, and had been replaced by a dark, sour man. Brunel decided that as a group he did not care for them at all, and scarcely felt any better about them as individuals. But he was surer of himself than he had been in Hamburg. He was playing at home now. They looked ridiculous in the tweeds anyway, standing in their melancholy semi-circle like monks about to pull the bells.

'We've got the guns in the estate-wagon outside,' said Keenor looking around professionally to make sure they were alone. 'So let's go, Brunel boy, and you can show us around.'

They trooped to a blue station-wagon standing in the forecourt, climbing in and arranging themselves around. Findlayson got into the driver's seat. Squatting down, Keenor looked at Brunel and said: 'Providing there's no ears on those trees up there we'll tell you all about it today.' He stopped to think and then, having reconsidered added: 'Well, not quite all, but enough for you.'

'Thank you,' said Brunel. Keenor squinted at each face. His ugliness, Brunel thought, was spoiled by the toffee tweeds he wore, and he had now become grotesque.

'You've seen most of these gentlemen before,' said Keenor to Brunel. 'But we'll do the round again because last time you passed out on us and you may not remember the names. It's important that you know everyone well. Because you're the errand boy.'

'Couldn't I be something else?' asked Brunel. 'Like the liaison officer. It would be the same job, wiping the toilet seats and that sort of service, but it's a nicer name.'

Keenor considered him with dislike. 'The toilet seats idea is not a bad one,' he said. 'Maybe we'll incorporate that in your everyday duties. This is Colonel Sergei Traveski and Major Andre Gorin of the Soviet Army. This is Major Jean Lestrange, who has been a special bodyguard of General de Gaulle during some difficult times. You know your very own Major Findlayson, I guess, and this other gentleman is Captain Verney Smith.'

Smith, Brunel thought, looked like a stoat that had died in a trap. His face was impoverished, thin, so narrow that there seemed hardly enough space for his eyes. The eyes were white, uncommitted and, at Keenor's introduction he bared his small teeth rather than smiled. Findlayson too had hardened in Keenor's company. Brunel could hardly imagine that this was the major he had seen in his underpants. He was driving the station wagon, taking it seriously up the wandering hill road to the roots of the forest, and he turned only briefly to look at Brunel. The face was like half set cement.

The Russians were as morose as they had been at the flat in Hamburg. Brunel realised that this was only to be expected. If they had appeared so unhappy during their recreation period they were hardly likely to be leaking with joy now. The one with the Josef moustache, it seemed, had let if grow further down his face. His huge cow eyes dwelt on Brunel for a moment and Brunel looked away with genuine fear that the Russian might burst into weeping.

Lestrange, the new man, the Frenchman, must have grown ill guarding de Gaulle. He had the complexion of the south but not the tan, and his eyes were like prunes. Given a few days sunshine he would probably have browned and looked sleek and quite fine, but he had the sort of skin that goes dead when it has been away from the sun too long. And it had. His thin hands were Oriental yellow and at some period, possibly during his service to de Gaulle, he had lost a middle finger.

Taken as a group, all in, honestly, without any hard prejudice, Brunel thought they were the most likely bunch of shitehawks he had ever witnessed.

'It's lovely to meet you all again,' he said.

They halted the car at all the places and clearings in the forest that gave a wide green view of the golf course, far below, and especially the hotel and its terrace. The sun was amber and stronger now, but up there it was cool in the trees, and pleasant out of them. At every platform of logs, at every picnic spot, at each hunting lodge, Findlayson stopped the car and they all lumbered or slithered out, depending on their physique, and attacked the lovely landscape with huge field glasses.

Brunel felt out of it. He stood aimlessly, shifting around, screwing his eyes through the lens of his spectacles trying to see what they were seeing. They rammed the field glasses against their faces as though they were drinking from them; grunted and swept them about with strange mechanical unison like a robot ballet.

'Brunel boy,' said Keenor eventually without taking

the glasses from his eyes. 'What's the distance between that clump of bushes and those guys farting around the little flag on the green blob down there?'

'I don't know.' answered Brunel reasonably. 'I can't see beyond the squirrel sitting on that branch over there.'

Rudely Keenor looked up, thrust his field glasses at Brunel, and grunted. He pointed down the chute of the valley. 'Down there,' he said, 'where those guys ...'

' ... are farting around the little flag,' completed Brunel. He got the correct focus and curled the glasses around, so that the greens and the browns flew across his vision and he was finally looking down on the group of golfers putting out on the fourteenth green. He could even see the ball, bright white and beautiful against the vivid green, rolling well from ten feet and dropping into the hole.

'Good putt,' commented Brunel.

'Good what?' said Keenor leaning towards him.

'That's the fourteenth,' replied Brunel. He swung the glasses again to where the small cloud of bushes sheltered the tee. 'A drive and a six iron.'

'Don't give me this ping-pong crap.' exclaimed Keenor. 'How far? So we can all understand.'

'Three hundred and forty yards,' answered Brunel, returning the glasses.

'Let's have answers like that in future,' grunted Keenor. He turned to the group. 'Right, let's move on.'

Findlayson drove on, the road becoming more primitive, squeezing its way between the slim trees and the fat rocks. At the extreme end of the valley, looking down the green length of the golf course, to the confused grey of Fulsbad, deep beyond in the distance, was one of the toy castles. It stood quietly among the trees, its little turret rimmed with battlements like strong teeth against the steady blue sky. The sun splashed against its creamy walls and its windows were slim and climbing to a mild point like good fingers.

'Nobody at home,' said Keenor obviously as the party grouped and stared up at the building.

'Not for fifty years,' informed Brunel. 'It's draughty. The tourist board keeps this and the others in reasonable repair, because they look attractive.'

A farmyard of grunts came from the group as they continued to stare up, as though expecting an archer or pikeman to appear on the battlements.

'They were week-end hunting lodges in the old days,' said Brunel determined to do the job. 'All sorts of things went on.'

'Like what?' asked Keenor. He had lit a cigar and he jutted his face so close to Brunel that he could feel the heat from its burning.

'Oh you know,' answered Brunel. 'Hunt the slipper. Beat your neighbour out of doors.'

Keenor, undecided, glared at him. 'Well they left this door open,' was all he said. 'Let's see.' He strode purposefully towards the arched door then turned. 'It's not dangerous, is it?' he asked. 'It won't fall on us, or anything, will it? We've got work to do.'

Brunel said 'Bollocks,' under his breath and led the way into the tiny castle.

Brunel went first and they followed him clumsily up the coiled stairs until they emerged at the platform behind the battlements. The huge green of the world fell away beneath them and then rolled like an estuary far out to where the small town lay in the distance. It hit Brunel in the face and he smiled to see the tuneful serenity of it. Keenor stood at his side, and eventually the others, when they had navigated the narrow entrance to the platform, and they all grunted.

'Brunel boy,' said Keenor with more softness, as though

the sheer wonder of it had even affected him. 'Something really big, really *big*, is going to happen in this dear little arseholing place. You must have been wondering what all this is about.' So far none of the others, not even Findlayson nor Smith, had said anything to Brunel or to each other.

'It did cross my mind,' lied Brunel. 'I've thought out all the possibilities, and nothing has come up. You *must* tell me, Mr. Keenor.'

Keenor said lazily: 'Let's get those weapons up and have a little target practice. I'd like to know our capability in that direction. Also, it would be interesting to see what the terrace of the hotel looks like through telescopic sights.' He glanced at Brunel to judge how the torment was having effect. Brunel obliged. 'Telescopic sights!' he almost shouted. 'You're not going to assassinate the wine waiter?'

Annoyance blotched Keenor's grey face. 'Knock it off, Brunel,' he said doing his habitual jerk-away. 'I can only take so much from you. We've got a job on here and we're not having any weak links.'

'You were going to tell me what it was,' Brunel pointed out.

'Get the guns,' said Keenor.

Brunel went down and brought back two rifles, one with telescopic sights and two pistols from the station-wagon. He handed the rifles to Findlayson through the narrow door at the top of the stairs, stepped out on to the platform and waited.

Taking the weapon with the telescope sitting on it, Keenor brought it up and turned it in a minor arc that Brunel guessed would cover the exposed terrace of the hotel about three hundred yards away. He lowered the rifle and put it against the moulding battlements, then picked up the other, an F.N.139, with a special recoil action, and a flash eliminator. As if on cue a deer, a dappled doe about a year old, wandered from the trees about a hundred yards to the left of the tower and padded across the grass in a wide pond of sunshine. Keenor gave an excited, muffled whinny and brought the rifle to his meaty shoulder.

Brunel stepped to his ear. 'Shoot and they'll get you,' he said icily.

Keenor's shoulders gave a jump of annoyance. 'Who'll get me?' he rasped, his right eye curling around towards Brunel although he still held the rifle steady.

'The forest rangers,' whispered Brunel. 'They count them.'

'So they count them.'

'One dead doe and all your plans here are a dead duck. They'll start asking who did it. Who you are. They'll find out.'

The spout of the rifle still greedily followed the deer, and Keenor's eye had gone back along the sight. Brunel thought he was going to shoot, but then he faltered and dropped the weapon forward.

His eyes seemed to have gone red as he looked at Brunel, but all he said, in a low mumble, was: 'Okay—target practice.'

No one moved for a few moments, but Keenor appeared to have them co-ordinated almost to a degree where spoken words were left unused. He inclined his fat head towards first Lestrange, and then Gorin, and they stepped forward to the old battlements. The Frenchman picked up the F.N.139 with a touch of flamboyance that Brunel was relieved to see. He had not, after all, submerged everything. Lestrange took the rifle and felt its texture and its balance as though it were a violin.

'Oui,' he murmured. 'Oui.' It was the first syllable Brunel had heard him speak.

'Take the three baby trees,' said Keenor nodding over the parapet. 'Left first, then right, then the middle.'

They were scarcely trees, slight and early without leaves, in a group like people at a picnic, at the foot of the dropping slope into which the men were now peering. There was a barrier of brown rock behind them, which is why Keenor had made the choice; it made them safer for target practice but it did not make them any easier to see.

Brunel screwed his eyes at them. His glasses were good. He could see much further than he would want any of the present company to know.

The marksmen would be shooting down at a sheer elevation. Lestrange brought the rifle up and simultaneously Keenor began talking to Brunel in a loud voice.

'*Well, Brunel boy,*' he shouted as though throwing his voice against a high wind, 'you're the last to know, but I'm going to tell you now.' The Frenchman, the rifle flat at his cheek, checked himself. Keenor said: 'Carry on, Lestrange. Don't let me stop you. Left, right, then middle. Okay? *Well, Brunel,* you're going to see some history made here, son. Real history. Nothing less than the re-unification of the two halves of Germany.' He stared at Brunel, then added, lower and confidingly, 'Which, you may know, have been separated since the Allied Victory in 1945.'

Bang! Lestrange let the first one go. Keenor didn't look, nor pause in his verbal stride. '*You can guess* that all the groundwork for this has been going on for a long, long time. It's been hard and kinda delicate, but our four countries have really got together this time, Brunel boy, and they are going to sign that paper. Right here . . .'

Bang! The Frenchman hardly moved with the recoil

of the powerful rifle. ' . . . in Fulsbad. This place has been chosen, Brunel, because . . .'

Bang! He let the middle one go more quickly. Brunel guessed it was too quickly. 'How many?' asked Keenor. 'Deux. Two,' shrugged Lestrange. 'Out of three,' said Keenor. 'Thirty-three and one third per cent failure.'

Brunel lifted himself slightly on his toes to see the three thin trees. Lestrange had taken a bite from the left hand sapling, hardly more than a nick, but white like a wound and clearly to be seen. The right one remained untouched, but the third bullet had lopped a foot or more from the head of the middle tree.

Looking unhappy, Lestrange handed the rifle to Gorin, who waddled to the parapet and set himself squarely like a man trying to hold a door up against a mob.

'Fulsbad,' continued Keenor loudly directing his voice towards Gorin, 'has been chosen because this thing must be done in secret. The Powers have decided that . . .'

Bang! Bang! Bang! Gorin streamed the three shots off like a man hammering in a nail. Keenor's eyes narrowed and he strode immediately to the battlements to look at the trees. 'Lousy,' said Keenor. 'One little nick. Give it to Findlayson.'

Gorin looked rueful and picked his nose. The rifle was handed over. Keenor returned to Brunel. 'Jeeze,' breathed Keenor quietly. 'Why are we making peace with them if that's how they shoot? Don't hurry it, Findlayson. Let's have some results, for God's sake.

'I like talking to you, Brunel,' said Keenor with sudden affection. 'These other guys, I don't seem to have nothing to say to them. Maybe you and me have got more in common. Let's get back to . . .'

Bang! ' . . . the treaty. The Big People have decided that the world mustn't know what a favour they're doing it. Nobody in the world, outside just a few of us, will know that the re-unification has been ratified until it's all over. *There's too many ...*' He had his eye on Findlayson.

Bang! ' ... outside interests. People who want the thing to be done, and those that don't. *There's plenty of ...*'

Bang! ' ... both, Brunel. How did you do, Findlayson?'

'Wasp in my eye on the last round, dammit,' said Findlayson wiping his left eye. 'Took a bit more off the middle tree though.'

'Late for wasps,' retorted Keenor. 'Maybe it was a hawk or a vulture. Anyway we're not woodchopping, we're shooting at targets. One-third failure again. I thought we had a good group here. Okay, Sergei, Comrade, you take it, and you then, Smith. There's plenty of wood left for everybody ...

'They thought they might sign the paper in some place like Berlin, but it's too hot, too fond of boiling over. There it would be too emotional. You know what I mean. Those people crowd people. They cheered Kennedy and they cheered your royal Queen, they cheered de Gaulle. They'd cheer Minnie Mouse. They just like hollering, *and getting emotional ...*'

Bang! Sergei had taken his time. 'So Berlin was out. Also out were all the other places like that. Other reasons too. They couldn't do it in Hamburg because the Bavarians would say it ought to be done in Munich. They couldn't do it in Munich because the Hamburg krauts would cry. So they've picked here. *It's quiet ...*'

Bang! Sergei had a good one and grunted. He was encouraged and did not hold the third shot long. Bang! He straightened up. 'Tre,' he grinned like a crack in the piece of wood.

Keenor leaned over and glared at the trees. 'Well done,

Defender of Stalingrad,' he said. 'If we need any trees shooting down we'll send for you. Give it to Smith.' Keenor caught Smith's pale eye. 'Captain Verney Smith,' he added with an exaggerated bow.

'It's quiet . . .'

Bang. Bang. Bang. 'Three,' said Smith straightening up. He handed the rifle to Keenor, who gave it to Brunel to reload. Keenor examined the trees through his field glasses as though he didn't trust Smith's word.

'Right, Brunel boy. To the firing step,' he said lowering the binoculars. Brunel sent the first round into the breech. It was an elegant rifle, just warmed from its immediate use. It had a firm feel, companionable, and a whiff of smoky smell came from it. He stepped to the battlements and saw what was left of the saplings. They stuck from the ground like a wicket for a rustic cricket match, their height halved, merging brown with the background of rock.

He brought the soft weapon to his shoulder and it snuggled there like a young brown lover. His cheek squashed against its wood. His eye went along the track from the backsight to the front, and down then, searching for the slender line of the left-hand tree, finding it and bisecting it with the nib of the sight. He turned his hands outwards to put an extra vice on the rifle. He took the first easy pressure of the trigger.

'*They guessed that nobody will ever crowd on this place at this time of year*,' shouted Keenor in his ear. 'So they picked it . . .'

Bang! Brunel felt the weapon spit the bullet out and saw the left-hand sapling divide at its centre as though someone invisible had cleft it with a blade.

He retrieved the bolt and pushed the second round into its hole. The same again . . . steady . . . sights . . . steady

... breathing regulated, not stopped ... take first pressure ...

'*So*,' yelled Keenor in his ear, 'that's what the plan is. Nobody will know until the treaty is signed and the Big People have *cleared out of* ...'

Bang! Brunel was pleased with that one. It went from the muzzle as though it knew where it must go, flying on with eight inches of the right hand tree travelling with it, and gouging out a saucer of soft rock from the wall behind.

' ... Fulsbad,' continued Keenor. He paused frowning at Brunel taking his time to re-load, sliding the bullet sweetly to its place of business. The rifle came back to his cheek again, familiar and warm.

'*At the Golf Hof*,' shouted Keenor. 'That's where the *signing* will *be*. And we are responsible. *Responsible*!'

Bang! Brunel wasn't going to budge now. This was a vicious one. It caught the middle sapling and grooved it like a nasty hungry animal, sending bark and splinters spitting out, and opening the small tree like the burst end of a comic cigar.

'Nearly missed that time,' commented Brunel giving the rifle to Keenor.

'Load it up, son,' said Keenor handing it back.

'We haven't left you much, Mr. Keenor,' said Brunel maliciously looking from the tower to the three split fingers protruding pleadingly from the hillside grass.

'It's enough, I guess,' said Keenor. He took the rifle from Brunel and gave it a whirl as though performing some minor but intricate drill movement. The men were all close to him now, watching his preparation and glancing doubtfully, hopefully, at the three skinny targets. Keenor set himelf up, shifted his feet, then shifted again, but was finally still and ready.

'Why is it *called Orange Wednesday?*' howled Brunel,

his nose almost inside Keenor's ear. He sensed the others stiffen, but Keenor did not move.

'Because,' rasped Keenor from the stock of the rifle. Bang! The left hand stump vanished. 'Because it was decided that each week from September onwards would have a colour, Brunel.' He moved the bolt back and in again almost sexually. 'Black, white, red, yellow and so on. Under this nomenclature, Brunel, the second week in November has . . .'

Bang! Brunel, Gorin, Traveski, Smith, Lestrange and Findlayson, went forward together from the hips like men with a gale at their backs. Seven pairs of eyes saw that the second stump had now gone. Brunel caught a movement high to the left and saw three squirrels going through the trees like monkeys.

' . . . got the designation *Orange*. Wednesday of that week . . .'

Bang! They just jerked up and peeped this time. The grass was short and uninterrupted as though the saplings had never been.

' . . . is the day when the actual signing will take place.'

He handed the rifle without comment to Brunel who mouthed something like 'nice shooting' but it didn't quite get out. 'We are here,' continued Keenor making for the hole that led to the stairs, 'to cover the area thoroughly and to anticipate any mishaps. But we are just the advance guard, the work party, Brunel boy, the delegations will have their own security people with them.'

'Oh,' said Brunel. 'There's more.'

'Sure,' confirmed Keenor putting the rifles in the rear of the station-wagon. 'A lot more.'

They completed their tour around the saucer of the golf course, examining every vantage point and its aspect of the hotel and the terrace, before finally taking the road that dipped into the town.

Brunel began to indicate that they could drop him off in the main square, but Keenor said: 'I've got a small task for you, Brunel. Just a couple of hours using your priceless local knowledge. I'll tell you when we get there.'

They reached the Golf Hotel again, having driven a full ragged circle that day, and Keenor held Brunel back in the lounge for a moment while the others, apparently having had orders, marched away glumly.

'I like you, Brunel,' said Keenor as though re-inforcing his previous reference. 'You are doing a great job just now. And don't forget, son, it's history being made here.'

He glanced up as though he hoped that this would have made some glow come to Brunel, but it had not. Keenor shrugged like a despondent missionary. He sighed. 'Okay, Brunel. I want you to get together with Prudence, you know, my secretary ...'

Keenor looked at Brunel steadily and Brunel just as steadily admitted that he remembered who she was. ' ... Get together,' continued Keenor. 'I want the full name, or title, and personal details of all the leading citizens in this town. Anyone in the public eye at all. Local politicians, busybodies, doctors, troublemakers, the managers of all the hotels, and places like the baths and the casino. The police, fire and especially the ambulance guys. Everyone you can think of, Brunel, who we might need, or need to check on, in any circumstance. Anyone who ever gets their name in the newspaper down here. If ever I want to find any of them, I don't want to have to go through the directories. Understand?'

'Yes,' nodded Brunel.

Keenor made towards the main staircase. 'I'll send Prudence down,' he yawned. 'She'll show you how to do things.'

No one could have said Prudence had come-to-bed eyes. They were been-to-bed eyes, shaded underneath, glistening too much in the pupils, too wet in the whites, and the skin beneath them a little sore and salty. Brunel had waited in the hotel lounge, watching an old man, thin as a stork, putting golf balls along the carpet from a wheel chair. He had six golf balls and when he had putted them all, with crafty accuracy, around the base of a potted fern, a hotel servant would come along, pick up the balls, and place them beside the old man's wheel chair again.

Brunel sat watching him swing the putter poetically – leaning forward so the thin club projected from near his nose, like a slim beak—and admired his consistency. Once, when the invalid had dispatched all six balls to the fern, no hotel employee appeared and the wheeled golfer just hunched there malevolently staring at the distant white company, apparently demanding that they return of their own small wills. Because he couldn't stand the suspense, Brunel got from his chair, after a minute and a half, gathered the balls, and shepherded them with the side of his foot, back to the old man. Nothing was said and Brunel tip-toed away while the balls were smoothed back to the pot. He felt glad the old man wasn't using a driver.

From the reception desk there came a nod and Brunel went over. A telephone was placed in his hand, and Prudence's voice said: 'Hello, Brunel. Keenor's given us some work to do.'

'He said you were coming down,' said Brunel. 'I haven't had any lunch.'

'We'll work better up here,' she said. 'Come on up. It's two hundred and one.'

'I'm hungry,' he said firmly. 'We've been miles overland this morning playing at bang-bangs.'

'I've sent down to the town,' she yawned. 'Ten minutes ago. To the Graf Zeppelin Hot Dog Bar. Half a dozen, with onions and ketchup.'

He went up to her room. Knocking once he opened the door and she was there laid out on the bare springs.

'It will smell,' said Brunel.

'What will?' asked Prudence.

'Hamburgers and onions. For God's sake this is a five star hotel. Bring stinking stuff ...'

'Rubbish,' she said getting up from the bed. She was naked and she turned away from him and walked over to the dressing table. Her back was a pattern of red weals, triangles transferred by the bedsprings. They faded at the valley of the small of her back, but rejoined redder and deeper at the big of it, in the flesh of her buttocks. Brunel screwed up his face.

'The place reeks of wintergreen and rheumatic liniments anyway,' she said. 'Nobody is going to notice a few onions.'

He closed the door behind him. Her body was very full, pink with appetite in places. He had frequently half-thought, half-dreamed, about the hour before dawn in Hamburg. She saw in the mirror of the dressing table what he had done to the door and she turned and leaned back on the glass top shelf so that it cut across her backside. She smiled her big smile which was much too big, but her pimples didn't show so much today. Brunel took his gaze off her and went to the window. It overlooked a russet copse and then the sweeping green of the eighteenth fairway. It was middle afternoon and the sun hung low giving the forest, beyond the golf course, a look of gentle fire.

'Have you been practising?' he asked.

'I don't need to practise,' she said.

'Oh, of course,' he agreed still looking from the window. 'It's just that your back is like some sort of wallpaper, where the springs have been digging in. I mean, you don't lie and sleep on them like that all the time, do you?'

He turned and she shrugged, then smiled. 'There's been no one else here,' she assured him. 'If that's what you mean. I was just stripped down and relaxing.

'Like they do in India,' suggested Brunel. 'On those beds of nails things.'

'I hadn't thought of that,' she answered as though it had given her an idea. 'No, I was, you understand, getting the bed warm for us.'

She was truly magnificently made. He took his time regarding her, letting his eyes and his now unresisting mind take in all her body while she stood still against the dressing table with the glass shelf continuing hard against the small fat of her lower mounds. The expression on her everyday gorgeous face, doll-like, looking like every sugary stereotyped lovely he had ever seen on the screen or in a magazine, nothing differently beautiful about it; the expression now was apprehension. It was as though she were very hungry and was afraid the food was going to be taken back to the kitchen. Her eyes were too round the blue, her hair too set and framing her face too well, and her lips too full and red.

'You're like a tutti frutti,' said Brunel cruelly. 'All lush.'

All lush, he thought for she did not answer but continued looking at him, and rich colours. She had full cream skin, except in the pink places, and her large breasts were indolent, sleepy, heavy, their nipples dull like closed eyes. Beneath them were deep shadows like black half moons, and her stomach was firm, not hard but firm like a good pillow is firm. In the crease of it her navel gave a half-smile, and then her trunk sharpened like a smooth spinning top, jutting down between the rounds of her legs, its apparent point caught and sunk in her small pubic garden. She had splendid legs; a tape measure would have confirmed their inched perfection, and a touch of the fingers would tell of their texture.

Brunel walked to her now and pushed the backs of his knuckles to touch the swelling of her left thigh. It was, as he expected, comfortably warm.

'Prudence,' he said looking at her face very near to him. 'You've got one huge fault. You're so perfect it's boring.' He touched her naked leg again. 'You're even the right temperature.'

'I'm just a lovely big girl,' she said kissing him on the chin, but not hard against him otherwise, just resting on him. 'And lovable.'

'That's the knock,' he admitted. 'Big, lovely and lovable. My God, why couldn't you have one eye or something, or a hanging backside, or skinny legs. Thank heavens for your teeth and that racehorse smile. It's a let-out anyway. But even that only shows up all the rest.'

'You're hard to please, Brunel,' she pouted. 'shall I grow a hunched back?' She pushed her long hand down the front of his trousers, like someone posting a letter. His hands went to her waist and travelled up under her armpits, his thumbs then extending and reaching to her lazy nipples. Then there came a double knock at the door.

'Graf Zeppelin Hot Dogs,' Brunel reminded her. 'Shall I get them?'

'No,' she said gently pushing him back towards the wire bedsprings. 'I'll go. We don't want Keenor to know we're working in here.'

Casually Brunel sat on the raw springs, leapt a little, and quietly transferred himself to an ample quilted bedside chair. He was out of view of the door.

Prudence wrapped a green robe about her like a satin pod and opened the door. Brunel experienced a moment of thin panic as it occurred to him that it could be Keenor in the passage.

But someone out there spoke in *sotto* German and Prudence's hands went out and returned full of Graf Zeppelin hot dogs, conserved in greaseproof paper and tin foil pot. She pushed the door with her painted toes and turned into the room, the robe now fallen open to show a steep chasm of body, bearing the unwrapped feast before her.

Brunel, at her suggestion, took his clothes off because of the excess of tomato ketchup which she thought might stain his shirt. She sat on the floor at his broad, naked knee while he reclined in the quilted chair, and they shared the sausages, dipping them into the pot and festooning them with hot brown onions and dribbling ketchup. Brunel was hungry after his morning in the open air, but Prudence munched with her mind on something else. His eyes were with his food anticipating the avalanching of the red sauce and the slivers of onion and catching them before they got away. But one onion slice, hot slippery and nicely browned, climbed around the back of the sausage he was attacking and dropped spitefully on to the fat of Prudence's left breast.

'Sorry,' said Brunel. 'Was it hot?'

She gave him a friendly look from his knee-level. 'Don't waste food,' she said. 'There are starving millions in the world.' Somehow she twitched an obviously well-trained muscle which raised the lump of the breast invitingly towards him. He knew then that he was all lost. It was like a brass band starting to play Souza down in his loins, thumping away giving him excitement and power. He bent towards her and picked up the segment of onion with his teeth.

'And the ketchup,' she muttered. 'It's very tasty.' He fell forward at that point and she rolled back on to the carpet, a steaming hot dog trapped somewhere between the flesh of their bodies. Brunel jerked out a childish yelp but she squashed the sausage with one crushing blow from her stomach, extinguishing it like someone desperately dousing a flame.

There was no making love *to* her. *With* her, yes. It was an experience that varied between a cross-country run and a storm at sea. At times they jogged beautifully through the splendid motions like people enjoying good fresh air and exercise. Then, at her instigation, although she was the lower partner, they would be caught and consumed by a thrashing fury; a fury that threw him and folded him, and stood him upright, kicked him in the soul, chucking him until he was sick and suffocating with the immense sensation, and the hot dog was pitifully decimated between them.

He had never realised that love was *so* physical. With this Prudence there would never be moments of quiet walking hand in hand, listening to birdsong, sharing food and drink, reading to each other and hot chocolate at bedtime. Nothing of that sort of love. All she wanted was screwing.

She blew up so violently, at one intermediate stage, that he had to fix her back on the carpet with all the strength in his broad fingers. Even then she wriggled briskly, until finally subsiding and looking up at him with her voluminous empty eyes. He had caught her in the vee-shapes between his thumbs and first fingers, pinning her wrists down and holding her still with the weight of his body.

'This *is* good, Brunel,' she said shifting dreamily. 'Where did you learn this one?'

'Boy Scouts,' panted Brunel. 'They get a cleft stick to keep a snake from lashing about, you know.'

'I am a snake, now?'

'Sort of. Why don't you go easily, darling?'

She closed her eyes. 'I would like to, truly I would. But I am like a fat girl with chocolates.'

'You're not fat and that's not walnut centre,' he replied.

'I will go slow, darling Brunel. Like a funeral for you.'

They began to ride in rhythm then, gently until it was like perpetual motion, each movement begetting the next, throwing it out so that it went oiled and easy, and provoked yet another. Her body was so accommodating that he did not miss the bed, even his knees were without discomfort, padded by the small cushions of flesh just above her knees. It was fine for a while, but then the tumult began again and this time he could not stop her bolting. Or himself.

'How do you feel, dear Brunel?' she mouthed close to his resting ear. His heavy head was across the bolster of her breasts, his body had slipped half-sideways from her. He moved his head but did not talk.

'How do you feel?' she repeated teasingly. 'Like a Boy Scout with a snake?'

He stirred. 'Like a man at the bottom of the sea,' he confessed. Then, after an interval, he added formally: 'And I have no further statement to make.'

They lay piled on the floor for some while. Brunel got the impression that outside it was getting dark and chilly. The room was contracting in shadows, so that it seemed to be creeping away towards the window.

'I read that someone had perfected a completely spherical jig-saw puzzle,' murmured Brunel his nose in her warm navel his lips brushing her pelvis with every word. 'Each piece had depth as well as ordinary flat shape, and they all sort of crunched together to make the whole thing. I feel just like one of those pieces fitted into you like this. Tell me some more about Orange Wednesday, Prudence.'

'We have not been on the bed,' she said with a sulk in her voice.

'Je—sus,' he breathed widening the holy syllables. 'I couldn't go through that wire torture now, honestly. It makes my knees so bloody sore.'

'One day,' she sighed like a pure young girl talking of pure young dreams, 'I am going to have a big room with a heavy beam over the bed.'

'What for?' he asked suspiciously.

'Some special thing,' she replied seriously. 'A special way which I have called in German "*Blokundtackel-unterhandlunder*".' She stopped him before he could voice his incredulity. 'It is as it sounds,' she said firmly giving the impression that she had to get a secret awful vice from her conscience.

Brunel repeated uncertainly: '*Blokundtackel-unter-handlunder*.'

'It means a block-and-tackle fixed to the wooden beam and rope and a harness for the man ...'

Brunel felt his face draining. 'For the man ...?'

'That is right,' she answered half turning away and looking at the ceiling as though examining it for strength. 'For the man. The harness goes around his middle and the rope through the block and tackle in the ceiling, and then ... and then ... I can give it a pull when I feel like it because I will be lying beneath with the rope in my hands.'

'My God, you're so ... unusual,' said Brunel inadequately.

'It would be nice,' she asserted. 'Very different and interesting.'

'Well forget me,' he said firmly, sitting up now and facing her. 'I'm not doing any fairy ballet for you. The man would look ridiculous.'

'Exactly,' she sighed. 'Shall I get a blanket to cover us on this floor as it is getting grey and cold? It would be black and warm under the blanket.'

He looked at her. How could she look so simple and be so complicated. 'Yes,' he said. 'Get the blanket. It *is* a bit parky.'

She reached for the blanket and covered them so that they grew comfortable and hot-breathed in the fug of it. Then they made love again, without frills, and she was very good and kept passive throughout.

'It's a shame you look so perfect, Prudence,' mumbled Brunel when they rested. 'Because you really are quite marvellous.'

Keenor walked into the room ten minutes later without knocking, looked around in the dusk, and walked out again without seeing them under the blanket on the far side of the bed. But by that time they were both asleep.

7

A dainty line ran from Brunel's big toe, through his
window, and into the infant river Agoos. It was a long
time since he had been able to fish. He was wandering
into sleep on his counterpane, with the window open
and the yellow October day very still outside. It was
almost like far times, he thought, before he had ever
heard of Orange Wednesday, or seen Keenor's hairy
belly, or felt the energy of Prudence.

'You,' he told himself, waking briefly, 'can now be
called "the Man From the Pru".' He grunted with dis-
satisfaction, and wondered if he would capture a trout
that afternoon. Frau Snellhort had promised to prepare
it for tea if he could quietly hook one from the
river.

'How many more are there?' he asked himself. A
legion, he answered honestly. Keenor there must be, and
the thought disgusted him; and the man with one arm
to whom she had said 'When I'm in your arm . . .' What
a wayward girl. All the Men from the Pru there must
be wandering now in bad repair throughout the world.
Prudence might not mean anything to any of them, but
they would never forget her nor experience the like of
her again. Some may have attained true domestic love
since then, Brunel thought idyllically, but because you
have found a nice pussy you would still never forget
that you had once been savaged by a lioness.

Even in her girlhood days, Prudence had told him, and he reflected on it now, she had felt the pressure. 'I had a good young boyfriend,' she had sighed. 'But every time he went away I always immediately looked for someone else, and always found them.'

'And he went away frequently?' Brunel had muttered in semi-interest. 'He travelled about?'

'Oh no,' she had whispered. 'He lived in the next street. I saw him every night. It was when he left me, when he turned the corner to go home, that was when I was hungry again, and I looked for someone else.'

Brunel was, however, far from sorry that he had experienced her. It was as though she had uncorked some plugged-up part of him that had badly needed unblocking. He had always, he now realised, had a guilt complex about women which he thought might have been provoked by the surpliced choirboys kicking his balls in on the gravestone so many years ago. He couldn't see why, but he thought that might have been part of the reason. And there was another part. One afternoon, when he was twenty, he had been sitting on a pebbled beach overlooking the murky sea of the Bristol Channel, sitting and watching the birds and ships moving across his view. He was on a lone cycling holiday, having come down from the Midlands to this shaded coast, and had spoken to no one for days. He was happily alone, stirring the old pebbles with his cycling shoe, and thought that perhaps he was the only human being on the beach. It was September and the summer had already gone.

Then he had heard minor voices coming from a depression in the pebbles and realised that a group of children were there. They were quite small, two boys and three girls, and Brunel had watched them run in bathing costumes down to the fringe of the sea, howling their voices against the brisk wind, flinging spray up with their toes, and running skillfully along the pebbles and the short sandy places.

They played with fresh energy for some time, then one of the little boys fell over, into the shallow water and one of the girls fell too in trying to pick him up. Brunel was halfway to his feet to run to them when he saw they were laughing in the cold water and in no need of assistance. But the girl who had fallen saw him begin to get up and stopped and looked at him. Then the children went back to their hollow and Brunel could hear them squeaking in Welsh voices as they dried themselves.

Brunel had all but forgotten them, squatting on the pebbles and wondering where he should make for next on his bicycle. Then, like a small fairy in a pantomime, the little girl who had fallen in the sea, appeared at his elbow. She had webbed hair and a splinter face and her arms and legs were thin too and red with the cold. She had dressed herself in a flowered dress of cotton and a little red cardigan that hardly fitted. Brunel stared at her.

'Mister,' she said in a high Welsh voice. 'I can't put my knickers on. I keep getting them the wrong way around.'

Brunel nearly fainted as she produced a pair of grubby pea-green knickers from behind her tiny back and held them out to him.

'Will you do it, mister?' she asked plaintively.

'Oh ... oh ... oh,' cried Brunel, grabbing at the pebbles to try to pull himself to his feet. 'Oh ... oh.'

He scrambled up as though an army of death-bearing creatures had just left the sea, and leapt away, and ran puffing up the beach in gigantic confusion The pebbles flew away beneath him and he stumbled to his knees twice, struggled up again, but eventually reached the road at the top of the beach. He lunged over the cross-bar of his bicycle, hurting his crutch on the nose of the saddle. Then he briefly looked back and saw the small girl, green garment in red hand, standing gaping at him, and her friends in the hollow wonderfully speechless at the spectacle of his flight. He touched the pedals and away he went, from that awful place, and pedalled hard until he had reached the Severn and was out of Wales forever.

Colonel Sergei Traveski was investigating the inside of his best boots. He did so cautiously, with soft fingers, because the boots had been placed outside the door for cleaning during the night, and you could never be sure what might be in them in the morning.

He remembered well a fellow officer pulling on his boots in a hotel room in Minsk and with the very action of tightening the laces on his right boot, firing a small toe-cap bomb which exploded and killed him. It was not a good sight, Sergei had decided at the time, to see a man who has been killed from the bottom upwards. When something like a toe-cap bomb goes off the force flies up like a volcano, blowing the front of the legs away and opening the base of the guts so that a quantity of them fall out. Sergei had watched the officer very conscientiously from a distance when he had tightened the laces because he knew what was about to happen. He had fixed the bomb.

So you could never be sure that someone had not thought it time that you were eliminated from the bottom. He always felt in his boots. Not that Major Gorin would be sympathetic to having to do any such action, but orders were irrevocably orders.

Gorin, if his assessment was right, however, was far too bovine, too Georgian for such subtleties. From him it would probably be a knife in the night.

'Gorin, Andre my friend,' Sergei said heavily. 'I think this American is a clown.'

'He is the sort who does not encourage trust betwen peoples of different nations,' agreed Gorin. 'I have not known anyone so discourteous since my drill sergeant at Stalingrad.'

'Volgagrad,' corrected Sergei.

'Volgagrad,' agreed Andre. 'But it was Stalingrad when I was there. And my drill instructor.'

'Now Volgagrad,' insisted Sergei. 'And he was like this Mister Keenor?'

'Indeed, Sergei. He could shoot a gun and, as the expression is, shoot his mouth, but that was all.'

'Perhaps it is as well Keenor is a clown. We do not want such people to be too clever. It is a shame, however, that he has not yet been able to fix us with some larger women. There are many in Germany.'

'There is time,' comforted Andre.

'Perhaps time tonight at the Casino.'

'The Casino. How do we explain that on the expenses dockets?'

Sergei flipped a superior Colonel's glance towards Andre, the Major. 'I have orders,' he said smugly, 'to report to an agent who will be at the Casino tonight. He will be at Table Number Four, always backing fifty marks a time on thirty-three.'

Gorin said : 'I have never been to a Casino. I have heard that they are very warm places, with thick carpet and chandeliers and the little wheels ticking around, and capitalist men and their beautiful women, richly gowned, and perhaps some of them fat. I think you can touch them near the tables.'

'We are going on the state's business,' reminded Sergei. 'Perhaps we will have some minutes for seeing the sights, perhaps not. We go there for orders. Remember much is to happen in this coffin of a town within the next few weeks.'

Gorin said: 'It is a pleasure, Colonel Sergei Traveski, to have worked and co-operated with you on this task. I have admired long your rise in honour and the esteem of the Kremlin people, and to see your methods now, and to know your friendship means a lot to a poor Georgian. I mean it sincerely, Comrade.'

Sergei rose, stretched himself on his toes and bowed theatrically. 'You say words that delight, dear Andre,' he smiled. 'I am glad that so much friendship and mutual trust has grown between us in this short time. Tell me, why is it you are feeling in your boot?'

Lestrange was playing at shooting Germans. They would always remain something of a novelty for him, perhaps because he had never seen one before he was twenty-one. Even now, after years away from L'A PEROUSE, he retained the childhood image of each German head topped with pointed brass.

He straddled a carefully placed chair, facing the pleasant, lace-curtained window of his room, overlooking the hotel terrace. He had a fat pistol and a slim rifle for his game, but they were not loaded because he could not trust himself. The pistol was for playing at close killing on the terrace, the rifle for targets more distant, away on the eighteenth fairway of the golf course. It was a good room and he was more than pleased with the window because as the groups of two or four innocent golfers came at the inherently slow pace of their game, up the long fairway, he was presented with a constantly changing choice of target, in a pretty variety of colours, at gradually decreasing distances. The Germans on the terrace were too close to be much fun, so he aimed for different parts of the anatomy with his pistol. Since returning to his window that sunny day he had eliminated three ears, pierced two jugular veins, entered the brain from eight different angles and shot off several complete sets of testicles.

He took up the rifle now. The rear sight always pleased him on this one. It was almost mystically in the shape of a cross contained in a circle. He had seen it held in stone in many churchyards. There was one on Lucille's grave on Ile St. Martin.

There were four golfers now dotted at the end of the green reel of fairway. Two in red sweaters, one in yellow, one in green. He lined up one of the reds. The other red would follow at a short interval, then the yellow at three hundred yards and the green at two hundred or perhaps two hundred and fifty yards. The only good thing about pretending to kill people was that the others did not run away. He was a choice marksman in sunlight, good in any light. He had deliberately failed to get top marks at Keenor's little shoot that day. The three shots had been released too quickly. He suspected that Keenor knew.

Most people thought, as Brunel had, that Lestrange came from the Mediterranean. His parents were from Vence, certainly, but he had been born after they had begun exile on St. Martin, in the Pacific, for some fringe political intrigue. La Perouse, the island's capital, a hot town, was his place of birth.

In 1940 Lestrange was seventeen and making a pig of himself with his first real lover at La Perouse. In those days, he remembered now, he was quite handsome inheriting his father's oily arrogance and tanned by the beach at his hometown. He spent a lot of time on the beach, never doing work for very long, but playing volleyball, swimming, going out in a big catamaran, and taking young girls out in the catamaran.

They were always young. Sometimes very young, even though he was only seventeen. The catamaran was not a sophisticated sailing vessel in those days—that came after—but the boat, which belonged to a hardworking friend of his father's, was beautifully strong. It was a twenty-five footer, its twin hulls shaped from native wood by the patient Melanesians, were exquisitely balanced, taking the longest rolling ocean with ease and confidence. The sail was tall and like a flexed muscle when the wind was in it; like a strong arm pointing at the aching blue sky. When they got into the wind beyond the shelter of the island then the catamaran would go like an unleashed horse, madly and gladly across the flying sea. Sometimes they would fish, fighting a whole day's battle with a shark, or screaming with joy as they battled with a leaping tuna. But sometimes that was too much like work and it was always hot. . . .

He had the first cherry red golfer flat against his sight now, covering the cross framework like a blot of blood. He took the pressure and squeezed the trigger and made a little sizzling noise with his pressed lips as he pantomimed the bullet flying on its way. The golfer walked on, bent to inspect a ball on the smooth fairway and took a wooden club from his bag.

... If Lestrange saw a young girl on the beach in those days, and she was from one of the French Colonial families who spent their vacations at La Perouse, and did not know him, he would ask her to take a trip on the catamaran with him. If she went she would be excited, out there, by the buffeting of the big seas, sometimes afraid, but he would always act the master and eventually bring the vessel around into a calm cove where they would rest and he would attempt to have sex with the girl. It worked for him a great many times, because the young girls were always so hot, breathless, and excited by the catamaran and the sea, and thrilled by the manly way Lestrange handled the strong boat. It was good to get them then and usually he found they wanted it because they were so shaken up inside themselves. But these he did not count as lovers, only incidents. ...

He was now in a position to kill the second red golfer, slightly to the right, making things more difficult and more enjoyable by being partly screened and shaded by a short aspen. The man was hitting his ball from the rough and Lestrange had only a third of his normal view of the target. He fired and killed the man just as he was making his stroke. The golfer clipped the ball well clear and walked to examine it sitting nicely in the centre of the safe grass.

... No, his first lover, that May of 1940, a half a world from France, was Lucille Benet, the wife of a middle official on the Governor's staff. She was thirty and almost every day he would see her walk bored to the beach, fling out a coloured towel and lie for a while in the sun. She never had anyone with her and at the same time each day she would go into the ocean and swim about for a while, letting the waves hit her, then get up and lie in the sun again. She made no sign that she had ever taken note of Lestrange, and he had never considered her for a trip on the catamaran because while there were young girls around he could not consider older women.

But one day, when he was straddled on the port hull of the boat, and she was swimming some distance away, she seemed to take a decision. sharply altered the course of her swim, and turned towards him.

'Will you take me for a voyage?' she said to him. She was holding on to the hull, her arms brown and freckled, and the tops of her breasts pushing just out of the water with tiny waves splashing in her top cleft. Her shoulders and her face were brown and there were a lot of freckles on her face too.

'It's fifty francs,' Lestrange said meanly . . . .

The yellow-sweatered golf man was clear and finely centred now. He was child's play for Lestrange, a bright yolk of an egg waiting to be spilled. Lestrange fired silently twice, hitting the man in the face with the first shot at two-seventy yards, and in the upper chest with the second as he kneeled forward on the ground. The golfer swung a flat wooden club so hard and well that Lestrange thought the ball was coming straight at him. He took fright and ducked behind the sill. But the ball was well short, curving down and holding to the edge of the eighteenth green by the terrace.

. . . 'It's fifty francs,' she had agreed. 'Perhaps the crew will be so polite as to help the passenger aboard.' He pulled her roughly out of the water, feeling hurt that he had bothered with her. When she was half-way aboard, and he was standing above her he could see the water from her spine scuttling down the crack in her backside, because her black swimsuit was very tight across there.

He tried some fishing that day and they hooked a big tuna and let it murder itself on the hook with sheer exhaustion before pulling it in. Lucille helped him heave the rubbery thing aboard, and her nails bit into the muscle at the top of Lestrange's arm while they struggled with its weight. He shrugged her off at first, but then she did it again, so after they had landed the fish he took the catamaran into the airless bay and they lay having the most profuse sex all the sunny, sticky afternoon.

She was like a love engineer, knowing every nut and bolt, cog and fly-wheel in his anatomy and hers. When she had their machinery working he imagined that even he, greedily hurried as he naturally was, could go on for ever. They were even co-ordinated with the slight movement of the sea beneath the boat. . . .

On the fairway the most difficult golfer was displayed for Lestrange, green against green it was true, but at two-thirty yards no problem. He lined up the rifle, only to be immediately disconcerted by the arrival in the sight of the yellow golfer. He lowered the weapon. The others were converging on the green golfer too, three killed men surrounding a living one, all bending down and gaping at his white ball. It was ridiculous to be baulked like this.

. . . Lucille was the first person he had ever killed. He did it after he had come to love her as only a young person can love an older one. In later years he always described it to himself as an unfortunate political accident.

He knew the matter so well that it sometimes went through his head like a film screened for the thousandth time, for his especial benefit, always the same details, but always somehow compelling him to sit through it until the end.

They were in the warm ocean and the war was then

a bad rumour from far away. Lestrange never looked at a newspaper and he sometimes laughed at unreal conversations about the war which he caught. He had never been to France, nor to anywhere outside the Ile St. Martin, so he had no picture of what terror might be happening there. He had never met a German. . . .

The shot golfers had now cleared from around his final target and he lifted the rifle. But the delay had spoiled the game for him. He realised how imitative, how impotent it was, like masturbating. He rested the rifle and watched instead. If he felt like it, he thought, he might finish the last one off with the pistol when they were putting on the grass.

. . . He had been making love to Lucille one morning, spread across the bottom boards of the catamaran drifting in the sheltered bay. She had patiently taught him not to conclude when he felt like it, but to breathe deeply and think of something else, something far away, at the big moment next to the really big one. In this way he could wait and she could wait too, stewing and simmering, before bringing it to the boil again.

Lestrange had experienced huge difficulty with this, not only because his had always been animal hurry, and the mechanics of this were so involved, but he could hardly ever find anything else to think about. He managed the deep breath very well, pushing his broad young chest into her hummocks, and lifting his flat wet stomach away from hers. But what to think about? How to take his mind away? He was interested in so little.

So Lucille would talk to him, steadying her dark-cupped eyes on his, as though daring him not to continue with the stoppage. She would converse about matters at the Governor's house, about her life, about the world. It was on one such breathless occasion, both half-drawn away from their union while both madly wanting to continue it, to finish it, that she spoke about the war. At first she whispered close to his sweating face: 'Don't. Be strong and patient. To finish now would be too bad, like committing suicide in the middle of a happy life.'

He liked to hear her talk because, unlike him, she was fluent with words and ideas. This time she said: 'The Boche have almost won in Europe. France is on her knees, you know.'

'That,' he had said coarsely, 'is my position too. Cannot we go on?'

She smiled a small, hard smile, because she was in control now. 'No. Wait awhile, infant,' she said. 'Let me tell you about the war. Breathe deeply now. Ah ... That is right. Now I will tell you. Soon France will surrender and a new government will be set up in an unoccupied sector. The Governor here and all of us will pledge our allegiance to the new government. We will do away with the British and the others.'

'Will that make any difference to us here in La Perouse?' he asked.

'None, my darling.'

'Can I continue now?'

'Please proceed.'

When she said that there was a close-up in the film rolling in his mind. The picture became very large and he saw her saying it very clearly. It was their final occasion.

When he next saw her it was during the brief fighting. The Governor had declared, as she said, for Laval and Pétain. Lestrange heard the mob and concluded that they were condoning, welcoming, the pact. He ran to join them, Frenchmen, Polynesians, Melanesias, all shouting and running, all going towards Government House.

Then he realised that they were calling the name of someone strange, a man, de Gaulle, calling it and waving burning brands and running through the streets towards the few soldiers at Government House. He went with them, suddenly afraid as though being caught on the scene of another's crime, but shouting 'de Gaulle. de Gaulle!' with them, and running under the fiery fists of the torches.

He saw Lucille being dragged from a small car outside the gates. Her husband was being killed by the mob on the other side of the car, and she was being torn from the door and stripped and beaten with wood and metal and hands.

He gaped down at her and her breasts, which his mouth had known so well, were pink with blood. She was wide awake still and she saw him and pointed at him and he knew she was going to scream: 'He is one of us too!' He could not allow that to happen because the crowd would have killed him, so he grabbed a stub of wood and struck her on the head with it before the words were formed. Her head went back as though he had broken a hinge in her neck and then all the men fell on top of her and he ran away. . . .

Up to the eighteenth green the four golfers progressed. The real recall of it all never failed to frighten Lestrange, if only a little, and he had no great interest in pretending to shoot the fourth golfer. So he spared him for some other day, struggled from the chair and went back into the shaded room. Yes, he had knocked her head back with a piece of wood, and so began his career as a devoted Gaullist.

There was no awful angush about it after all this time. He was forty-two now and, as he always told himself, you did many strange things in the days when you were young and foolish.

It was ironic that they should have sent Verney Smith to watch Findlayson. Findlayson thought so.

'Imagine them sending you of all people,' he said. He had said it before, mercilessly repeated, in the preceeding weeks. Smith's privately pale eyes had watered at the repetition of it.

'Yes, imagine,' he agreed. Findlayson was sitting on the stool of the dressing table in his hotel room, leaning back by some control of his muscles as comfortably as though he were relaxing in a heavy chair. He had taken his brown officer-issue boots off and his mildew coloured socks were on the top of the dressing table so that their unpleasant undersides were reflected in the mirror. Smith was sitting on the corner of the bed and Findlayson was looking at him in the mirror.

'I mean it's bloody ludicrous, when you think of it,' continued Findlayson. 'Me, twenty years of blameless, not to say gallant, military service, and you, old boy, the biggest crook who ever had the nerve to put the Queen's uniform trousers on his arse.'

'Nobody knows that,' said Smith, his expression unaltered, his eyes still clouded. 'Only you and I.'

'Yes, but I mean,' chortled Findlayson. 'Sending *you* to watch *me*. I mean, what a fucking cheek, old lad. You who, I know but nobody else knows, put a few thousand quid in his back pocket over that war surplus deal in Alexandria before we cleared out. I didn't have any of it, although I could have dished you, old boy. Any time I could have dished you. You'd still be counting the years now. But I didn't. And they send *you* to watch *me*!'

Smith said: 'You know they do this now and then as routine. Give someone an aide to keep an eye on them. It's just a security check, and especially with a thing like this Orange Wednesday rubbish. Don't worry I'll give you a virgin clean sheet.'

Findlayson hooted: 'You will! Marvellous! Terrific! Oh, thank you, kind captain.' He got up from the dressing table and walked menacingly over to Smith. Smith sensed that he should not get up, so he sat there like a boy, head down. Findlayson got hold of his ear, but only gently. 'Just you mind I'm going to give *you* a clean sheet, Smithy.'

'Oh Christ,' said Smith. 'What are you worried about? I *told* you why I was here, didn't I?'.

'After I'd made a shrewd guess,' said Findlayson. He let the ear slip through his fingers like an expert testing a piece of fabric. Then he walked back to the dressing table again, resumed his former posture, and picked at his teeth, examining every crevice in the mirror.

'Anyhow,' he said meditatively, 'what if I do stray? What if I forget my years of training and loyalty to a King, a Queen, and that crappy little country across the water? What if I let the ackers dazzle me, old boy, like they dazzled you in Alex?'

'You wouldn't,' said Smith simply.

'*You don't know me,*' exploded Findlayson. He hushed his voice, then: 'You don't know me at all. Not now. Years ago I may have been an easy push, sonny, but with the time going by, and the army getting into the shitstate it is, perhaps I've changed. Maybe I'm in the market for someone to come up to me and to say: "Listen British soldier, I'm acting for some rich West German industrialists, and we don't want to take on that impoverished and indoctrinated thirteen million from East Germany".'

He turned to face Smith: 'There are plenty like that, you know. Plenty in West Germany. The only grudge they have about the Berlin wall is they didn't get the contract to build it.'

Smith sniffed. 'I'm aware that there is a trend of feeling like that,' he said.

'That sounded nice,' grunted Findlayson. He mimicked: 'I am aware that there is a trend of feeling like that. Good old official Smith. Trend of feeling! Ha! They'd be glad to pay, to get somebody to kill for it, old lad. Very glad. They don't want this treaty signed. And there are the others who feel the same because of various political quirks and fancies.'

'You seem to have surveyed the field,' suggested Smith.

'You don't have to dig very deeply.'

'Any offers?'

'Bollocks, old boy. Do you think this is Alex? We're not selling cold tanks and surplus egg custard to the Gyppos now.'

'What are we doing, exactly?' asked Smith. His eyes and his white face had hardened now as though his senses had been roused.

'Well, I'm watching Orange Wednesday, and you're watching me watching Orange Wednesday. That's what we're doing.'

'But, after twenty years loyal service to a King, a Queen and crappy country, as you put it, you could be open to offers?'

'I would hardly confess to you, sonny, even if I were. So stop pushing it and shut up.'

Findlayson rubbed his fingers across his eyes. He looked straight in the mirror at Smith again, hesitated, then spoke as he yawned. 'Smithy, how much, exactly how much, did you make from the Alexandria fiddle?'

'About twenty thousand,' admitted Smith. 'Net.'

'Ballsing up a thing like Orange Wednesday ought to be worth a lot then?' he said.

'More than tanks and egg custard,' said Smith.

'Twenty thousand,' repeated Findlayson reflectively. 'And you're still in the service.'

'Why not. Haven't you seen the advertisements. It's a fine life for a man.'

A tug on the line looped to his toe opened Brunel's eyes like a marionette's. He jerked up from his flat position on the bed and sent his hands towards the line to pull in the fish.

But it wasn't a bite. Standing at the bottom of the bed, playing at the string and looking decently embarrassed was a man, wearing a pale grey sweater and trousers almost the same colour. His face was so earnest and open that he could have only been an American dedicated to something.

His hair was fair and short like a rug, and his expression became loaded with concern when he saw that Brunel was awake. He reached from somewhere indistinct and thrust a waddy pad and a pen towards Brunel.

'Sorry to wake you,' he said with bright anxiety, giving the string a final pull as if to make sure that Brunel did not fall back again. 'My name is George Bone. I'm an American student. I'm travelling all over Germany.'

'Good for you,' said Brunel. He yawned and detached the line from his toe. He looked around for his socks.

' ... and I wondered if you would care to add your signature to this petition I'm compiling.'

Brunel screwed up his face. 'What's it for?' he asked.

'It's not *for* anything,' said the man. 'It's an *against* petition, if you get me. It's *against* the Re-unification of Germany.'

Brunel went to his office the next morning and, as though

129

his body had missed the habit, he fell asleep across his desk very quickly after drinking a portion of medicinal port wine, soaked for an hour in prime liver. The cat, smelling and remembering the treat from afar, wheedled in, ate the liver, and flopped stupidly drunk on to a catafalque of moribund files, causing them to collapse like ancient dead suddenly exposed to the air. The cat, and Brunel, slept on. Brunel had a dream of terror in which Prudence was hoisting him naked to her ceiling while Keenor fired short bursts from a sub-machine gun around his lower limbs, Otto pranced a chestnut roan about the room, and an American voice, disembodied, kept howling at him to sign a petition for the re-unification of Vietnam.

He awoke, clothed, to his surprise, but shivering at the badness of the dream, and took the remainder of the medicinal port, a large portion thick with dregs of liver, and drank it. Normally he left that bit, but he needed something. He felt it do him immediate benefit, running warm inside him. There was a lot of it, but it was soon gone, and he stretched himself, filling his clothes, feeling much better, more confident, and grandly certain that he was strong enough to defy Keenor at any time.

He went out into the chilly day, walked to Otto's cafe, and brightly asked Hilde for some coffee. While she had gone for it Prudence, like a prowling cat, came under the trees and sat down opposite him.

'Well,' Brunel shrugged. 'It *is* a small town, I suppose.'

'I followed you,' she confessed. 'From the baths. What were you doing in your office? It's Sunday.'

'Having a nightmare, or whatever the daylight equivalent is,' he said. He felt the extra mouthfuls of medicinal port working around and filling him inside. He felt good, slightly rebellious. He somehow wished Prudence had been Keenor.

'Were you trailing me for your boss?' he asked.

'For myself,' she said. 'I know you always come to this place—I have my own intelligence service, you understand.'

'What would you do without it?'

'I wondered why you came here, that's all.'

Hilde appeared with Brunel's coffee and her child's face became tight and touched with little lines, suddenly womanly, when she saw Prudence. Prudence looked at the girl steadily.

'Another coffee, please, Hilde,' said Brunel, unaware of the exchange. The pimple in the valley of Prudence's nose was a bit purple today. It must be the cold, he thought.

'*Ja*,' grunted Hilde, still looking at Prudence. She turned quickly and went back into the cafe.

'She's too young for you, anyway,' said Prudence.

'Oh, much too young. Freckles too. Can't stand freckles.'

A vague collection of men and women were moving heavily along the street. Brunel watched them stop and form a circle immediately on the road outside the cafe. It was as though they were about to play a game. They wore nondescript clothes and expressions. The smallest of the men, a little fellow bent half-round like a mole and with a mole's tapering nose, had a side drum at his waist and one of the women, an angular lady, had a dulled saxophone. These two began to play in praise of Jesus, and the others began to sing.

Prudence grimaced. 'I think we're just in time for the collection,' she said.

Good,' said Brunel still defiantly. 'I Shall contribute. It's a worthy cause.' He suddenly felt annoyed with Prudence for following him and half wondered if Keenor had instructed her. He *really* did not like Keenor. He was sure and decided about that now.

'There's a nice American chap at my hotel,' said Brunel daringly while the playing of the praise went on. 'He's a sort of elderly student. A campus nut, I suppose you could call him.'

'So?' she said.

'He's collecting signatures,' continued Brunel smugly. 'For another good cause. He thinks so anyway.'

'What's that?' She was leaning forward, immediately suspicious.

'It's a petition . . . against the Re-unification of Germany,' he ended triumphantly. 'I may sign it myself.'

Even in his new confidence he was shocked by the whiteness that swept across her face 'That's bad,' she whispered. 'That's terrible. Have nothing to do with that, Brunel. If Keenor . . .'

'If Keenor what?' said Brunel, now leaning forward too 'I'm sick of Keenor and all the other rubbish. The more I think about this business the more I realise how bloody ridiculous it all is.'

'But it's *not*,' she urged. 'It's serious. And any stupidity by you or anyone else will be serious. Please believe me, Brunel.'

'Are you going to tell Keenor about Bone—this American nut?'

'I won't tell him anything,' she said. She was starting to get up from the seat. Brunel was astonished at the change in her. 'But for God's sake don't be crazy, Brunel. Don't attract attention to yourself. I know what I'm saying.'

Hilde came out with the coffee and at the same moment the leader of the religious group approached

Brunel and politely asked him if he would care to testify before the assembled witnesses. A large grin settled on Brunel's face.

'Of course I'll testify,' he said, staring at Prudence. 'Glad to testify at any time.'

'Don't. Please *don't*,' said Prudence. 'Don't attract attention. Keenor will . .'

But Brunel was up. So was Prudence, backing away down the street as though he were about to destroy himself with a hand grenade Brunel glowed and grinned again. He went to the centre of the forlorn circle who turned thin expressions on him.

Brunel plunged into his testimony. As he shouted he threw his words towards the retreating Prudence. white face still towards him as she went.

'Support God and Jesus!' bellowed Brunel defiantly. He stopped there, stuck for a moment. He saw Hilde giggling into her hands by the cafe table. Then he shouted on, bravely. 'Yes, God and Jesus . . . the old firm!'

His testimony was received with a huge indifference, which was not surprising since it was delivered in English Soon the little religious band moved off with the mole-man drumming at their head. Brunel returned to the cafe table. He sat down and made to pick up the coffee intended for Prudence.

'Do not take that,' warned Hilde. 'It was for her. There is a strong laxative in it.'

'That's a nice thought,' he said without emphasis.

'Why did you do that?' she asked nodding towards the road.

'Give testimony?' he said 'Oh, I felt the Call. Some of us do, you know. Anyway I wanted to do something just to prove I'm still me, I'm not just a number, clicking over as *they* like.'

'They?'

'You wouldn't know them.'

'Is *she* one of them?'

'Prudence?' He decided to lie. 'No. Just a cousin visiting here.'

'A cousin?' said Hilde, brightening, but at once unsure again.

'My mother's sister's little girl,' said Brunel. 'She's leaving soon.'

'Good,' said Hilde vigorously. 'I will get some more coffee. I have some secret news for you.'

She went and he stared, red-eyed with apprehension, at the door until she returned through it. 'What news?' he croaked, certain that it could only be calamity.

She bent near him and he felt her clean breath after the heaviness of Prudence. Her hair had dropped again and she was so close to him that two strands of it became connected to his right eyelash, looping between him and her like mooring ropes. 'Tomorrow,' she said, 'in the early evening my father's friends, you know the bang-bang club, are meeting in the forest. A man from Munich, a special visitor, will be there. I do not know what will happen, but I know the place where they will be. You are interested, Brunel?'

Brunel felt another ton press on his mind. 'I'm interested,' he nodded hazily. 'I have to be, I'm afraid.'

'We will go,' she promised. 'But we must be there early, so that we can find a spot to watch. I will wait for you outside the town on the road that is away from the golf course. You know it? By the funny shop that sells Graf Zeppelin Hot Dogs.'

'I know the hot dogs very well,' grunted Brunel. 'I'll sniff my way to the shop.'

8

The autumn had been so dry, following the arid summer, that the grass, the ferns and the lying leaves in the forest were brittle like ash. They walked up the paths by some way she had known since childhood, through hidden bowls and twice across falling streams, until they had reached the roof of the forest and they could see the full blue sky through the trees. Brunel held her small hand over the more difficult places and on the third instance she refused to let go again so they walked like that.

He felt very old with her. As old as the splintering forest. As old as age, as worry, as old as responsibility. His big fair face had dropped into a growl when she declined to release his hand, and he kept it like that although she took no notice except to glance quickly at him and sweetly grin. When they attained the biggest trees that overruled the rest of the forest, Brunel was puffing a little as his heavy legs reached the final mound of moss. From there he looked straight out and he felt he could have counted every tree.

'Young girl, I am an ancient,' he said, sitting monkishly his fringe on his eyes. She laughed at him. 'You are thirty-three on the eighteenth of December,' she said. 'This I know.'

'That's ancient,' he nodded. 'Ancient anyway when

you're climbing about like a ten-year-old. Where is the place?'

She turned against the clear cloth of the sky and he found himself staring at the lovely young shape, her legs back a little like a pony's, her stomach out, pushing against her tight skirt, her girl's breasts lying small but heavily under her sweater, and her golden arm pointing out to a remote valley beyond the next treeline. Her face and hair were facile, fragile, set like some artist's model for a vision of youth. He felt dirty and horny and ashamed of himself.

Hilde said: 'The place where they meet is over there. It is not far, Brunel.' She turned and caught him looking as he was and it shook her to see him like that, making her quickly afraid.

Brunel felt sick when he saw that she had caught him. 'Let's get down there,' he grunted getting awkwardly to his feet. 'We will need to find a decent place to watch before it gets dark.' They walked and sometimes jogged down the opposite back of the hill. He had his hands rammed like stakes down into his pockets to keep either one of them away from her fingers. It was quite difficult going through the trees and the dry, fallen branches and twigs, like forcing a way through a crowd of spectators standing on a mountain and breaking their toes underfoot. But they reached the flat below the slope, then up a gentler incline where the trees had been harvested a few years before and young saplings were growing. At the ridge of that ascent she stopped and nodded down to a saucer space, fifty feet below, which had been completely cleared of big trees, leaving only their stumps squatting on the grass. Because the heavy shade of the forest had been taken away the grass had grown thicker, and the forest flowers and shrubs more healthy, and some there were still in bloom.

'This is the place, said Hilde, looking down with wrinkled disgust. 'This is where they will meet. You will see, Brunel.'

He began walking slowly, like a dog, around the perimeter of the bowl. 'Let's have a rummage about,' he said. 'Somewhere for a good view of the show.'

He had taken his hands from his pockets now and she, no longer with any fear, took his right, slipping her fingers into it easily. 'It fits well,' she said looking up at him. 'Like a new key going into an old lock. There, does that please you? I have called you "old".'

'An old lock an an old door,' he said conscious of the small coolness of her hand. 'A creaky old door. I feel a lot older than thirty-two this afternoon. Are you sure that's what I am?'

'I saw it in your army pay book,' she said. 'When I searched through it one day to see if you had any pictures of a wife or little children or a sweetheart.'

'You're a pickpocket and a spy,' he said without emphasis. 'You must have been disappointed that there was nothing doing.'

She smiled. 'Nothing. Just a photograph of you looking very thin and funny in long baggy shorts, on a bicycle. You were very young then. As young as I am now, and so funny you looked. I prefer you now. Much more.'

'What else?'

'Did I find? Nothing of importance to me. It was some months ago and I hardly remember. Oh yes, there was another photograph of an old pastor.'

'My father,' he said. 'This looks like the sort of place. Let's see.'

It was a shapely culvert of tough grasses with a wall of ginger dry heather screening it from the clearing below. In the first part of winter it probably drained the rain into the lower area and made it a pond, and later, it would hide the snow in soft secret until far into spring. Brunel slid into the culvert and stretched himself along it, so that through the ferns he could see every sawn tree stump below. Hilde came down the smooth grass with an unstoppable slide, and laid herself out alongside him. He jumped like a criminal.

'No! Definitely no!' he said savagely. 'We can't. Not like this.'

Because the sides were so confined and steep she was pressed close against him. 'But how will I watch?' she asked slyly the words forming themselves an inch from his set mouth.

'You *won't* watch if it means like this,' he said. 'For God's sake child turn it in.'

'Turn it in?' she inquired. 'What in?'

'Stop it. Pack it. Finish it. Kaput it. Understand?' He levered himself away from her sufficiently to give himself room to crawl from the little ravine. From the top he turned and she was still stretched out there on her stomach, her skirt half way up the backs of her upper legs. Her legs, shaped and smooth like pieces of fawn soft wood, well planed.

'Hilde,' he said heavily, 'come on out.'

She turned her face upwards, sulking, then shrugged and climbed from the place without any help from him. He turned away like an annoyed schoolmaster, kicking spitefully at the twigs until they were lying injured all about him in the grass. He circled a graceless pirouette and lowered himself down on to the roots of a birch. The long-striking sun was on its trunk making it shine like a sword. He leaned back against the bark and felt the mild, slanting warmth upon his face. Hilde walked sedately to another tree ten yards to Brunel's right and sat down also.

They could both see easily into the clearing from their

places. Hilde without turning said: 'The tree stumps look so strange. As though some elephants have been here and gone away leaving their feet behind.'

He laughed and they turned their faces to each other. 'Can I come and sit at your birch tree?' she asked.

'There's no space,' he pointed out. 'It's a thin tree.'

She got up, her legs opening like springs, and went to his tree. 'I will sit at this side and lean on it,' she said. She did so lying back on the silver wood, her slight shoulder touching his heavy arm and her hair straying over to the skin of his neck. 'There,' she said smugly. 'Plenty of space. If two more people came they could have the other two sides. Four against a tree. You see, you cannot have everything for yourself.'

A red squirrel made a movement on a log twenty yards away. 'See it?' whispered Hilde with a child's delight.

'I can see it,' he said dully. 'There are not many red ones left. The grey squirrel, the American, has taken over the trees all over the world.'

'You should not hate Americans,' she admonished.

'I don't,' grunted Brunel. 'It's their squirrels I don't like.'

She giggled on her side of the tree. 'Brunel,' she said, and he felt the brushing of her hair on his neck-skin, 'do you get all your strange thoughts from your father, the pastor?'

He snorted: 'The most unwise man I ever knew. Ignorant black men in Africa learned from him that God is Love and yet he went down into the grave screaming for Jesus to catch him—or else he wouldn't believe in Jesus any more.'

'Perhaps Jesus caught him,' said Hilde optimistically.

'I doubt it,' shrugged Brunel. 'He hit Eternity with a dull thud, Dad did.'

She said: 'Tell me, then, about when you were very youthful. When you were a boy and later to when you had those little knees in the bicycle.'

Brunel shifted against the tree. He lost the feel of her arm, but she moved also so that it was against his again. 'The only thing dramatic or traumatic I remember from the first bit, when I was a boy,' he said, 'was being beaten up across a gravestone by some choirboys still in their black and white rig-out. The second era, the bicycle years, is mainly recalled by the memory of a little girl on a beach holding up her green knickers and asking me to put them on for her.'

'And did you? Oh no, that's stupid. Of course, you did not.'

'No I didn't. I ran away.'

'You should have done it. It might have done you good. The young are older than you think, Brunel.'

Brunel shook his head. 'No. The only good this would have done would have been the fact that she would not have had to hobble home with two little legs in one hole I ran and I'm glad I ran.'

They left it there. They sat then and watched the sun trying to thread its way into the thicker forest on the distant side of the clearing. 'Do you love your country, Brunel?' she then asked. 'Is England as they say, so green and so peaceful?'

'Sometimes green when the soot has drifted away,' he answered. 'At peace when we're not fighting to keep it green. When we fight, your lot particularly, we always tell ourselves it's for that. We seem to think there's some special magic which we have alone, some secret in keeping meadows verdant—a favourite word, one they always use in poems and things—and keeping sheep grazing and having cottages and lanes so quaint and quiet. Nobody else has got it, you understand, or we don't think they have, and we always kill people to protect it. It's part of being British.'

'If you're a pacifist you should not be a soldier,' she argued from her side of the tree.

'Oh, I'm no pacifist,' he said. 'I'd fight. And especially I'd fight you lot. It all has to do with history, see. Anyway it's easier like that. I'm all for the easy way'

'When you were a boy didn't you go into the country and hunt for rabbits and that sort of thing that boys are supposed to do?' she asked anxiously as though searching for something good.

She sensed him shake his head. 'When I got to my funny knees stage, as you call it, I grew to like the sea. It's cleaner and less occupied than the land. I used to cycle all over the place searching for it. We lived slap in the middle of England and I would go out of my house in the morning and just point the front wheel in any direction and the pedal until I came to the sea. This was mostly in the autumn and the winter so that there wouldn't be a lot of Englishmen or Scots or Welsh gits paddling in it. Oh yes, I've seen more of the sea from a bike than some people have from a bloody boat.'

Hilde was going to say something but she felt him about to go on. He said: 'When I was about ten we lived at a town called Stoke, a deathly place where they make cups and saucers. All the week this dump would be coughing out smoke, all sorts of pretty colours, mind you, but smoke, nevertheless. And on Sundays all the people would rush out into the country to give their lungs a treat. And there would hardly be a soul left in the town. The smoke would clear so you could even see to the end of the street and the sun would filter in and it used to be marvellously quiet. I used to go right *into* town and sit in the middle of all that peaceful ugliness. There was a canal full of yellow water, as if all the world had been washing its sores in it. But it hardly stirred on a Sunday and the sun looked all right on the thick water and I used to sit there looking for sharks.'

'That was strange.'

'Yes. The other kids, who went off to the country on Sundays with their mums and dads, used to say there were sharks and conger eels in the canal because the effluent from the factories made the water warm and tropical. I never saw any, of course, but it was all right.'

Hilde said sternly: 'I am surprised you do not love your country.'

'Oh I love her right enough, now I come to think of it,' said Brunel. 'It's some of the games her children play I don't like. The country's all right.'

'We all play games,' she whispered. 'Look at these foolish men we will watch here tonight. What a game that is. I want to kill my father sometimes for his foolishness. And yet . .'

'And yet?' asked Brunel.

' . . . It is most difficult. One evening when your Queen was here, Brunel, I went with my father to the house of Fritz Heyer, his friend who will be here with him tonight, to see your Queen at the Schloss Bruhl at Bonn. It was on their television. It is a poor house. Frau Heyer is deaf and says nothing. She is tattered and old and her two sons were killed, the first on one day the second on the next day, during our war in Russia. Herr Hayer is a stupid old man, fat, with his dinner always on his woollen waistcoat, and the house is as they are.

'And we watched on the television, Brunel. And it was just like in former times. All the German soldiers, hundreds and hundreds, all with the same face, marching. No, not marching, tramping. Tramp, tramp, tramp. You could imagine the people beneath their feet. Slowly they went, in long, long ranks. And there was no music.

Only the drum beating. And they carried burning torches and the eagle on a standard, Brunel, hundreds of torches shining on the round parts of their helmets.

'And your Queen was all in white, Brunel, and they marched for her. But they were marching *not* really for her. But they were marching for Germany. The people there could feel it, you could see how the old Germans in the crowd stood up stiff and so brutal again. And even in the room you could feel the thrill of the soldiers and the torches and the drum. You could feel that this army could go on marching from that spot and never stop until it had won the whole world—everything.

'My father and Fritz Heyer had got to their feet, fat bellies out and sweat on their faces, and were upright and proud and staring at the soldiers. But then worse. Frau Heyer, who had not heard or spoken for years, whose sons were dead ... then she got to her feet and behind the table, standing there all dirty and loose, but her eyes were shining, Brunel. It was for her too they marched.'

'And you?' asked Brunel quietly. 'What did you do?'

Her voice was very small now from her side of the tree. She said: 'I ... I looked at my father and he told me with his eyes to get to my feet and I did. Then we all put our hands out and said "Heil Hitler." I did too, Brunel. *I did too*. I ... I   think perhaps it was because I was so afraid of my father at that moment. Or perhaps I could not resist the thrill of it. I, who wish hurt to no Jew ... to no one ... It must be something inside us, Brunel.'

Her young head leaned over to him and he could feel her tears on his neck and wetting down inside his shirt.

The darkness was collecting now and there came a quick sound from the forest on the other side of the clearing.

'Don't cry now, Hilde,' Brunel murmured into her white ear. 'We must hide. The cowboys have arrived.'

He rolled smoothly into the culvert and Hilde rolled after him, so that they were again wedged together in its narrow base. She was pleased with what she had accomplished and she grinned across her face still smudged with badly wiped tears. Brunel mouthed some words at her without making any sound, but it was too late to make her hide elsewhere. They would have to lie together until whatever was about to happen in the clearing had been completed.

It always seemed to him that she was so fragile against his bulk. And they were so tight he was afraid he would crush her against the hard earth side of the channel.

They could hear the cowboys now, clearly and without stealth, coming through the trees. Brunel was only three-quarters on his stomach. His right side and his leg were on the rise with the girl slotted under him. She was more or less face down, looking with difficulty through the screen of ferns, her head at his shoulder. He was aware of her feel all the way down. Her toes were hard across his lower ankle, one shin ran straight against the muscle of his calf, and one knee was like a small wooden ball pressed into the side saucer of his knee. From there her body had performed a half screw movement and the choice segment of her upper left leg and one buttock were tucked into his groin. He felt himself involuntarily growing down there and wished to God she had kept away.

Their half-bellies were flat against each other, but nearly quiet as though each was listening intently to the other. One warm pudding breast was lodged under his right armpit.

Her breathing and his, unco-ordinated, set up a small movement so that their points of contact were always in tiny motion. Brunel could never remember feeling so uncomfortable.

A light, like a firefly, wandered through the far trees. It was the final phase of dusk now and the man on the horse who appeared was just a dented shadow. He paused at the clearing and the horse sneezed wheezily.

'It is Herr Gotten, the milkman,' whispered Hilde. 'Only his horse sneezes that way.'

'Quiet,' ordered Brunel. 'No more talking.'

She nodded and moved her body half an inch up his, which for him was half an inch in six places. He closed his eyes to let the spasm pass. The horseman, a small lantern at his stirrup, went down to the clearing. Others followed, mounted shadows breaking from the trees, eight in all, walking their horses about the dish of the clearing like riders in the circus ring. The dusk was dissipated now and it was completely night. Two men were at the centre of the area dragging pieces of wood together. A match showed their stooped faces for a moment, then they had a fire going. The others sat in their saddles and watched the light grow. It grew apace because the wood was easy and dry. Soon Brunel and Hilde could see the men and make out their faces.

The group represented the first funny thing that Brunel had ever seen connected with politics. Ferocious, futile, fearful, but funny. Jokes on horseback.

More logs were dragged to the fire by the two dismounted men, but the others remained on their horses. The light grew in area as though someone had turned up the wick of a lamp. Brunel looked from man to man and horse to horse. The horses, except one, were thin and the men, except one, were old, some fat-old, some lean-old. Otto was near the centre of the group, his black boots shining in the firelight. It had not occurred to Brunel before but with the contrivance of the cowboy club they were also able to wear brown shirts.

There was an expression of stout doubt on Otto's broad, shining face. His cowboy hat was pushed from his forehead, with the lace engaging the third of his four chins. His neckerchief was wandering around his throat. His guns were slung so low that to reach them would have meant falling from the horse. The horse was a mouldy hack, angled and boney, standing with its eyes tightly closed. It was either tired, thought Brunel, or it couldn't take the glare of the fire.

Next to Otto was the grey milkman, Gottan, whom Hilde had identified, patting his tubercular mount, and then three others in a line, like a spiritless James gang, self-conscious in their disguises, and unhappy on horseback.

Beyond them was a tiny old man wearing a single, heavy, genuine Colt in a huge and fancy holster, the combined weight of which pulled the frail wearer heavily to one side. The seventh man, mounted on an uncouth mule, was the leader of the forest rangers who counted the deer in the winter and who had showed such animosity toward Brunel.

Then there was an eighth cowboy, an ornate young man in a goucho's frills and leathers, riding a glowing stallion. It was towards him that Otto had directed his doubtful expression and the others were regarding him with similar unease.

They seemed to expect something from the young man on the stallion and the old men grew visibly tense when from his saddle bag he withdrew a folded banner. Brunel thought Arthur's Knights might have had that eagerness when he drew the wondrous Excalibur from its scabbard.

The banner had an extendible pole which the young man deftly whirled and ran out to full length. He thrust it into the ground arrogantly, but the earth was hard and bounced it back with equal arrogance. He blushed in the firelight, then selected a cracked spot and turned the pole squeezing it down until it was firm. Then, pulling a silk string, he released the banner and it rolled down, jerked to a halt, and revealed a head and shoulders portrait of Adolf Hitler.

'Our Founder,' grunted Brunel drily.

The old timers looked at the out-fashioned face in all its cruel comedy. Each seemed to find some steel in his back and sat straight and fine while they raised their flat hands and said a muted 'Heil'. The ceremony was spoiled and terminated because the frail man with the single heavy gun toppled from his horse, the action of raising his arm having set him off balance. But they all dismounted then, anyway, and two of the cowboys kindly set their friend on his uncertain feet.

Looking through the dead tracery of the ferns into the firelit scene, Brunel felt he was viewing a hellish farce through an ecclesiastical window.

Most of the men had climbed from their horses out of consternation for the fragile fellow who had toppled. Now they all dismounted, including the young man from the fine stallion.

'Who is he?' whispered Brunel, his lips touching Hilde's ear.

'Never have I seen this man,' she said. Then the man answered them. He had squatted on one of the tree stumps and the others sat around like boy scouts on the others.

'My friends,' he grunted, 'I bring you the good wishes

of your brothers in Munich and in all the Bavarian centres of operations. All the time we grow in strength and in ambition. We are the seeds of the Great Germany that will follow before long. We will sprout quickly, and people will know that we are growing, and what we stand for. They will know where our inspiration is from. Adolf Hitler would be the ruler of the world today if it were not for the treachery and moral weakness within the Third Reich. A fine old man he would have been now. . . .'

Brunel felt the girl trembling. Or it might have been him He was not sure. He pushed his face into the earth in front of his nose partly because his neck was tired and partly because he wanted to take his eyes from the fire-lit scene. Hilde put her face down too and turned it frantically to him so that even in their immediate darkness he could see the frantic expression in her young eyes. He found her hand underneath his body and held it.

'The mistakes that were made in the past will not be tolerated again. Everyone who remains will be loyal.'

'Who remains? From what?' wondered Brunel.

'The victory of the P.R.P. party in Hesse, in *free* elections, and the many other signs from different parts of our Fatherland have shown us that the people are ready once again.' He looked about at the little gathering as if undecided whether to confess something to them. He apparently decided to do so. Brunel remembered his father using this technique in taking Christ to the savages in Africa. Your audience felt it was getting a bonus, that you were making it a gift of something no one else had known. His father had always hammed the hesitation so heavily that even as an infant Brunel had wondered why, simple as they were, they could not see it was never spontaneous. The Munich man's hesitation was slightly less protracted now, but not by that much. He bent his face reverendly and dipped in a sudden surge of confession into what he was going to reveal.

'When I was ten years old,' he said solemnly, 'The Führer came to the town where I lived to inspect our war effort—a complete battery chicken farm housed in the local synagogue. And he walked to me and put his hand on my head.' There was a murmur from the small audience as though a sacred relic had been disclosed. Brunel thought the Munich man was going to take off his goucho's hat to show them the spot. But he refrained and remained with head hanging down filled with the famous memory.

'I have never forgotten it,' he stammered. 'At that moment, little as I was, I felt that somehow he had chosen *me*.'

'He did. He did,' muttered the others moving their old heads.

There was a silence of a minute or more while they digested the episode. Then, pulling himself together, the younger man said: 'And that is why I come to warn you to be ready. To work to get yourselves into positions of authority and power, no matter how localised, so that when the time comes all our friends and all our resources will be in the right places. Work, and talk, but talk carefully; get others in sympathy with you. One day Germany will be one nation again ...'

He paused and Brunel put his mental brakes on to buffer the collision of the next words he expected. But they did not come. Nothing about Fulsbad.

'One day,' the speaker promised, 'we will have our own land to ourselves again, and we can push out and reclaim those places which are dear to us—our Lost Territories, and then perhaps further and perhaps further still.'

'War again then,' said Otto sitting on the stump

in front of the Munich man. Brunel felt Hilde start.

'War again,' confirmed the young man with a hard smile. 'We cannot fulfil our destiny without fire. Fire is good. It takes away decay and gives man a fresh start.'

Otto fidgeted with his left firearm. Brunel thought, 'If he pulls the trigger he'll shoot his toe off.'

'Does that answer your question, sir?' asked the Munich man of Otto.

'Yes. Yes,' mumbled Otto. 'Smoke and fire. Yes, yes, sir.'

'Good.' The visitor looked around and smiled his cemented smile. 'It is a delight to find a group that has discovered the secret of getting together, of meeting easily, and of wearing uniforms. I congratulate you,' he said. 'You have surmounted a great difficulty that groups experience in all parts of the country. The uniform is nice too. I must suggest it to other places. We have, of course, a very big cowboy club in Munich. Unfortunately this has nothing whatever to do with us. They are real pretending cowboys. They ride and shoot and call "yippee" and swing ropes. They are quite crazy.'

The visitor had obviously finished. There was a little fidgeting, then the man Brunel now recognised as one of the forest rangers, rose and came awkwardly to attention in his spurs.

'Sir,' he said with embarrassment. 'As social secretary of the month I wish that we should show our appreciation of your visit by singing the old song of the Munich Storm Troopers. We have rehearsed it specially.'

The visitor looked doubtful. 'Very thoughtful of you,' he said. 'But is it not dangerous to sing here? Someone could find us.'

'We have adequately drilled our precautions,' said the ranger smugly. 'Ready, gentlemen. Please rise.'

They stood up in the firelight and in undertoned

voices that made them sound like dying men, they sang:

> 'And now the day of revenge
> Is coming nearer, and the Leader
> Calls us to war.
> Then out of need and shame
> We shall raise the Swastika ...'

Brunel and Hilde could not believe what they were seeing and hearing. The company paused, ready to roll into another verse, and at that moment a day bird, frightened by the singing, almost collided with a dozing owl in a tree. Their quick quarrel, high in the dark, stopped the singers in the first breath of the new verse. It was Otto who gave the quick signal and the entire company changed key and went softly singing:

> 'Home, home on the range,
> Where the deer and the antelope
>   play ...'

9

Keenor and Prudence were resting. Because he had insisted, the mattress had been re-bedded on the springs and they were lying out on it. The half light, after-sleep was on Keenor, and Prudence, white and naked, lay considering him glumly. To others the mound of his stomach, with its coarse tundra of stiff hairs, might seem repelling, but she was a strange woman and although the seeing of it did nothing for her, primitive contact with him was like having sex with a warthog. She found it dangerous and diverting.

'You're very tired today, chief,' she said sulkily, looking closely at his lower anatomy.

'Pooped,' he mumbled. 'Pooped.'

'That thing especially,' she grumbled, flicking her finger spitefully into his groin. 'It hasn't got a spark left in it.'

Keenor's chrysalis eyes opened a segment. 'Hell,' he said without taking his voice above a groan. 'What d'you expect, honey? I'm a tired man. I just said, didn't I?'

She nodded towards the part she had just flicked, and said sourly. 'I remember seeing an old walrus in the Hamburg Zoo on a hot summer's day. He was flat out, exhausted, lying there wrinkled and limp. That's how that looks right now.'

'First time I've heard it called a walrus,' muttered

Keenor without rancour. 'Why don't you try throwing it some fish.'

She snorted like a mare. But she calmed quickly, moved down closer to him and began a minute inspection of his stomach hairs, like an expert grading a barley crop.

'Shit,' sighed Keenor. 'You don't know all the trouble I've got. In two days the big boys will be moving in. All the security joyboys, expecting the whole place to be nice and swept up and clean for them.'

'Isn't it?' asked Pru, going on with her interest.

'Hey!' jerked Keenor. 'Take it easy. Have a look at them, okay, but for Christ's sake don't pull them by the roots. I hurt easy.'

Pru apologised. 'What's your worry then?' she asked.

'My worry? I wish I knew. I wish I could definitely fix it down. But I can't. It's Wednesday today, right? Next week it will be Orange Wednesday. But I can't guarantee everything is going to be okay. It wouldn't be so difficult if I could trust anyone. With Americans I'd know where I was. I can handle Americans.'

His voice took on a soft, reflective tone: 'Pru, did I ever tell you how I got this job with Special Precautions Office? I got it because of getting top grade, Pru. Full Marks! Maybe I'm not heavy with brains, but I'm shrewd, which is what you need to be. I always got full marks with the C.I.A., when I was there, so the S.P.O. grabbed me.' He turned to her in sudden, confiding enjoyment She thought he might be about to recite a verse. 'I'll tell you something, Pru, I was the only guy to get full marks at the C.I.A. over the Bay of Pigs operation.'

'You were on that?' asked Pru, surprised.

'No. That's the point. I took my leave when they did that balls-up. And when I came back everybody was blaming everybody else, and the President was yelling. *and I had nothing to do with it, Pru! I wasn't* there. I was in Elizabeth, New Jersey. When I got back I was the only one they couldn't pin it on. I still had top grading. So I got my transfer and promotion.'

He puffed at the memory. It was the first time she had seen Keenor on the fringes of happiness. But immediately it all fell, shattered, from his face, like a window falling out.

'And now this,' he said. 'The Frenchman's a killer for sure. I don't trust him. The people in Paris wouldn't let us see his record at all. They just sent him as he stands, with their love and assurances. Assurances! Aw, hell! He could shoot a hair from a fly at a thousand yards, yet he missed when we had a little shoot in the woods the other day. And my own contacts in Paris tell me that somehow he scraped around an indictment after the Ben Barka killing. How did he do that?'

Pru said: 'Maybe he was on leave, like you and the Bay of Pigs.'

'Shut up, Pru,' said Keenor. He scratched the garden of bristle she had been investigating. 'Then one of the Commies is going to smudge the other out before this thing is over. I've never felt so sure of anything in my life. I've had them watched. They spend half their time expecting to get knocked off. They even search their boots. Looking for toe-cap bombs, I guess. Very decisive the toe-cap bomb. Ever seen one go off?'

'If I have, I've forgotten,' said Pru.

'Stop gagging. I'm telling you. When one of those things explodes it knocks the bottom out of your barrel. Right out. All your guts fall on the floor.'

'I've never seen one, then,' decided Pru. 'I would have remembered.'

He looked at her with disgust. 'If you weren't such an almighty grind I wouldn't keep you on the staff,' he said. He sniffed when she made no response. 'Now these other two, Findlayson and Smith. That's another great pair. Smith has been sent to watch the other guy, I'm sure of that. All I need on this jig is someone who needs watching.'

His face was twisted with the contemplation of his difficulties.

'The walrus is down to a baby seal now,' commented Pru sadly.

'Honk, honk,' murmured Keenor. 'Now we also have the white knight, this guy Bruno . . .'

'Brunel,' corrected Pru. Keenor glanced at her sharply. 'What do you know about him?'

'That his name is Brunel,' she said simply.

'So it's Brunel. He was named after some guy who played bridge, or something crazy. I can't figure him. I don't know whether he's dangerous or just a nut. I think I'll keep him as dangerous, though.'

'You won't tell the security people about this will you?' she asked. 'It sounds as though you have no confidence in your crew.'

'I won't tell 'em, because I had this group wished on me from outside, and there's nothing I can do about it. No, I'll tell 'em that we've done the job. Given the area a phase-one survey, found it okay, and put it in their lap. I want to have full marks. But, my God, this is a nutty town. I saw some guys riding on horses, in cowboy rig-outs. Yeah. Cowboy rig-outs! Anything to dress up, these krauts. Stop pulling those hairs, will you.'

Three books were piled before George Bone. They were two sturdy volumes, *Butterflies of Central Europe*, and *Castles of the Rhine* and a thinner one *Jewish Opinion in Germany, 1939–45*, and they reached his chin level from the table at Herr Snellhort's hotel. Mr. Bone was eating leek soup, the plate sitting on the books; the soup being scooped in a flat movement into Mr. Bone's mouth.

'Books are always useful,' observed Brunel, nodding from his side of the table. It was early evening, the best time in the little hotel with dinner by oil-lamp and the munching shadows of Frau and Herr Snellhort flying across the walls as they served the single table. There were no other guests tonight. There rarely were.

Frau Snellhort had promised a good dinner 'to take the cobwebs away', a phrase she had taken at some time from Brunel and which, he noticed, she used proudly and increasingly whether the circumstances fitted it or not.

'Economy,' observed Bone, 'is the essence of a long and easy life. The Chinese eat their food from mouth level, you know, shovelling it in with the sticks, straight at the gullet. This fancy stuff you see with picking little bits up a time is strictly for the China Town Restaurants. The people, the peasants, the low-low and kow-tow, all that category, they get it down into it as quick as they can in case they die of starvation before it hits the floor of the belly '

'I thought you said it was the essence of a long and easy life,' said Brunel grimacing at Frau Snellhort as she ladled more leek soup before him, leaving a hot greeny trail of it across his wrist and saying it would take the cobwebs away. 'The Chinese have never had it very easy.'

'The Chinese,' breathed Bone happily as though Brunel had fed him a welcome philosophical thought. 'What people! What people!'

'Why don't you organise a petition for or against the re-unification of China,' suggested Brunel helpfully. 'A job for the rest of the winter term, for you.'

He couldn't understand how Bone could be forty, which he patently was, and still be a student. The American with his intent face, his grey campus jumper split by orange lightning and a huge octagonal letter 'O' in the same colour, his fair student crop, and his brain loaded with splinters of fact; most of it dead and useless. He never finished an argument or embroidered a thought He might, in a few fleet sentences, set up the scaffolding of some highly promising concept of life, then deliberately knock it down, dismiss it with some unconnected argument, or forget about it altogether in the course of two breaths.

Now, like some hero of a mental melodrama, he leapt deftly out of China, and back into the oil-lamp presence of the Snellhorts' shadowed dining room.

'Brunel,' he said, watching his smudged leek soup plate hooked away by Frau Snellhort and immediately replaced by a red mess of goulash transferred from Herr Snellhort mouthing away in the background. 'Brunel, friend, can you give me one, just one, valid reason, why you refuse to sign my anti-re-unification petition?'

He had said it before and each time Brunel felt like an invalid suffering a quick relapse. He was tempted to give as his one valid reason his desire not to be killed by Keenor. Instead he said: 'The same reason as I've said before, Boney, and that is my Queen doesn't allow me to sign things. I'm a serving soldier. Nothing doing.'

'And I've told you that soldiers are the one section of society who will sign anything,' argued Bone. He had thrust some of the Snellhort gloulash into his mouth and the red gravy was stretching down his chin like the overflow from a punch in the teeth. 'They sign chits and leave tickets, and leave passes. Anything.'

'But not political documents,' replied Brunel keeping cool. He thought the goulash gravy looked disgusting on Bone's chin, and since the American showed no intention of stopping the flow Brunel let his gravy dribble down too They sat conversing like two fanged monsters. Brunel said: 'A soldier is not an individual to that extent. Anyway perhaps I'm in agreement with the opposite view to your petition.'

'What!' exploded Bone in the peculiar American way of detonating over everyday things. 'You *agree* that the two halves of this country should be re-united?'

'I might,' said Brunel amiably. 'Anyway, get stuffed, because I'm not signing. And I'm not arguing any more either.'

'Okay,' agreed Bone. He switched with agility 'I guess you've been to plenty of these hunting lodge parties, eh, Brunel. Lots of laughs?'

'No,' answered Brunel. He decided to wipe his chin after all. The feel of the gravy was causing him more discomfort than the American was obviously experiencing from the sight of it. 'Not only never been to one, Boney, but I didn't know they had them.'

Bone, having defeated the Englishman, wiped his chin carefully. 'What have you been doing around here all these months?' he asked 'All the teenagers go to these things up in the forest.'

'I'm nearly thirty-three,' grunted Brunel. 'That's possibly why they didn't let on to me. They don't want the old folks to know what goes on.'

The barb was lost on Bone. 'There's a party tonight, Brunel. I'm going. You come too'

'Shall we wear our bobby-sox?'

'Outdated,' grunted Bone.

'I can't do the twist.'

'Outdated.'

'And I take cold if I eat ice-cream cones.'

'Your girl-friend is going.'

Brunel stared at him with fright he could feel sharp in his own eyes.

'You know,' smiled Bone beguilingly. 'The sweet one from the cafe. Aw come on, Brunel boy. Maybe I am the school sneak. But it's a small town and you can't miss much. Walks in the woods and all that. Fine. So you've been rolling her . . .'

'She's about fifteen,' said Brunel tersely. 'And we haven't been rolling. Anywhere or anything.'

Bone looked upset. 'Sorry, Brunel. Don't take it that way.'

Brunel saw he was genuine. He nearly said: 'I know her father . .' but he changed it as he said it. 'I know her family,' he said. 'She's a child.'

'Sure, they all are, we all are,' said Bone without malice. 'Anyway, a lot of the college children are going and some great kids on leave from the Panzer Division at Luneburg. Someone lends them a lodge and they make hay for a while. It helps the winter along.'

'Won't you feel a bit out of it?' suggested Brunel. 'You must be all of twenty.'

Bone ignored it. 'They won't mind. I've been invited anyway. They want to hear about American campus life. The girl from the cafe, the one whose family you know, asked me to get you along. She said you wouldn't go if she asked you. Anyway we'd be good company for each other.'

Brunel laughed 'She asked you did she.'

'As you're a friend of the family.'

'As I'm a friend of the family.'

10

The hunting lodge was curiously shaped, high and narrow, with a long ridged roof, and leaning forward on a forest ledge of rock, isolated, like the ark on Ararat. Bone and Brunel went up on the forest road, eight miles of whirling trees and suddenly obvious chasms, as passengers of a cherry-faced Panzer gunner, who had a motor cycle combination. Brunel, never a confident traveller, crouched in the coffin sidecar and squeezed his eyes to buttons every time the eighteen-year-old hung on to the final six inches of a bend. Bone was on the pillion, his right hand lightly on the young man's shoulder as though he were guiding him. They were shouting a conversation against the uproar of their journey, short exclamations from each, but Brunel could hear nothing.

Squares of amber light at the back of some black trees, and a grand finale skid of the motor-cycle on the lip of the rock ledge, told Brunel that they had arrived The young rider hailed someone distant and flapped his heavy gloves. Brunel carefully climbed out of the sidecar on the motor-cycle side, since to leave it in the normal way would have meant dropping unchecked five hundred feet over the shelf.

There was a Volkswagen mini-bus on a flat gravelled section outside the wooden lodge, with some more motor-cycles, and a German army scout car with the black cross on its side. The distant sound of other vehicles came up through the hills and trees. It was about ten o'clock and it was cold in the forest.

Brunel nodded towards the Bundeswehr scout car. 'Someone's risking a brush with the commanding officer,' he observed.

'Kids,' said Bone affably 'Same the world over.'

Kids they were. Young kids. Even the half-dozen soldiers, fresh as peaches, with fair hair and clear eyes. Strange, thought Brunel, to see them like this, harmless lads in field grey, when the picture he had always carried from his wartime childhood, the message of his comic books, was of the German soldier hard and brutal, booted, curled-mouthed, hate behind the eyes and always a rifle butt behind the blow. To him then, also, they had been much older too, bitter and grey and full of death. And yet these young, clear boys were soldiers also, and with bigger and better tanks. But boys. Could his comics have been wrong?

There were about thirty or forty others there now, students and others from the town Brunel recognised the sweet girl from the cake shop. Then he saw Hilde on the distant side of the room laughing with the young man who had brought them up on the motor-cycle.

She was smoking with affectation a tiny cigar and had a drink in her left hand, which gave Brunel a strange displeasure. Her skirt was short and she wore a white sweater and big ear-rings. She looked about as she talked and laughed and saw him. She said something brief to the young man and walked across the floor.

'Brunel,' she said. 'So the ancient is here with the little ones Come and meet my friend Gunter.'

'We've met,' explained Brunel, nevertheless crossing the pine floor with her towards the young man and the fire. 'He brought me here. I hope he drives his tank slower than he does his motor bike.'

'It was of no importance,' smiled Gunter, who caught the end of the thought. 'I do not drive the tank. I am with the *kannon*.'

'And how is your *kannon*?' inquired Brunel conversationally. Some beating music was coming from a portable record player across the room Hilde had gone to get him a drink.

'The *kannon*, he is beautiful,' said Gunter seriously and fondly, as though referring to an elderly clergyman. 'Twenty-five millimetre, double recoil, you understand, forty rounds in one minutes only. I keep it very nice. Very nice.'

It was a big room, all wooden like the inside of a gigantic packing case, with only the fireplace of stone. The windows were high and tangled among the tarry rafters and beams, smoke hanging about them like curtains. More people were there now, squashing in. Brunel could hear Bone's voice somewhere against the playing record, lilting an American college song, the chorus reprised by a choir of harsh young voices making hard work of the sung English.

Hilde came back, sliding expertly through the crush, and handed Brunel a full pint of red wine in a thick glass. He grimaced and she glanced at him guiltily. Before he could make any observation she said: 'Brunel, Gunter has been in your country.'

'Good for him,' said Brunel. He thought he knew what would follow now. Every time 'your country' meant London, and in his whole life he had spent only half an hour in his capital city and that was changing trains. He tried to forestall Gunter.

'Paddington,' said Brunel nodding in the manner of a friendly expert. 'Marble Arch, The Elephant.'

Gunter doubtfully screwed his face. *'Nein,'* he said.

'Piccadilly,' burst out Brunel, and then, almost blocked. 'Paddington,' again.

Gunter rolled his blond head. 'Brynglas Miners' Welfare,' he recited carefully. 'Pant-coed Bricklayers Arms. That is good. Plasdewydd Quarry for taking the young ladies in the summertime.' This was apparently a joke because he laughed.

'England?' queried Brunel.

'Wales, England,' confirmed Gunter. He thought a moment and then added: 'Taffy boy-o,' slapping Brunel on the back.

Hilde said: 'The Panzers they go to this place for training.'

Gunter said: 'It was no good. The sand got into my *kannon*.'

'That Welsh sand does,' agreed Brunel. 'Bloody terrible for the *kannon*.'

Suddenly Gunter lost his cherry look, he stood up squarely and said to Brunel gravely, 'My *kannon* is good. It points East.'

'Why?' asked Brunel suddenly chilly. He was half way down the wine in the thick glass.

'Because that is where it points, my friend,' said Gunter deliberately. 'It is a good *kannon* in the tank. Twenty five millimetre, double recoil . . .'

' . . . Forty rounds per minute and you keep it very nice,' finished Brunel for him 'You told me before.'

Puzzled Hilde was looking at something in Brunel's face. 'Brunel,' she said. 'He is only a young man.'

'With a *kannon*,' said Brunel. He turned to go, conscious that the wine was soaking into the sponges of his gut and mind.

He filled his mouth up again, though, letting it run first down the ducts of his teeth and gums, then clumsily feeling it squirt from the corner of his lips. As he turned he found himself confronted with Bone.

'This is Gunter,' Brunel said slowly to Bone. 'He has a *kannon*. He keeps it nice and it points East.'

Gunter gave a short bow. He seemed unable to detect Brunel's mood. But the talk had wiped the boyishness from his face and his eyes were stiff and military now. He was bulky and truculent and Brunel remembered now seeing him in a comic in his childhood.

'Why keep the *kannon* nice?' asked Bone. 'Why point it anywhere? In that way some military fool is going to expect you to go out and use it.' He had slowed almost to a drawl and Brunel saw that he too had a thick glass in which now only remained a short wedge of wine. Gunter stared at the American.

'I recall,' said Bone abruptly, as though beginning a lecture, 'being a sight too darned clever when I was in the United States Marines.' Brunel, who was still about to go away, as he had been for some time, stopped again and returned. Others had joined the group by the fire too.

'We were playing a game,' said Bone. 'A childish game where some of us had to hide and the other guys had to find them.'

'Hide and seek,' said Brunel drunkenly helpful.

'Thanks, friend,' said Bone. 'Camouflage training. You know?'

'*Ja, ja,*' said Gunter with military enthusiasm. 'We also hide the tanks . . .'

'And I, being a too-clever guy, hid right under the feet of the platoon trying to spot us. I could have touched their pants. I was in a kinda ditch, behind a little bit of scrub. They found all the other guys that were spread out in the distance; just too easy that was. But they couldn't find me. And when I came out, boy, was the sergeant-instructor pleased. "You're a born com-bat-man, son," he said to me. I was pleased too. And the Commanding Officer was pleased when he heard. And the next thing I knew, friends, I was on a draft for Korea, where they were fighting in those far days.' He looked at Gunter. 'Don't be a born soldier, son. To hell with the *kannon*. Keep it dirty and don't point it.'

Gunter blinked but said nothing and Bone drifted away easily, taking with him a sort of core of followers, to some other part of the big wooden room. They be-gan to sing the Whiffenpoof Song, the Germans sitting contentedly about Bone's feet.

Gunter went away and Brunel said to Hilde: 'That Bone is like a sort of tee-shirt Jesus. Wisdom and words and people following him around. Why are you drinking like that?'

She smiled unhappily. 'It is good wine, local wine,' she said.

'Your old man wouldn't like you drinking like this,' he said with firm intentions, but unsure whether the words were emitted firmly or not. 'And you were smok-ing when I got here. Like a roll of brown paper.'

'Shut up, Brunel,' she said. '*You* sound like an army Jesus.' She went away from him, slim and hurt, and he filled his bulky glass from the wine bottle on the table. The wine had muscles of its own and his strength was sapping. There was a lot of dancing and shouting going on now and the place was foggy with smoke. There was an indistinct group in one corner, but Brunel could hear Bone's accented voice.

'Yeah, sure. Eichmann was a snerd. I was there, sure I was. In Jerusalem when they had him on trial in a glass box. I went every day for a month. It was too hot outside, so I used to go and watch it. Oh boy, that guy was no good even to the blessed memory of the

Führer. He never made any fight. He wasn't even a good bit of sadism for the Jews. That was Eichmann.'

'Was he like that, then?' a girl asked. 'Did he not stand up straight before the Jews?'

'Balls,' said Bone amiably. 'He just sat and listened. He looked like some little guy at night classes. He did you no credit at all, friends.'

Bone surveyed all about him, apparently surprised that they were hanging so intently on the recollection. 'Oh, come on,' he said encouragingly. 'We're talking about a snerd. This is the character who complained that at the first Jewish execution he attended he felt sick because some Jewish kid's blood splashed on his uniform. Then he told them, the judges in Jerusalem, I mean, that he remembered this place well because there was this nice railroad terminal there. It was built in the reign of the Emperor Franz Josef, and he had always liked the things from that era.

'And he described the railroad station, friends, and said it was painted a pretty yellow and it had arches and statues and all crap like that. Then he said he went along to another place where they had been killing Jews that day and they'd buried them and he could see their blood welling up from the ground like a spring.' He looked around him. 'How can you tell about two lots of murder and put in a railroad station—painted yellow and with cherubs—slap in the middle of it?'

'Adolf Eichmann,' said Gunter standing tall, looking down at Bone, 'was a brave and famous German. I salute him.'

A vacuum of silence took hold of the young people. Then a voice: 'He was a man who, like the others, took a knife and cut all the self-respect from the heart of this country. Took out its dignity and threw it like offal in the dust. Eichmann was a poor German.' It wasn't Bone saying it. The voice which had answered for him was near the fringe of the group. Bone looked up with his pale, distant eyes. Gunter swung about sharply. Brunel had moved to the group and turned too.

The young man who had spoken was slouched and reedy, his eyes like tunnels in his face. These eyes were regarding Gunter, the youth from the Panzers, with a half-hidden calmness. 'I believe what I say,' he said to Gunter.

'Fool,' retorted Gunter in a low hard voice. Brunel could see him plainly now marching in the drawings in his comics. Then he repeated: 'Fool. Who are you?'

'I do not know you,' said the other young man. 'I have only come to Fulsbad this year. But they have told me you are in the Panzers.'

'I am,' growled Gunter. 'I am proud to be.'

The slouched youth moved, without shoving, through the people before him and stopped an arm's distance from Gunter. Bone was squatting on the floor almost under their feet. Hilde had come to stand alongside Brunel. Brunel looked at her and decided that, perhaps, she was just on Gunter's side.

'My name is Werner, and I am pleased to meet someone who is proud to be a Panzer and drive a big tank.'

'I fire the *kannon*,' corrected Gunter.

'Even more destructive,' encouraged Werner as though it were a good point. 'Which way is your *kannon* pointing, Gunter?'

'East,' Brunel broke in drunkenly. 'He told me it points East. Over there.' He extended his finger towards the West. Changed his mind and pointed the other way.

Hilde laughed at him and he scowled at her in confused annoyance. Most people had the heavy glasses in their fists loaded with the ruby wine. Werner whirled his about the bulb like blood, drank deeply and wiped the drops from his strong, jutting chin. Gunter had said nothing more and had remained motionless except to glance at Brunel when he had interrupted. The rest of the group shifted uneasily, watching the confrontation. The music was still coming out like some animal voice in the background and some of the young people were still dancing at the far end of the room. A girl, who had swallowed too much of the wine, was giggling and crying in short alternating bursts. From the fringe of the crowd a boy turned around fiercely and told her to shut up as though she were spoiling something good or sacred.

'The Panzers are fine,' said Werner with a quick smile. He had the gaunt looks and accentuated eyebrows of a male ballet dancer and his face was always moving into an expression or away from one, like a rough reedy pond empting and immediately refilling.

'They are fine,' nodded Gunter.

'Honourable in battle and with a brave history,' agreed Werner. 'But this is all the better reason, my countryman, why they should not be used by cruel and ambitious men for destruction.'

'Fool,' grunted Gunter. 'Pacifist fool.'

'A pacifist, yes,' concurred Werner willingly. Then he shouted: 'Everyone here—in this age group and in this country most of all—should be a raving pacifist.' His tone dropped at once. 'Anything for peace. Anything to stop the marching and the death,' he said. He took a step nearer Gunter. 'You and your Panzer tank and your *kannon* are old and silly, my friend. Left behind by events.'

Gunter hit him with his wine glass still hooked in his fist. Werner took the blow high on the cheekbone and fell down across Bone's feet. 'My *kannon* is good,' said

Gunter with finality. The glass had shattered in his palm, thick though it was, and the wine was now running with blood down the front of his trousers. He looked at the two streaming reds as though wondering from where they could have come. Werner apologised to Bone, got off Bone's feet and on to his own. The skin on his higher cheek had burst like a flower, red and with ragged petals. His channelled face was grey. Brunel looked at Gunter and saw him every inch a young German, the broad, heavy face, the close fair hair, almost golden in the lights of that wooden room, the excited blue eyes and the full mouth.

'So,' said Werner. 'We must fight. This is what you want?'

'This is what I want,' confirmed Gunter.

'In the way of this region?' asked Werner. Blood was running in a thin streak from the wound on his cheek-bone, like a stem to the flower.

'Of course, in the way of the region,' said Gunter.

Brunel was squeezing his eyes together in a drunken attempt to sober himself, as though he could himself press out some of the wine that was swilling in his belly. He had some shadowy idea that he and Bone, as the older people present, should stop this but he couldn't frame the words with sufficient conviction, and he could not step forward without staggering. Bone made a move from his place on the floor but that was only his contribution to the general motion to make room for the fighters.

'What is ...' Brunel began, looking at Hilde, 'this thing about the region?'

'It is hateful,' she said in a frightened way. 'It is ridiculous and brutal. One will get badly hurt. Perhaps both.'

Bone sidled to them. Drunk as Brunel was, he could

see that Bone was drunk. He had been fine sitting on the floor, but standing up had revealed his limitations.

'Might be interesting,' he slurred, holding on to Brunel's arm and Hilde's narrow shoulder. 'A little local colour, Brunel. Like American students fighting with fraternity pins.'

'It is stupid,' repeated Hilde. 'Some mad tradition.' She watched sullenly as Gunter and Werner stripped to their waists. Gunter's chest was pink like the bright flesh of a little pig and there was a small copse of fair hairs on its crown. Werner's stomach, revealed as he bent and pulled his shirt away from his body, over his head, was arched like a cobra's neck, but his chest was narrow as a plank and he looked cold standing there watching Gunter.

'A long time ago, years or centuries, I don't know,' continued Hilde, 'there was a law in this region that men must not fight. There were hard punishments. It said that the people here must not raise their hands against each other. But men *must* fight, of course, especially German men. So they obeyed the written law and did not raise their hands. They tied them behind their backs and fought instead with their heads and their necks and their faces. It is brutal and childish. This is what they will now do, Brunel.'

Her voice slowed at the last part of the explanation, like a guide repeating something which long ago ceased to interest. She was close alongside him, hooked on to the arm which also supported his thick wine glass, holding like an apprehensive child.

'There is nothing will stop them,' she said resignedly. 'No peace. Only when Germans are beaten do they make peace. You have noticed that?'

'I've noticed,' agreed Brunel. 'You're not the only lot, dear. Wars are never stopped when they *could* end. Only when they *have* to end.'

He was trying to calculate how many tracks the long-player then on the turn, would run. Vaguely he recalled another, different noise only a minute before, and thought there must be at least fifteen minutes playing left in this one. That would last the fight, he thought, unless somebody took it off.

Nobody took it off, in fact two girls, thin as twigs, continued to dance in the short distance throughout the whole of the contest, never missing a beat for cries nor the crack of heads, nor blood itself, always on the rhythmic bounce and on the draw-away in accurate time.

Gunter seemed to be glowing. They had made a rough oval, not a circle because of the long character of the room, and he was posed and poised at one narrow extreme of it. He had a thick waist for a young man, but his chest was thicker, bulging now with his body's internal preparations for the battle like an engine getting up steam for a fast run. Because he was so pink the muscles at his arm and shoulder junctions looked fat, but Brunel guessed they were hard. Apart from the crowd of light hairs on the prow of his chest he had shorter hairs, lying flat and not so discernible across his breast area and his nipples, in this hair, were like small pressed, gold coins. There was blood working about in his neck, blotching the area about his jugular, and his face was bright from his stubby chin to the crest of the short fair hair framing his forehead. He stood like hard, shiny wax, waiting for them to tie his wrists, ready for his bullet head to do battle.

'Strength through joy,' muttered Brunel to himself, surveying the youthful Panzer gunner. He had drunk even more wine now and had reached the stage where he felt he might fall down at any moment. Even the saying of the three words intended for no one in particular required a careful building up of syllables, a definite putting and cementing into order, like a conscientious bricklayer constructing a little but important wall. He could see Bone some few people away, also adopting an unsure attitude, pursing his lips and screwing his eyes fiercely in that curious sort of test that men apply to themselves to see if they are really drunk or if their senses are just pretending.

At the other blunt point of the egg-shaped arena, the young man Werner was also waiting for them to tie his wrists. He seemed taut with nerves and tapped one foot to the background music coming from the record player. His trousers were shabby and ill-creased and the singlet he had now replaced over his starved chest was grey with dirt, almost inky at the edges below his armpits. He seemed to have everything opposite to Gunter. His face was wild and unsure, already blemished with Gunter's fist and wine glass, his neck was chicken-thin and corded with veins, and the sinews of his arms hung visible like the cables of a suspension bridge.

'Gunter will kill him,' whipered Hilde.

'He looks thin,' said Brunel with an expert's careful phrasing. 'But perhaps he's wiry too.' He remembered the euphemism from far back. At school they always referred to weak, skinny, children as wiry.

A self-appointed referee, a hard-faced young girl, now moved forward into the fighting area. She was short and square with a marathon-cyclist's legs. Her hair hung straight, black, on all sides, cut like steps into an ugly fringe. She said something, gave an order in German, and it was obvious that she would be obeyed.

Brunel did not catch it. 'What did she say?' he asked Hilde. He began turning his head down towards her face as he asked, but it lolled dolefully and of its own weight;

it seemed that only string were holding it to his body. He checked at the sensation, straightened it out again, and asked the question looking straight ahead with military rectitude.

'She said,' explained Hilde a little more cheerfully, 'that they must take their boots from their feet. It must be in good spirit. No kicking.'

'That's what I call sportsmanship,' commented Brunel. 'I mean, they can't do much damage with their heads can they?'

A pair of helpers at each end were now securing the wrists of the two youths with lengths of electric flex. No one had been able to find sufficient rope and the string they discovered was too fragile for the fight.

'You were right,' said Hilde seriously, 'about wiry. They put it on now, you see.' Brunel did not correct her. He watched the attendants tie the wrists with the devotion of nurses bandaging wounds. Both Gunter and Werner were barefoot now; Gunter's feet fat and clean and Werner's oddly aged, but with barbed uncut toenails.

When the fighters were ready and facing each other the music stopped abruptly, but only for a moment. The two stick-thin girls were still shadow dancing somewhere at the back, but they cut, changed the record, and began again, to a sharp, jerky beat, in a quicker tempo.

Bone went over to Brunel in a curious rolling motion. Brunel nodded towards the dark direction of the restarted record player. 'I thought it might be *Deutschland Uber Alles*,' he grunted. 'They like to observe the proper things.'

Bone said pedantically: 'Like to have a bet on the fight? Who do you fancy?'

Brunel turned his head, found it lolled again,

so straightened back once more. 'You ought to stop this, friend Yank,' he muttered. 'You started it.'

Bone admitted: 'I know. But nobody could make them quit now. I couldn't. A fight is like a good lay for a Hun, they'll go on till they're finished, no matter what.'

They began then. Both contestants moved towards the middle, thicker part of the space, and the girl referee took two paces back and watched them anxiously as though needing them finely balanced before she would permit them to fight. It was strange to see them ready to attack, bereft of their arms. They were comically awkward, waddling with their shoulders as though their legs were useless too. Brunel had a quick picture of the men he had seen floating in the medicinal pool and he wondered if they ever fought private contests. Then there was Pru's one-armed lover. How did he fight? Half of German manhood, when you thought of it, were out on a limb, yet they still fought. Perhaps, as Hilde had said, it was something in them.

Werner, perhaps anxious to put himself on even terms for the initial punch from Gunter, struck the first blow with his head. Gunter seemed to want him to give that one, like a tennis player deliberately throwing away a point to level a wrong line decision. He did not try to pull out of it and Werner's thin head hit him square across his fat cheek.

'Very sporting,' observed Brunel.

'How?' asked Bone.

'Taking that clump. Made up for the first one.'

Bone said, like an *aficionado* explaining to a novice: 'Gunter let him do it because it's bust open that cut on Werner's cheek again. Werner led with that side of his face.'

Brunel nodded, disappointed. 'He should go southpaw,'

he said. 'Turn the other cheek, and hit him with that.'

The fighters had resolved into a bending dance, almost mystical, the movements from the waist, the trunk angled to fit into an attacking position. First one would bow one way, then the other, trying to get their heads into striking pose, like storks in a courteous love ritual. Brunel had never before realised the full importance of arms.

Gunter, as might be expected, had his feet firmly apart on the pine floor, like well-fed rats, moving them slowly and only after obvious deliberation for the next manoeuvre. Werner's was a more mobile, but lightweight, attack. A movement from the hips and shoulders, a dark, gypsy dance. The technique came rapidly to Brunel, fuddled though he was. It was no game for defensive tactics. The antagonists had to come to a pact to attack each other. For one to do so, while the other side-stepped, was hopeless, for the attack was so necessarily clumsy that almost any evasive action was bound to succeed. It was an ideal way for two brave or angry men to fight, or for two cowards. *Both* had to fight to make a fight of it. Cowards could indulge in a marvellous non-battle until they reached the point of exhaustion, but no hurt.

But Gunter was angry and Werner was brave. Their initial slow whirlings, stranger because they were coinciding with the half-beat of the music still coming from the darkened end of the room, did not take too long.

Werner swished his body like a lean whip and flung his head into the final inches of the vicious movement. Gunter jumped with surprising grace, his pink feet leaving the floor like those of a quickly-rising angel. The blow only caught the extremities of his lips and the tip of his nose, bending both sharply right, and provoking a snort from the young soldier. He landed flat on his feet again and the head of a trickle of blood emerged from his right nostril like a timid animal venturing from a burrow. Gunter felt it crawling out. He involuntarily moved his tied hands attempting to put them up to test the blood. A vivid fury took hold of him. He straightened from the bending pose and threw himself bodily at Werner, taking him off-balance, and smashing into his head and neck with violent swishing of the fair head. It was like a man nuzzling a lover, but speeded up and hardened ten-fold, the swinging of the face a blunt, swift weapon.

Werner took one blow on each side of his jaw, the first ramming his head sideways to the left, the second flinging it back the other way. His eyes, by some curious misconnection swung the opposite way to his head, rocking, brightly startled, right and left at the same pace as the blows.

The girl crouching near them, the referee, had a sickly violent expression on her ugly face, like someone hidden and watching an orgy. She was ejecting short breaths, spitting them out through her teeth, like an American cheer-leader. Her legs would fly wide apart, and then close again like scissors, and her body movements, though oiled and definite, slipped quickly and frequently into wriggling contortions.

The two huge blows had sent Werner spinning away from Gunter, reeling and bending, and pulling his head right down into his shoulders as sure protection from further assault. Only the two had landed though, and Gunter had, in his own excitement, missed his immediate opportunity. He was standing off, snorting like a prize pig, his eyes alight with what he had achieved.

Werner, as though he were spring loaded, came at him like a ram, head slightly down, hitting him full in the face with the tangled dome of his head. Gunter screamed and went backwards, Werner falling unchecked on top of him. They rolled and writhed around the floor, in the open space, then among the feet, like snakes in a pit, striking out with their heads, then lying full-length, six inches apart, and smashing short blows at each other. The two brittle girls who had danced throughout, stopped, looked at the fighters, and then went together, hand in hand, to change the record. They may have chosen at random, in the dark, but however it was, the final throes of the fight were squirmed out on that wooden floor to the accompaniment of silvery strings and a Strauss waltz.

There was a catching, lilting melody, all spring woods and flowers and sunlight, while Gunter was leaning across Werner finally smashing his face. Werner had taken a violent collision of ears much worse than Gunter, and had fallen back on the floor as though paralysed. Gunter could only crawl by then, but he knelt, almost tenderly by Werner's side, and proceeded to rain head blows on the other youth, his head rising and falling viciously like a hen pecking corn. Before Bone, pushing aside the girl referee, who had just accomplished her orgasm, reached Gunter to pull him away, he too flopped forward, lying across Werner and forming a rough cross. There was blood smeared on the pine-wood boards, and some of the girls were weeping. Many of the young people began going towards the door. Brunel felt the wine crushing him down and he slid into a corner, hitting the floor and almost pulling Hilde down with him. He forced open one eye and treated her to a full, foul smile.

'Thank you for asking me,' he said. 'It was a lovely party.'

II

When he woke Brunel was hunched in a huge, soiled, salmon-coloured armchair. He knew immediately that he was still at the lodge because he could hear its wood creaking in the forest wind. Before there had been too much noise—first the music and singing and then the fight—to hear the wind, but he imagined it must sound like this all the time when everything else was quiet. The effect of the raw red wine was hanging over him like a dry drape. He shivered dustily as soon as his senses returned, but it was only internal shivering because the room was warm. There was a stone fireplace, smaller than the one in the big room, but the same shape; some logs had been burning in it for a long time because they were subdued red, cushioned on grey ash, with a small flame sometimes waving from them like a solitary hand.

Someone had taken his tie away and he buttoned the top of his shirt in some attempt to stop his dry shivers breaking out. His shoes had also gone and he looked about, but not moving his head too far, to see if he could see them. He couldn't. From his chair, without turning, he could see what he imagined must be about half the room, because a big, black beam, a central beam, projected over his head, and he could feel there was another deep part of the room behind him. Amber lamplight was coming from somewhere and he could not see the lamp. He felt too bad, too hard at his middle, too brittle at his outside, to turn then, so he sprawled quietly, taking in the part of the room he could see. There were unkempt books and furniture, and solid curtains against a low window, all dim and old, and a table very dusty except for a clean wide track scored across it by a girl's white slip. The slip had been thrown across it carelessly and had slid, but held to the far edge of the table, hanging down like a small, threatened avalanche.

Brunel attempted a minor movement in the salmon-coloured chair and found that it answered him with a squeaky swing of its own. It was on a swivel and by pushing out his foot he turned it grumpily a quarter of a circle and saw Hilde lying asleep, full naked on the bed.

It was a broad, wooden bed, with an impressively high back, carved like an altar, and a turmoil of bed-clothes, none of which was covering the girl. The lamp he knew would be there was three feet from her; a hideous squat lamp with startled birds of paradise on its yellow shade; but its light shone on Hilde.

She was so peacefully asleep, lying face down on the untidy sheet, so naked, that Brunel felt himself choke. He wanted to turn the chair, to jog away from her again but the simple action was beyond him. She breathed regularly, her face turned from him, the hem of the sheet lying primly across her lower legs as though they, of all her parts, should be hidden.

All the primary innocence that she had was there displayed at that moment. He had always thought her pretty in a small, awkward way, a child's way really, he supposed, and he enjoyed her youthfulness and her serious talk.

But now she lay for him to see, to inspect guiltily.

Perhaps she had planned it like that before she slept. He glanced to the left and saw that the slim middle bolt on the panelled door had been pushed home. Only she could have done that.

She had undressed carelessly, perhaps dreamily, because her few clothes were thrown about the room. Apart from the slip on the table her shoes were hung, one on each bottom bedpost, and her stockings over the top posts as though it were Christmas. He could see her sweater spreadeagled on the boards, half under the bed, its arms thrust out, like a headless swimmer.

Brunel was four feet away from her, grey as a waxwork in the big chair. He felt dry and old and foul, but the light from the hideous lamp was touching her sweet skin and he allowed himself to sit and watch.

Her hair was tumbled and had fallen into whirling shapes about the pillow and her gentle neck. At one place it had opened into a little fan, at another curled into the shape of smoke, and then become fringed and ordered like the straight end of a fine brush. The parts in shadow were dark and promising as velvet; the parts in the light were touched with copper.

A segment of her neck showed through the full hair, a pale stream, a tributary, running from the niche of one ear, straight down into the splendid light brown estuary of her shoulders. Her arms were raised, slightly higher than her head, the same distance each side. The hands and eventually the long fingers curved inwards as though she had fallen asleep while dancing.

The stem of her backbone was deep set, a long narrow dish, perfect slim inches of channel reaching down to the pink bald heads of her backside. Two triangles of white, one on each mound, were superimposed where her summer swimsuit had been. Her legs, brown again, thrust out beautifully from there, moulded well, and lying slightly apart.

While Brunel studied her, a tiny moneyspider, minute but mobile, emerged from the deep crack separating her buttocks and marched cheerfully up the long valley of her backbone like a hiker walking through glens. He was a wicked black and seemed to have his head in the air as he went. Brunel leaned forward in his chair, half-expecting to hear the little fellow singing. He was travelling at a good rate and within half a minute had accomplished the valley and was climbing ebulliently under the disarrayed patterns of her hair.

Hilde stirred immediately and, nowhere close to waking, rolled on to her back. Brunel could feel his face was damp and his throat was so full of dirt that he could not swallow. Once again he dared himself to turn the chair away, to look anywhere else, but again he failed to find the resolve to give one small push.

The treasure of this girl was all there for him to see. She smiled distantly and her nose moved in her dream. Her face, without the constant mobility of her eyes was confiding, guileless, and sprayed with small pale freckles across the nose. Her lips were opening slightly now, and closing again, as though she wanted a drink; her chin was a bud and her neck a sapling.

Brunel had never seen a young girl's breasts before. He had ever known they were like that: like dainty blancmanges topped with fairy pink, but firm and set, waiting for the birthday. He found himself muttering something which he did not quite hear. Then the moneyspider appeared, still travelling happily, like some Disney creature, over the round of her shoulder and in an unremitting line straight to her left breast which he proceeded to climb with all the bursting confidence of an alpine expert. Brunel wanted to scream. He moved to bend forward but realised there was nothing he could do. The spider was having difficulty near the summit and he paused. Brunel would not have been surprised if he had produced a tiny ice-pick. The nipple was curved up and out a little, before it converged to its round-pointed head and the spider had to climb under and over in one determined rush to attain the top. This he did and stood surveying the world of Hilde's body from the apex of the little mountain.

Brunel followed the spider's line of view, down the slope to her stomach, flat and smooth and brown as a lonely beach at low tide, with the navel hole at its centre like the burrow of some small sand animal. Her legs, now she was on her back, had pulled away from the white sheet, and he could see them from groin to big toe. They were slightly pulled up, minutely arched, so that the smooth dunes of her thighs sloped down to meet the beach of her stomach, and between them was grouped her pubic puff like a sea anemone washed ashore and dried.

When he had been looking for the sea, in his younger days, his bicycle days, he had sometimes found a solitary shore like Hilde. Usually it was late in the year, quiet November, a monochrome day with no movement on the untouched beach and the only sounds those coming from within himself. After all the ugliness he had faced in these past weeks, Keenor, and the windows of women in Hamburg, and the gnawed limbs of old men in the baths, and the blooded heads of the young men in battle that very night. after all that here was loveliness and tranquility and most certain innocence.

He had forgotten the spider, however, and now, having balanced like some small circus show-off on the nipple for some time, it jogged, slipped, and finally slid down the lower slope of Hilde's breast, and then continued on its carefree tramp down the rest of her body. 'If it goes between her legs I shall wake her, get it out and stamp on it,' Brunel promised himself as he watched. 'Squash it up.' The spider, of course knowing nothing of this threat, proceeded busily across Hilde's stomach, into her navel dimple, out again and headed unerringly for the wedge of her thighs.

'No,' whispered Brunel, nearly away from the chair. 'No. Not there. To the left, you bastard, to the left.'

Hilde was awake when he looked at her face to see if she was awake, considering him with dreamy amusement while he waved his arms like a traffic policeman at the spider. He was bending over her, away from the chair.

'Who is this bastard who must go to the left?' she inquired sweetly.

'Sorry,' said Brunel aghast at the situation. 'It was a spider He's ... he's ... sort of ... gone down there.'

He pointed desperately, suddenly wondering whether he had really seen it, or imagined it, and she curled with joy, covering her face with her girl's hands and laughing behind them. 'Oh, Brunel,' she said quietly, 'I sometimes wonder which of us is the child.'

He stood now, head down with his own awful misery. He said: 'You are the child. *Definitely*.' He felt he was full of thick bubbling hot water and when she told him: 'Put your hands on me, Brunel,' he reached out and placed them lightly, one on each pure and naked shoulder.

She was half sitting up now, lodged on her pointed elbows on the bed. He had screwed up his eyes and was trembling.

'Why are you afraid?' she asked.

'For you,' he said simply. 'Nothing must happen to you.'

The bolt on the door must have been thrust into a weak or badly screwed receiving end, because the entire door flew in at that moment as though an explosive charge had been fired behind it. It was Keenor's shoulder that did it. He stood there rubbing the joint and in the background were some other men. Keenor looked at Brunel and the girl, frozen in their separate but loving attitudes, and then concentrated his greedy eyes on her exposed chest. His hands stopped rubbing his shoulder.

Brunel moved. *'Get out, Keenor!'* he cried leaping at the man. *'Get out! Get out!'* He took Keenor with the full force of his rushing fury, throwing him out like a drunk from a bar, slamming the door and throwing two older, stronger bolts at the top and bottom.

He shuddered back from the door, panting and very frightened. 'Against the wall, Hilde,' he urged. 'Against the wall, darling. This bastard will shoot through the door.'

'This bastard won't shoot through the door, darling,' said Keenor's voice oozing thinly through the keyhole. 'I just want you both to come out, that's all, Brunel son. Don't try the window. It's a longer drop than you can manage—about five hundred feet. I guess.'

Brunel glanced at Hilde and she nodded confirming the drop outside. He called towards the door. 'Just wait, Keenor. We'll be out in a minute.'

'When the chick is dressed?' asked Keenor, enjoyably, through the keyhole.

'Yes,' said Brunel. 'And don't spy through the keyhole either, old mate, because I'll ram a pencil through it and into your eye.'

'Tell her to get dressed,' said Keenor sourly. 'She's got two minutes.'

Hilde had been standing quite still against the wall. Now she came towards Brunel with her customary young assurance. 'Who is this?' she whispered. 'Somebody very powerful?'

'He's the most powerful man in the world at this minute. He's got a gun,' said Brunel. 'Get your things on, Hilde.'

She smiled sadly at him. 'So many things I know nothing about,' she shrugged. 'I thought that you had been so strange these weeks. Is it something to do with war?'

'Much worse,' grunted Brunel. 'It's to do with peace. Come on. Get into your clothes. Your slip is over there.'

She pouted. 'I know where it is.' She went to the table and took the white garment from its edge. 'And here,' she suddenly smiled, 'are my little things.' She went to the chair in which he had been sleeping and took a ball of white silk from the seam of the back and the padded seat. Brunel stared at her without understanding. 'I put them behind your head when you were sleeping and drunk in the chair,' she explained sweetly. 'For a soft pillow.'

Brunel felt himself blushing. She stopped with the silk like a rolled kitten held in her hands and took a step towards him, looking into his face with gigantic seriousness. 'You remember the beach and the little girl and her pants,' she said. 'You told me, remember?'

'Yes, I remember,' he nodded.

'Now you put these on for me,' she asked. 'I want you to do that, Brunel. Will you? For me.'

Almost choking he took the white silk ball from her, and felt the superb richness of the simple garment on his fingers and the palms of his hands.

As he took it Keenor snorted from the other side of

the door. 'I'm getting nasty, Brunel boy. One minute left.'

Brunel did not reply to him. They were standing inches away from each other, entranced in what they were about to do. His body felt tensed and powerful as steel. Her quiet eyes were fixed on his face as she waited.

He moved a fraction closer, holding out his hands and slowly and gracefully, like a little pony, she lifted one leg. He put them on this leg, waiting for the toes to emerge through the silk and then gently drawing them over her ankle.

'Now the next,' she instructed as though he could not possibly know. She lifted her right leg, through the hole. Then Brunel with his fingers drew them up her long, young stems, the inside of each thumb travelling first over the skin, right up to the join. He eased them over her lovely buttocks and then helped them as they slipped up over her lower stomach. They were in place then; she was wearing them. He turned with huge self-reproachment from her and called: 'I'm coming out now, Keenor. The girl will be a minute. Nobody must come in or I'll kill them. She'll be out before long.'

He unbolted the door and opened it slightly. Keenor was standing back, a revolver aching in his hand, black hair plastered down, the white parting like an arrow. Two men in civilian suits were just behind him. Brunel went out. Keenor grinned a fat grin. 'Frolics with little girls, eh, Brunel?' he said.

Brunel felt like hitting him, but he didn't want any shooting. So he said calmly: 'It's my only pleasure, Mr. Keenor.'

12

Keenor pushed the cat from the desk with such hard unpleasantness that Brunel frowned. It furred up, but decided against retaliation, and padded away with a sneer. It went to lie across the harmless feet of Hilde sitting on an old wooden filing cabinet one side of which had been gnawed into holes by machine-gun bullets loosed may years before.

'Consorting-with-known-Nazis,' spelled out Keenor. Brunel was standing and the single dusty light was shining directly on Keenor's sticky black hair. The other two men were sitting among the moribund documents in the background, one of them reading Brunel's recipe for correct preparation of anti-anaemia port wine. The other one had taken a file at random from the shelf and was engrossed in an account of a useless patrol raid near Alsace in the autumn of 1944.

Brunel had never been in his office at four in the morning and he did not like it. It looked very moribund.

'Nazis,' repeated Keenor. 'An operative group, and *you* were consorting with them. *Her* father for one.'

Brunel felt Hilde begin to get to her feet. He asked the question for her and she sat down again. 'What have you done with him?' He looked closely at Keenor as though their roles were reversed and it was he who sat with the gun and the questions.

'Nothing,' grunted Keenor surprisingly, but with such obvious disappointment that Brunel knew it was the truth. 'Nothing as yet. We're looking for Otto Furter. He's farted off somewhere on a horse, dressed like a cowboy, so he shouldn't be too difficult to locate.' He grinned at his own pun and then turned on Brunel again.

'*Nazis*,' he said for the third time. 'And *Commies* too.'

'It's a fine combination,' admitted Brunel, astonished. 'Who are the Commies I've been consorting with?'

'Well let's try the name of George Bone and see how that fits,' snarled Keenor. 'You know this agitator?'

Brunel was stunned. 'Agitator?' he said. 'Christ, the man was staying at my hotel. What could I do, tell him to go East? I didn't know he was a Communist.'

'Didn't know,' mocked Keenor. 'Aw come on, sonny. How about this Anti-Re-unification petition. You knew about that.'

Brunel didn't think Prudence had told Keenor. But you could not be certain with Prudence. 'What's happened to Bone?'

'Farted off,' admitted Keenor reluctantly. 'Before we could even get a look at him.'

'In a cowboy suit?'

'*Shut up, Brunel!* I've got *you*, and I've got *her*.' He nodded nastily across to Hilde. 'That's okay to go on with. I want to know everything you know.'

Brunel felt fearful and felt a sickness go to his

face. 'She . . .' he began. 'That child knows not a thing. .'

Keenor hooted 'That child. Hey, that's bloody great! That child! You big sporting bastard Britisher. Protecting the young!' He paused and gave Brunel a glance that a disappointed schoolmaster would give a pupil who had let him down. 'She's *not* a child, Brunel. She wasn't a child a couple of hours ago when you were screwing her up at the lodge. She didn't look a child when you were helping her on with her silk pants in the room.'

'Bastard,' said Brunel.

'Yah, I peeked. I was naughty.' He regarded Brunel again with dark seriousness. '*You* don't know,' he said 'You *can't* know the pressures and the responsibilities that lie on me In twenty-four hours they'll be signing that treaty here, and I'm the guy who's supposed to have the whole place vetted and clean. All the security clutch are moving in.' He nodded at the two men now both reading files in the shadows. 'And now, right *now*, I get wind that one of my own men is in with reactionary groups.' He looked deeply hurt. 'I always got full marks, Brunel. Always. Nobody's ever known me not to get full marks. But I'm not going to this time. This will be the first time I haven't got full marks. I think I'll take you out to that bloody forest and nail you up somewhere. I'll have you crucified.'

'It's been done,' said Brunel. 'Years ago.'

Keenor looked sorry for him. 'Too smart, that's your complaint, Brunel. Clever, smart, funny, funny.' He snorted. 'Consorting with Nazis!'

'And Commies,' Brunel reminded him.

'Yeah, Commies too,' acknowledged Keenor suddenly

absently, and apparently not seeing the sarcasm. He hunched on the desk apparently putting together a big thought, then he brightened and said: 'I've got to know it all. Everything you know. *Everything she knows.*'

He underlined the final sentence so heavily that Brunel felt a shiver building up inside himself. But he kept it in, pressed it down so it would not shudder free. 'So, let me guess, you'll have to torture me,' he said. He tried to emphasise the last word without emphasising it.

Keenor had a truly nasty smile. He could not have smiled pleasantly if God or someone of equally high standing, had walked into the room. Now he smiled at Brunel and then Hilde. 'It's a great idea,' he said.

'I'll tell,' said Brunel simply. 'Everything we know.'

'No you won't,' answered Keenor quickly. 'I'm going to get out of you more than you would tell your own mother. I don't let anybody bugger up my chance of getting full marks on this operation without paying for it. Come on, friends, we're going to take the waters.'

In all her life after that night experience Hilde could never swim in the sea, nor in a river nor a pool. The water terror which Keenor forced upon her smothered her with a fear that never went away. Before that night she had swum every day in summer in the pools that the small river Agoos left and fed in the meadow country beyond the town, where the forest ended. She was slim and agile in the water, swimming with sleek strength, diving from a place where they had fixed a plank out from a fallen tree, and rummaging about in the deepest cellars of the ponds where the biggest of the fish hid from the sun. But after Keenor had finished with her she was always afraid.

Throughout all the whole time of it, the hour or the two hours, or the half an hour, she never knew how long, she tried to throw her mind away from that fantastically terrible present; to throw it wildly, like a saving rope, far from her, hooking it on to some small thing of the past that she had liked or loved and had sufficient remembrance for her to take some of the horror away.

Keenor left the two shadowy men behind him when he took Hilde and Brunel down to the medicinal baths. He did not want them to realise what had happened to him. He had taken the thin steel handcuffs from the security men, put them about her slim wrists and Brunel's thick wrists, and then told the men to remain behind and enjoy themselves with reading the old files.

They went along the clammy corridor, dark as only marble can be dark, cutting out light as though there never had been light. The hot water cocktail fountain was still throwing up in the entrance, sounding in a silence. Brunel had never noticed it made a noise before; not a watery noise either but a regular mechanical gurgle like a coffee percolator or someone dialling on a loose telephone dial. He and Hilde, their held wrists behind them, went down the corridor with Keenor prodding their spines with the nose of his gun or the heavy finger of the other hand. He never spoke but grunted like a shepherd's dog, harrying them down the stairs to the baths, pushing Brunel roughly and Hilde more gently, using his hard hand flat against the slight swelling of her short skirt at the back.

Keenor must have returned to the baths since the day he and Brunel were in the pool with the maimed men, thought Brunel. Either that or he memorised light switches very well. He turned on a cluster of small lights hung in the roof, and then, with a strangely happy look on his ugly face he turned a single white beam down on to the small side pool where the wooden ducking stool squatted at the water line.

All the steam of the day was gone from the place now. It was dead and without spirit like the void belly of a furnace holding only cold ashes.

'We must take our shoes off,' said Keenor like a guide conducting tourists round a mosque. 'They spoil the floors and the baths people don't like it.' He bent and took his own brown shoes off, leaving them at one side and pausing and rearranging them minutely so that the toes were completely in line. Then, standing with smiling carefulness out of kicking distance, he took Brunel's shoes away, and finally Hilde's, holding her foot in his hand for a few moments and running his fingers over it.

'Listen, Keenor,' said Brunel desperately and hoping he sounded genuine. 'I can tell you plenty of things. I was with the Nazis up to the ears. I've been with them for years. And I know about the Reds too, because I was infiltrated into them for the Nazi lads. I've decided to tell you everything, Keenor. It's only fair to you.'

They had walked to the side of the little pool now. Under the single light the chair on its ratchet looked like an engine of execution. The water was emerald, very still. Keenor turned to Brunel and mimicked: 'I've decided to tell you everything, Keenor. It's only fair to you.' He punched Brunel with huge force in the stomach. Every muscle in Brunel heaved, trying to get out of his mouth. He doubled forward and while he was bent Keenor casually pushed him backwards into the pool.

Brunel had wondered if the water remained at its daytime warmth all the time. It did not. It attacked him with its bitter iciness as he struck it and gnawed at him like a maneater all the way to the bottom tiles. He rolled about in the basement of the terrible tank, the light coming through the freezing green, numbed and shocked. Almost by reflex, and with what seemed his last second of strength, he pushed his legs against the bottom and sailed slowly up through the aching water again. His head came through the skin of the pool and he heard Hilde screaming for him, his name crashing in huge, high echoes about the marble-tiled spaces flying along pitch dark corridors and howling over the other pools, settled as death in their tiled squares.

She saw his head pierce the surface and tried to go after him, fighting like a vicious puppy to get away from Keenor. But Keenor wanted Hilde in the chair, and he merely held the handcuff chain at her wrist and let her fight. Brunel was making noises like a bullfrog, trying to call to her with reassurance, trying to keep his balance and his mouth away from the water.

The steel at his wrists was cutting through the skin and into the sinews. He could feel his flesh ragged and broken. Because he had no balance with his hands held at his back, his trunk kept turning in slow circles so that his head was above and beneath the water alternately, his eyes full of the naked glaring light or the engulfing green of the water.

But after the first panic he began, surprising himself, to think lucidly, and his first thought was the optimistic one that at least the freezing water had acted as a quick antidote to Keenor's punch. Even if he were due to drown within two minutes he no longer felt sick. He knew that the one chance he had was to reach the side of the small pool and to hang on to the water-level handrail with his chin or his feet or even somehow with his imprisoned hands, even though they were behind him. He kicked towards the far side, away from Keenor who watched him with interest while tightening a short leather strap as a gag across Hilde's mouth. He forced the girl's tongue over the top of the strap with his thick finger and thumb, keeping her teeth open with the mass of his hand, so far open that she could not even bite him. His other hand pulled her over backwards from the chain of the handcuffs, and held her down, like a captured young seal, while the thong gag was fixed.

He picked her up then, while Brunel bobbed like a mooring buoy by the distant rail. He took her, not fighting now but weeping, over to the wooden chair and sat her in it. Holding her powerfully across the stomach with one hand he fixed around her the broad straps that were used in working hours for fastening rheumy ladies to the seat before lowering them to the benison of the water. The old ladies were regular paying customers, and not one had ever fallen from the chair into the pool because the straps were good straps.

Keenor looked at the girl with the satisfaction of a man occupied with a difficult hobby, as though, at last something had gone right for him. He turned and saw Brunel wallowing painfully by the rail on the distant side. It was an excellent pool for this sort of operation. He had thought that from the time he first saw it. There were no steps. No one would ever get out from it if his arms were tucked away out of use.

He called cheerfully across to Brunel, like a true friend: 'Hold on, son. I'm coming to help.' He waddled around the edge and reaching down caught Brunel's fair hair. He trawled him along to where the rail terminated with an ornate, oval knob. Reaching carefully he got two fingers, and then his whole hand on the chain of the handcuffs behind Brunel's back. Then he heaved with his great strength, brought half Brunel's body above the surface and deftly hooked the chain of the handcuffs over the final knob of the rail. Brunel found himself face down, hanging behind by his wrists, projecting into the pool, with his feet against the tiled sides, but his nose just clearing the water. He was fixed there, hung out, like the carved figurehead of a ship.

Keenor leaned over and patted him. 'I always got full marks for forced interrogation, Brunel. Never less than full marks.'

'I'm going to kill you, Keenor,' bubbled Brunel, his mouth hardly clearing the water.

'Consorting with Nazis,' answered Keenor like a quarrelsome child, backing away along the side of the bath, towards the chair and Hilde. 'And Commies,' he added thrusting his head forward with petulant emphasis, as though clinging to an excuse for what he was doing, and what he was going to do. Then he turned and with a few anxiously-hurried strides made for Hilde.

Brunel watched him, in the way that Keenor had intended he should watch, move close and greedily to Hilde. Her young eyes went around to him, not fierce now, but with a soft despising light in them. Keenor patted her legs in an almost fatherly fashion, liked it, and so went back and did it again, but slower. He put his fingers against her skirt and her sweater as he tested the firmness of each of the chair straps.

The chair was on a pulley and ratchet mechanism so that it could be raised or lowered, straight up and down, into the pool. The operation took some time because the aged people who were put into the water when it was nicely warm in the daytime were too infirm to stand more than a gentle journey. Keenor released a lever and pushed a button. Brunel knew then he had been back and learned since the day they were there together.

Hilde was lowered into the bitter water, inch before inch. Brunel closed his eyes because he could not bear to see her face when the water caught her. His exposed head felt quite separate from the rest of him; his whole cold body below seemed like some strange, numb tail. Hilde sat still and stiff, very bravely, while her feet went in, although she knew from the first bite of the water how terrible it was to be. It travelled like green ice up her slim legs, kept apart by the straps, so cold that by the time it was at her knee her entire body was shivering in the chair. Her eyes closed as she waited for what must happen next. It happened with all the cruel sharpness of a sword, another notch down on the ratchet, another inch into the water, and it came shooting up the creek between her legs so cold that it made her tremble and scream.

Three noises were sounding like animal voices around the empty place now. The crying, sharp and low, of the girl, a hard breathing and grunting from Keenor standing, eyes eating her, and gruff sea-lion barks from the feeble Brunel in the water.

As she went down, as the level caught her thighs and back and then her waist, as it put all its wet cold fingers under her skirt and then her sweater, Hilde threw her mind away from it with a huge effort.

Despite the freezing water creeping up her, there was sweat on her face, and tears, and she screwed up her nose and mouth and eyes like a wrinkled nut, and forced away the present and remembered being a little girl, one day, when her father took her to a space in the forest where a tall carpenter worked in a hut. She was four then. Otto had held her hand all through the trees and told her that the carpenter was a magic man and made tables and chairs for the forest people. She remembered how delighted she had been because that day they were going to collect a rocking horse he had made for her. Actually he was not a magic man, but he had once been a German cavalry soldier, in the first war, and, for fun, he mounted the rocking horse himself and rode it, swishing about on each side with a spokeshave, pretending it was a sword, and he was, once again, an Uhlan warrior. He was very tall, with a white moustache, and he laughed roughly as he used the imagined weapon, which had frightened her a little, but she remembered it as a good day because the forest was clean and new with spring and she was with her father and she went home with her rocking horse. . . .

The water had pinched her chest, shrivelling her breasts, and frozen her shoulders now. She was very strong within herself and she could not faint. There was a point where the chair was supposed to stop. It sometimes stopped for the rheumatics patients after it had only gone into the water a short depth. But Keenor let it go on. He never asked any questions about her father, the Nazis, or anything else. He merely stood beside her like a conscientious engineer at a vital machine, and made his own private noises.

When the level was at her throat she mentally fled again to the winter when she had learned to ski. Then the snow was piled in the streets of Fulsbad and she had gone with the other young people up to the slopes beyond the trees. She was thirteen at the time and she remembered how the butcher's son, Klaus, had tried to kiss her when he helped her up after she had fallen in a drift. And the ski-ing! Oh, how that had been. A young girl's dream of enchantment, flying down the steeps and over the humps, suddenly endowed with the gift of balance and ability after many failures. She could see herself now, red and rushing, with the air flying away from her ears and cheeks, and the shouts of her friends on the slopes. . . .

The water went over her face, to her forehead, freezing and shocking every muscle. It was not for long. Keenor began to manipulate her out of the pool. Up came the chair and she was still upright, still clenched in the straps, her young clothes sticking to every swelling, every flat, every hole in her body. Up she came further and the green cascade flowed from between her legs and then she was free of it, shivering in the air and now with warm tears running over the iciness of her cheeks.

She could never remember how many times he did it before she lost consciousness. Her mind had been occupied with the Easter Fair, with the skipping games they had enjoyed at school, with the autumn dance in the Town Hall, with the day she had gone shopping with her father in Munich, with the picnics of half a dozen summers, with the recent hour she spent lying beside her beloved Brunel in the culvert in the forest. . . .

At six in the morning the man who always arrived first at the medicinal baths, a coughing boilerman who started the fires and the stream, saw the lights and went in and found Brunel and Hilde. She was still in the chair, clear of the water but unconscious. Brunel was on the last seconds before drowning, his head lying in the water while he hung from the pool rail by the handcuffs. The boilerman pulled them out. He was a simple man and he had seen people faint on hot days and knew that you gave them drinks of cold water. To these two frozen beings, then, he logically brought each a cup of hot water from the cocktail fountain. Then he called the Fulsbad ambulance.

13

After six hours Brunel got dressed and walked out of the hospital. He was on his way to kill Keenor. He still felt the chill of the pool upon him, a cold lying over him like a skin of frost, thicker below the armpits, and in the gathering of his groin. He thought that killing the American would make him feel much better.

It was Wednesday, Orange Wednesday. The wounds of Europe were to be healed that afternoon at the Fulsbad Golf Hotel, stitched with pen and ink across parchment. Brunel cared nothing about Europe, whether its wounds were healed or whether it got deadly septic poisoning. His was a small personal wish.

He walked down through the town. It was not at its best in that month. The sweet autumn light had gone now and the place sat dumbly, like one of its own visitors, in the dun November day, the old buildings suddenly senile, the roads too steep for them to stand upon, slippery with a smear of rain. The trees rattled now and the sky was sad. As Brunel walked to get his gun to kill Keenor the nice old clock struck mid-day.

At his hotel Frau Snellhort chose this day to meet him with a complaint. 'Is not this hotel good for you now?' She placed her working hands primly across the front of her apron. 'You go away and are not in your bed. All the time you are out. There is no fishing from you these days. I make your breakfast today and you are somewhere else. It was good breakfast.'

Brunel looked at her wearily. 'I didn't feel like breakfast today, Frau Snellhort,' he said. 'I am very sorry. I have a cold.'

She turned in a feathery huff. 'This week also,' she sniffed clinically, 'you have had *no* bath.'

Brunel all but cried out aloud at that. But he had to get on with his murder so he patted her hurt shoulder and went up to his room. He decided to take his service revolver, which was a good one and to which he had given great care, rather than the powerful rifle. The rifle could not be concealed and he honestly fancied shooting Keenor at close range because he wanted to see the look on his face. He opened the door of his bedroom. He found his stomach disturbingly level with the small black hole of Otto's Colt revolver. Otto, still in Western frills and leathers, was hunched on the bed, gripping the implement with frightening lack of skill.

'Put it down,' said Brunel.

Otto put it down. 'I am in fear,' he began. 'I am hunted down by Americans or some sort of men like that. They have put some of the cowboys in a prison. I don't want to be in a prison.'

Brunel felt a presence behind him, in the passage outside, and turned quickly upon a conciliatory Frau Snellhort holding before her a cup of black coffee.

'To take the cobwebs away,' she recited in her recent usual manner, displaying a forgiving smile with her lonely teeth.

'Thank you,' said Brunel hurriedly. He took the coffee from her but kept her outside the door because he imagined she had not seen Otto. He gave the coffee to Otto who was staring at it with fierce envy. 'She doesn't know you're here?' asked Brunel.

Otto said he had crept in when the front of the hotel

was empty. He had recognised Brunel's room by the Waikiki shirt left across the bed. Brunel picked up the shirt and regarded it fondly like a memento of days that would never return.

'What is this about cobwebs?' asked Otto, his nose in the coffee steam. 'She said about it.'

'She's always saying it,' said Brunel without interest. 'She thinks I'm stuffed up with spiders.' He took the cup from Otto and drank the final mouthful of coffee himself.

'Listen Otto . . .'

'Where is Hilde?' said Otto as though he had been waiting to ask. 'She was with you?'

'She's back at the cafe,' lied Brunel. 'Listen, I've got to tell you about something important. You can be of great help to me.' He hesitated then added: 'And to Germany.'

Otto seemed unsurprised and said simply. 'I will do anything.'

'Well listen,' said Brunel. Then he told him that the day was Orange Wednesday, that the Big People were to sign the Re-unification Treaty at Fulsbad Golf Hotel that afternoon. Otto stood up, his bulky face shining. 'But this is *so* good, Brunel. Here in Fulsbad! Just think of that!' He sighed and sat down. He said slowly: 'Our nation will be together again after all this time. Germany, Germany once more.'

'There's a difficulty,' said Brunel. 'There's a man who intends to prevent this signing. He is going to stop it, I know, if he can. We must go up to the golf course, to the hotel, and we must *get* him. It's no good going to anyone official; it will be too late. You know all the ways of the forest, Otto. We must go together and not be seen.'

Otto looked doubtful. 'But with such a matter

of importance is not the place surrounded by an army.'

'No,' said Brunel. 'That is the point. There are guards, of course, security men, but no army. Everything has been done so secretly that anything massive like that had be left out. They couldn't keep it quiet and make it big.'

'It is so astounding,' murmured Otto. 'If this was not you, Brunel, telling me, I would not believe it. But, imagine, here in Fulsbad. It will be famous.'

'Not if this man stops it,' said Brunel craftily. 'I want to get up there, and I want you to guide me so that I am not seen. We must do something about this man. His name is Keenor.'

On Orange Wednesday, an hour before it got light across the Fulsbad golf course, Colonel George Burroughs, a talented American officer in charge of the full security operation surrounding the signing of the German Re-unification Treaty, drove up the forest road from Fulsbad. He reached the Golf Hotel half an hour after Keenor had returned with his two men. He had some breakfast and called an immediate briefing of all the security and communications officers attached to the operation. They sat in the billiards room at the hotel with Burroughs sitting like a carefree boy on the edge of the table, rolling the red ball against the sponge side and catching it on its return. He never looked directly at the ball but went over each man in the entire company with a detailed eye during the following hour. Keenor watched Burroughs particularly closely, wondering how you got to be like that, in full command and power, at forty. He would have thought it difficult to have attained sufficient marks at that age.

Burroughs said: 'You might be excused if you thought that the security of this Orange Wednesday operation has been handled in a strange way. It has. But of necessity. It was essential, gentlemen, that we kept the main activity of the plan right away from this area. We wanted no excitement here. This place was chosen because it's quiet and that's how we wanted to keep it and we did. So what we have here today is what you might call a pre-fabricated security set up, organised from my office in Frankfurt and transported down here for one appearance only, as they would say in show business. It has been a huge job, but I think it's going to work. It had better.'

He looked at Keenor and his small group sitting at one side, the Russians, Gorin and Traveski, Lestrange, the Frenchman, and the English officers, Findlayson and Smith. He wondered what had happened to Brunel. 'The advance party, under Mr. Keenor, here, has been on the spot, working quietly for some time, and from the reports I have been handed it seems that the ground work has been well covered and we have nothing to worry about on that score. What happened to the other English guy, Mr. Keenor? The man who knew the locality from the start?' Keenor thought he was going to stutter, but he trod on it in time. 'He's deployed, sir. Doing a small routine matter I want clarifying.'

'Okay,' nodded Burroughs. 'I wanted everyone accounted for.' He sighed as though he felt tired at that early time of day, and pushed the red ball more slowly at the billiard table cushion. 'Now, let's get to today's detailed arrangements. You all have fixed orders about the part you must play in this pretty important gathering here. When you have memorised those orders they must be returned here to me for their destruction. That is before we leave this room.

'Now, briefly, this is the overall plan. Five separate helicopters will bring the Big People—American, British, Russian, French and German—to this hotel at three this afternoon. They will put down on the golf course itself, in already designated order. The signing of the treaty will be brief. We want the V.I.P.s in and out of here in one quarter of an hour exactly. They'll come up to the terrace just outside here, and meet there. We have one official photographer to take a group picture. They will then walk into the library of the hotel and sign the treaty, shake hands all round, another picture, and then out again to the choppers. By the time the world knows it is truly at peace they will be tucked up in their beds. Okay?'

He was watching the two Russians closely and decided he didn't care for them. He didn't like the Frenchman either. Nor the two Britishers. 'The officers of Mr. Keenor's advance squad, who have worked so well together,' he smiled, 'will each have a separate area of the surrounding forest as their responsibility. They will act as guides and advisors to you and to the extra security guards who are being drafted in at this moment. We don't want to move an army in here because of the obvious requirement for secrecy. But guards there have to be, of course, and these, numbering in all just about one hundred, will be spread through the wooded areas, and on some points of the golf course. My own special staff, and the personal security men of the V.I.P.s will be the only ones permitted on the terrace or in the hotel. Anyone else will be shot. Make no mistake about that. The hotel staff here—the hotel is normally closed at this time of the year anyway—are members of various security groups so we have no worries there.

'One other general point. It's possible, more than possible, that there will be people coming into the forest today on perfectly legitimate errands, and these people will have to be dealt with carefully. Our observation system, as worked out by Mr. Keenor's boys, is very good. We can see most of the surrounding area from our posts. But any people coming into the forest must be stopped and detained. No one's to do any shooting out there in the trees. Is that understood? One false shot and there's no treaty. The V.I.P.s know that if any trouble happens, and depending on how I view the immediate situation, they will scram out of here in the helicopters, double quick. And it's taken years to get the treaty worked out. So don't let's spoil it on that count. Any accidents and I'll want to know who went wrong. Okay?'

He went over the detailed deployment of the various groups and the men of Keenor's nucleus who were to be their liaison. Then he smiled. 'Let's see that Orange Wednesday is a successful day,' he said like an advertiser. 'Any small details, any routine things you want doing, then Mr. Keenor has a first class secretary who is around the building somewhere right now. She's the lady with the big tits.'

The day was dismal cold and lay like a grey cloth over the hills and the forest. Some tepid sun in the early afternoon lit up the elderly face of the town. But it never touched the higher ground.

On the rim of the golf course, in the bunched trees, in some of the hunting lodges, and in all the little white castles, the security ring was formed. It was done well and quietly and on a day like that there were not many wanderers in the forest. The deer standing together in the gathering cold watched with surprise the activities of the men, mounting guns, slinging telephone wires through boughs, marching silent and solemn patrols from empty place to empty place. The deer had never realised that there were so many men in the world.

'I swear those things are counting us,' said Findlayson carefully distributing a groundsheet in the floor of a hollow of red leaves. He placed his beautifully clean rifle just as carefully on the canvas. Smith glanced at the deer. 'Haven't had venison for years,' he said.

Findlayson looked out from the hollow, down the green chute of the valley flank, to the bed of the golf course, and across the exposed ground to the terrace of the hotel. He rolled his field glasses across the breadth of view, across the screening trees at the other side, the evergreens still thickly clothed, the others almost black with the massive entanglement of boughs and trunks. Then down to the eighteenth green with its belly-button hole, and the flag very still in the chill windless day. Across the terrace then, now moving separately like officers on the bridge of a ship, solitary figures doing appointed tasks in readiness for the arrival of the Big People. A little elevation of the glasses and he looked directly into the expansive glass windows of the hotel library where the treaty would be signed. They were fine glasses and he could see the shining table with its pads and pens and its carafes of water. Surely they wouldn't need a drink of water after merely signing their names, he thought. Finally he turned the glasses past the hotel to where the trees began again, climbing up and around the rim of the course, thickening all the time until they were part of the wintry forest holding up the sky.

'If I should die, think only this of me . . .' mused Findlayson carefully bringing down the field glasses.

'Who will die, this day?' recited Smith.

'Whose is that?'

'Smith,' said Smith. 'Me. I made it up. Just now.'

'Lyrical,' said Findlayson. 'What I was going to say was that if I should die, think only this of me, that deposited in the Dresdener Bank at Stuttgart is an envelope, traditionally sealed and secret. If someone today decided that my time had come, then this envelope would be forwarded to the S.I.B. and opened.'

Smith scanned loftily over the landscape, at first apparently trying to see everything without artificial aid. Then he put the large glasses to his small eyes.

'That's a bit unoriginal, isn't it?' he said. 'I wouldn't have thought that of you.'

'Unoriginal? Yes, I suppose it is. But effective, don't you think?'

'Most certainly,' answered Smith. '*My* envelope's at the Deutschbank in Munich.'

The deer had ceased to find in them a curiosity and had moved away, deeper into the stronghold of the trees. A party of the newly arrived security guards, all German, were moving up the thin path to the hollow where the British officers awaited them.

'Here come the krauts,' said Smith. 'Why couldn't you have seen a sight like that in the war. My God, we could chop this lot to bits from just here. Have a peppermint,' he added, offering the packet.

'Thanks. Do you think I've got an arrangement about today; something I haven't told you about?' asked Findlayson.

Smith said: 'No. You haven't got the guts.'

At noon Lestrange drank some black coffee and ate a sausage sandwich then walked, thoughtful as a dog, up the inclined road towards his place in the forest. He had no humour in him but it occurred to him with quaint irony that this afternoon, of all afternoons, he would be in virtual command of a platoon of Germans. They were up there now, waiting for him to go to them, waiting for him to guide them and put them into their positions overlooking the eastern extremity of the course. His own small army of Germans.

It was not a good day for him, though, because he had heard from friends in Paris, real, true friends who feared him, that the Ben Barka matter was creeping, reeking from its grave again. He had escaped very well until now, sidling around some greasy corners when others had been pinned. But once again like that night in La Perouse, he had to admit to himself that for all the best motives he had backed the wrong side. He had thought in the kidnapping and murder of Ben Barka, the Morrocan rebel leader, in Paris in 1965, a plot involving political assassins and co-operative policemen, he would be with the *safe* people, the security men who planned it, the odds-on winners in any eventuality. But the explosions had all gone off in the wrong directions. The arrests and trials had take place. People had made confessions. Lestrange did not feel safe that day.

Not that he *knew* anything would happen. Nothing for certain. But all his integral alarm system, sensitively wired all these years, since that first murder, was vibrating. He was unwilling to act on uncertain fear, however, and running, at this place and juncture, he knew would be foolish and fatal. But he would not be surprised if someone awaited him, and would not have to wait much longer.

That afternoon he felt like killing even more than usual. It was a day of the right texture, an empty day, grey, and with no feeling in it, withdrawn and silent and almost telling him to kill for the sheer effect it would have on the monotony. He had his best rifle, lying comfortably and comfortingly across the soft wedge of his palm, and his pistol, like a pet, buried in the holster at his hip. He felt well, usually, with these two friends. But not now.

The German security guards, keen and fresh as a sports team and anxious that the day should go right, were waiting for him when he gained the top of the slope. There was one senior man who had been with the occupation army in Orleans during the war and spoke French with some searching of memory. Through him Lestrange ordered them to their set positions which Keenor had worked out on the operations map. There was an *Oberleutenant* in charge of the party but Lestrange ignored him.

Some rock had forced its head through the dry cold grass at that place, sitting like a stray gravestone under the conifers. It was quite flat, but with a step projecting up at one end, like a headstone. Lestrange lay his rifle carefully at an angle, the barrel resting on the higher stone, and then looked out and across the deep vale to the hotel.

Some men were rolling white coils, like fire hoses, and he knew these were the canvas strips that would be laid out on the golf fairway in the form of crosses, the alighting points for the helicopters. He studied the terrace. From his position at the eastern end of the golf course he had a view of only part of the paved area, but he could see the swimming pool, winter empty and yawning like a subway entrance. Keenor came out on to the area and Lestrange brought up his rifle and sent a single imaginary shot to quickly kill him.

Gorin and Traveski dropped carefully but heavily from the jeep which had taken them up the difficult road to the toy castle. This was to be their place. Their place and Keenor's too, looking down perfectly through a channel in the trees to the hotel and the terrace as they had done on the morning when they had competed in marksmanship.

The two Russians, in dun-coloured field jackets and floppy trousers, each took a rifle and a pack from the back of the jeep. Gorin then banged eloquently on the side of the vehicle and it went off to turn in a space at the far side of the little castle and then returned down the hill towards the hotel.

Keenor would be with them later. He had appeared on the terrace and strolled up and down like a man on holiday taking the air and the sun, except there was no sun on that day. Then he had gone over some delicate details of the operation plan with Burroughs, before starting on a tour of the perimeter, careful as a nurse making sure that numerous children were settled in their beds.

The door in the face of the small castle was hung with a heavy metal handle, but it turned easily. Traveski looked minutely over the solid wood at the back of the door like an antique dealer assessing a discovery, nodded with satisfaction, and then clumsily followed Gorin up the bending stairs to the open roof.

Traveski looked at the flat, unbroken sky, heavy across the trees, and then used his field glasses to examine the golf course valley, then bringing each detail of the activity on the terrace close to him. Burroughs was on the terrace now, drinking coffee from a large mug, using a clip-board and its clinging papers as a tray. Traveski kept the glasses constant for a moment to admire the pistol at the American's hip in an open holster. He had watched it closely that morning at the briefing in the billiard room and thought how much he liked it. But the day was not good. The light, he knew, would fold away very quickly by four-thirty, by which time, of course, it would all be finished for good or evil. But the vagueness of the light now, even as he looked through the glasses, worried him.

'Today,' he said to Gorin, 'the German sun should be here. After all, friend, it's their day of fulfilment. It should shine for them.'

'Isn't the light good enough, Sergei?' asked Gorin.

'Good enough,' shrugged Traveski, then asked himself a question aloud: 'What is good enough? It *must* be good enough, whatever it is. There will not be another hour like the one that will be here soon. But the sun would be nice.'

'What is the vision like through the rifle sight?' asked Gorin.

Traveski said impatiently: 'I am about to look, friend. I can tell you without even putting my eye to it that it will be worse than the glasses.'

'I realise that.'

'Good. It shows you appreciate the situation. I was beginning to wonder when you would be of some help.'

'I cannot arrange the sun for you.'

'Today,' answered Traveski evenly, now at the crouch and looking through the rifle sight, 'We will be in harmony, friend Gorin. Working together, in agreement. So that everything will be satisfactory. You understand?'

'I understand,' nodded Gorin.

'I think that you must now use your skill as a carpenter and arrange the wedges for the door.' Traveski emphasised the word 'carpenter' and it hurt Gorin, for once, long ago before he joined the service, he had been a village carpenter. He knew that Traveski had seen it at the very start of his dossier and he was upset that it should be mentioned now. After all, it was years ago. A man was entitled to forget his past.

Sullenly he opened the pack that he had placed beside his own rifle, took out two cheese-shaped pieces of wood and some tools, and went down the stairs tunnel. Traveski could hear him working on the stout wood of the door and knew he would do a good job because he had high recommendations as a carpenter.

Traveski settled himself on his broad stomach, shoulders almost against the parapet wall, lodged to the right of one of the lump teeth of the castellations. This was the best place. He brought the rifle up from his flank, gentle as a man drawing a delicate lover to his side.

He pressed his grained cheek against the cool feminine smoothness of the wood, felt his hard hands holding very firmly, but without strain or emphasis. Then, lastly, his big Russian eye rolled up and along the blue steel of the beautiful long neck of the rifle, to the nipple at the far end. He had unclipped the telescope sight as a precaution against damaging it in these preliminary settling movements. Everything was good, he decided at last; everything except the sun not being there.

From the hollow where the stony steps went down he could hear Gorin working and singing some innocent Georgian song. Gorin was going to become an encumbrance at one point in the day. He would be essential, vital to the work, especially now Keenor was going to be with them, until that point was reached. But afterwards it might be difficult to preserve him. For one thing it was far simpler to hoist one man, like himself, into a helicopter, than to take two. No, he was certain, there would come a moment when Gorin would have to be expended.

Traveski felt for the telescopic sight in its comfortable case where it slotted into red velvet like a surgical instrument. Then he decided that this was too casual, so he laid down the rifle, pulled himself to his knees and occupied both hands with taking the sight from its little soft grave and clipping it on to the trunk of the rifle. They went together like a baby at the breast of its mother. He called to Gorin, quite softly, to stop singing the Georgian song. Then he went down on to his stomach behind the wall again and this time brought the rifle up to his shoulder, felt its wedge and balance, and looked down the bright eye of the telescope. The flag on the eighteenth green jumped towards him and he could see sharply the edge of the cupped hole in the grass. That was not bad at three hundred yards on a day with no sun.

14

There was a slow bus that went once a day to the forest villages, making a wide, ragged round of a journey from Fulsbad and back to it again. Brunel and Otto went from the Snellhort's hotel and caught the bus as it came around the corner, slowly having just sidled over the narrow river bridge. It was a very old bus, painted Mediterranean blue, and its interior hung with an ancient damp smell, which Otto said lingered from the war days when the vehicle was used to collect wood from the forest for the garrison in the town. They had replaced the seats when peace reappeared, but the years had only slightly lessened the green smell of elm and aspen and the sharp spice of conifers.

Otto was still in his cowboy suit but the bus never filled with passengers until it reached the forest villages, and there was only a violently dirty old woman to see it. She knew Otto from childhood, it appeared, and they conversed for a long period of the journey. She told him how much she liked his new suit.

'There is a good place,' whispered Otto to Brunel after several winding miles. 'It is not far from here. I have known it since I was a little boy. We played soldiers and battles in this part of the forest.'

'Germans and English?' asked Brunel.

'Sometimes,' nodded Otto. 'Usually Germans and French. It was more enjoyable.'

Brunel felt rough now. Sickness was lying in the pool of his stomach. His body still had a cold skin over every part. His eyes felt weak and his muscles were stiff as iron. But he had his revolver, lying beneath his service battledress blouse, in the ungainly canvas holster and tucked firmly into his belt. It seemed that just there was the only part of his flesh that was warm. It was past noon and Otto had said it would take them about an hour to get craftily through the forest to the perimeter of the golf course.

The conductor, a tatty man who, Otto said, had been one of the wood choppers working on the bus during the war, and had stayed on, kept up a complaining conversation with the driver for most of the journey, and only as they were about to get off did he take the coins for the fare from Otto. Brunel had no money at all on him. He thought that his loose change must be at the bottom of the pool in the Fulsbad baths. When this was all over he thought he might even go and ask them about it.

There was a minor milestone standing like a hunched midget at the roadside where they left the bus. They stood by a ditch, lined with its first run of winter water coming from the higher ground, and waved to the old woman and the tatty conductor as the bus went off to its first village. On the milestone it said that Fulsbad was ten kilometres distant. Otto led he way into the fringe of the forest that began immediately at the roadside.

At first there were wide spaces between the trees with brambles and bracken and some tardy, pale blue wild flowers. The path was clear and easy, but within three hundred yards the real forest suddenly crowded on them like a belligerent army refusing them further progress.

'From here it is more hard,' said Otto choosing his English, as always, with apparent care. 'But even although it is hard, it is easy for us because no one will see us. There is a little way through the forest and no one, except the hundreds of children from this area, knows of it. I will lead you, Brunel.'

Brunel looked at the plump old man in his ridiculous fat cowboy suit and his hanging holsters, his folded face bright with the hope that he was doing something for Germany. 'Otto,' he said, stopping the first step Otto was making into the thicker forest.

'Yes, Brunel?'

'Otto,' Brunel began again awkwardly, 'We are going no further unless you make a promise to me.'

'What promise is this, Brunel?'

'I want you to show me the way. Just so far. To the place where I can find my own way to the golf course. That is all I want you to do. When we get to that place I want you to promise that you will turn back and return here to the road. You promise?'

Otto dropped his eyes. 'I wanted to be there, right there in the place, Brunel, on this day of days for my little town and my country. Is not this possible?'

'Definitely not,' said Brunel firmly. He leaned towards the elderly cowboy. 'there is a very good chance that you might make a terrible mess of the whole thing. Then Germany will never be re-united.'

'In that case,' said Otto bravely, 'I will return to the road. There is a bus from the villages at two o'clock.'

'Good. That's understood then.'

'It is understood.'

Otto turned and waddled into the guts of the forest. It was heavy and difficult, but he found the thin track after some looking about and followed it like an elderly setter on an ancient scent. It must have been years since he had been there but he was very sharp, finding the ways through the brambles and brown bracken, walking with no great hesitation in a sure direction through the trunks, and making little satisfied indigestion noises as he picked up each piece of the track.

Brunel felt very ill now. He was shivering deep in the caves and rivers of his body and trembling at a different tempo on the surface. Twice he tried to throw up the sickness, projecting his neck and head out like a cockerel but it stuck in his stomach. His feet and his hands might have been miles distant from the feel they gave him. His knees ached and now he had violent earache too, beating in both drums. When he was a boy and did not dry his ears out after swimming he used to get pains like that. The gun, however, still felt warm and full of latent life tucked into his belt. He kept trying to imagine the look on Keenor's face when he turned up to kill him.

They had been going quite well for fifteen minutes, making very little noise, and not getting lost at all, when Brunel saw a file of men coming from their right, moving through the trees with novice difficulty. He caught Otto's shoulder and forced him down like a child pushing down a jack-in-the-box.

Otto realised what was happening and tumbled softly on to his round stomach, well submerged in the undergrowth. Brunel went down too, lying in the depths of dead and dying forest tangle, but feeling his legs and arms grateful for the respite. He watched two minute black insects walk busily along the stem of a fern and return within seconds carrying one of their kind between them. Brunel wondered whether he was dying, dead, or drunk. It was surprising how little humans really knew, he thought, of the amazing world about them.

The security patrol coming through the trees stopped twenty feet away from their hiding place. They grumbled and made jokes in German, about the forest and about fairies and if the local girls could ever be brought this far into the trees. They were obviously having a break, a stand-to, before going on. Brunel heard a voice tell them they could smoke. Only a stranger and a fool at that, thought Brunel, could tell his men to smoke in a dry forest.

Otto was lying commendably still a few inches ahead of him, his solid backside sticking up like a rump of earth. Brunel had cramp, but only in his fingers and his toes, so he could manipulate it away without great trouble. His eyes were necessarily on the rough grass and ground immediately under his nose for most of the time, but he rolled them up at intervals and could just see the tops of the security men's forage caps, and the tips of their shoulder-slung rifles, sticking up over his horizon like the roofs and chimneys of a village.

Then, describing an arc like a tracer bullet, the red cigarette end of one of the patrolmen flicked absently away, came to land in the brittle leaves and bracken six inches from Otto's trousers. Brunel's sickness nearly came up as he saw it pitch. In seconds the industrious red ash had spawned a finger of smoke and busy flat flame. It seemed to look about joyously and then spread itself, burning apace among the dry leaves and ferns like a glutton going through a feast. It was very close to Otto's trousers and the double event of the patrol spotting the smoke and Otto feeling the flame was only a few moments off.

Brunel took the risk and thrust his hand forward to Otto's shiny boots. He gave a short twist and the old man's walrus head came slowly around and saw the jigging flames.

Brunel was staggered with admiration by Otto's immediate action. He firmly but quietly rolled on to his side, thrust his hand down and released the zip of his cowboy trousers. Then he brilliantly urinated all over the little flames, swishing quickly, efficiently, copiously, but still quietly over the burning area. He pointed his hose up and down and then performed a little zig-zag, killing every knot of fire. By the time he was finished the flames were finished too.

The security patrol moved away through the trees. 'That,' whispered Brunel, 'was marvellous. I'll never know how you lost the war.'

Otto was getting awkwardly to his knees in the undergrowth and adjusting his dress with a dignified movement of finger and thumb. 'Perhaps,' he grinned ponderously, 'it was because we chose the wrong weapons.' He pointed whimsically down towards his crutch. 'In any case I never think that we lost. It was merely that we failed to win.'

'Come on, you old Boche,' said Brunel. 'Back on the trail.'

They trudged on, pushing their way through the tangled places, finding small flats of water lying hidden under leaves and pine needles, and eventually following the treeline that led them up high, and immediately quickly down into the clearing where Brunel and Hilde had watched the meeting of the Nazi cowboys.

'Strange place,' commented Brunel. He wished he had brought a bottle of brandy with him to put some heat into his cold guts. 'Just like a fairy meeting place. Somewhere they meet and sing their fairy songs.'

Otto stopped suspiciously just ahead of him and Brunel saw his fat neck harden, but he changed his mind about saying anything, and moved on solidly.

They had been walking for almost an hour, having twice more had to lie on the floor of the forest growth because of the arrival of security patrols, when Otto stopped just ahead and Brunel, halting obediently, saw a spear-shaped section of continuous green through the trunks and knew they were near the golf course.

He was glad they had arrived. He thought the walking would make him warm, would inject some movement and energy into the chilly corridors of his body, but it had not. He felt ninety-per-cent corpse, his body hardly hearing the instructions of his brain, his feet icy, his hands purple, his chest aching with an unseen weight, his pipes all frozen. He still had earache too.

'Right,' he said. 'Lie down, Otto.' It occurred to him that it was the sort of instruction given to a dog. 'Stay put until I've gone down into the valley and then off you go back to the road. Now you understand that, don't you? You promised.'

'Ja. Ja,' grunted Otto, his chins folding and unfolding several times as he performed the two syllables. 'I will catch the bus, Brunel. Good luck to you, my son. Germany is proud of you.'

Brunel patted Otto's large head and was surprised to find it warm to his palm. 'I'm off then,' he said inadequately. 'Cheers.'

'To you also, cheers,' replied Otto. He crouched forlornly behind a berry bush and watched Brunel move forward. Then he, quite genuinely, remembered that the two o'clock bus did not run on winter Wednesdays.

At the time that Sergei Traveski was recruited to assassinate his own prime minister he was busy building a rough model of the Kremlin for the amusement of his children on a beach at the Rumanian resort of Marmia. It was the second week of August and it was hot on the Black Sea. Sergei, his nice wife Maria, and his delightful children Peter and Natalie, were on the beach building the castle. He had just accomplished a difficult assignment in arranging the murder of two dissident political figures in the picturesque agricultural country of Eastern Russia and he was enjoying his leave. A saggy red swimsuit in flannel hung about Sergei's loins, his son, aged eight, and daughter, aged six, were fine brown in the sun, and Madam Traveski sweated a bit in her white imitation silk slip.

Sergei built a splendid sand Kremlin on their first day at the beach, but some waves demolished it within a few hours, so the ever-careful Russian sited in twenty yards further back at the next attempt. It would not do to have too many Kremlins washed away by the Rumanian sea. You never knew who might be watching and what construction they might put on the demolition.

As it happened his caution was justified. He was completing the final embellishments, carefully with wet sand applied with a wooden ice cream spoon, when a shadow moved over his work.

'You have these two domes in the opposite positions,' said the man. He wore a big white shirt, open at the neck but linked at the cuffs and light grey holiday trousers of inferior design and material, held up a snake-buckle belt. His feet were bare and had sunk into the fine sand, lying like half submerged hogs. The finger which pointed out the architectural inaccuracy was curly with baby black hairs.

Traveski looked up and saw that he did not know the man. 'It is only very rough work, you understand,' he said feeling a little ashamed. 'Tomorrow I will build another and put the matter right.'

He knew the man wanted to talk. They walked away together in their bare feet, down to the shore line where children splashed, girls in bikinis rolled in the sun, and youths did hand-stands and other showy gymnastics. They talked against a velvet sea-wind full of the unique echoes of summer on an open beach, shouts and laughing and other enjoyable sounds.

'Traveski,' said the visitor gently. 'There is a feeling in Moscow and some other centres that, like your delightful sand-castle, something is not right with the Kremlin. I speak not of architecture, of course, you will understand, but the people within the building—the leadership.'

Sergei had learned, very long ago, to make no immediate contribution to a suddenly terrifying situation like this.

'Huh,' he said making his big toe run a liquid furrow through the wet, shiny sand.

'The leadership, as we of a certain group, understand it, is preparing a major concession to the Capitalist Powers. Nothing less than the Re-unification of Germany with a great many of our previous demands unmet.'

'It's the Chinese,' said Traveski.

'Everybody today says "It's the Chinese",' complained the man.

'It's a good saying,' answered Sergei, feeling a little surer now that the visitor had revealed his inclinations 'It does not commit the speaker.'

'We *are* committed,' said the man seriously. '*You* are also committed, Traveski. My group have investigated you quite thoroughly and let me now tell you that you *are* committed. We have chosen you as an instrument of the course we propose to take. If you join willingly then the rewards, Sergei, will be great for an ambitious man like yourself. If you have no sympathy then we must take action to see that you cause us no trouble. Some people in the highest places would not iike to know how you have been involved in several political adventures. Perhaps you recall the toe-cap bomb prank you played on the officer at Minsk. There are people in power this day, Sergei, who would rather have that man living than you.'

Traveski nodded miserably. Two children, a perspiring boy chasing a giggling girl, dashed through the sand between the two plodding men.

'What is to be done?' he asked.

'The Re-unification treaty is to be signed in secret, in Germany later this year. It has the code name Orange Wednesday.'

'Nice,' nodded Traveski. 'I like the name.'

'Our leader will travel to this place to sign this stupid document. His section of the party is determined to do so. We want him eliminated before he has signed. Then we er ... evacuate you ... and after certain changes within the Kremlin we blame the Germans for the killing. No treaty, back to our normal relations with the West, and forward with Communism.'

They talked the length of the beach and Traveski said he understood that there would be further contacts made to him in Moscow on his return. Then the man patted him on the shoulder, left him, and turned to the sea, paddling along in the shallows and eventually taking two children by the hands and walking away with them. Traveski thought the man must consider himself unusually lucky to have an assignment which also provided a holiday for his family.

He returned to his own children. 'We are waiting

for you to finish the Kremlin,' Natalie told him.

'You must learn these things yourself,' Travesk
said regretfully. 'Your father may not always be
here.'

15

For the final hour, strangely, after all the preparation, there was not much for anyone on the security side to do. It was like setting up a house for a party and then sitting in a vacuum, wondering if any of the guests would arrive. Burroughs kept flicking the switches of his radio circuit, like a man playing with an electric train set, keeping a regular and dull conversation with the security men about the forest area. The bunch of diplomatic men were busy as charwomen in the writing room, waiting for their masters to come in the helicopters. Keenor wondered if Prudence could spare ten minutes on the springs. For the first time since he returned to the hotel that day he thought about Hilde and Brunel.

He began to worry a little. He was solidly certain that both were waterlogged and dead when he left the baths that morning. But the arrival of the early boilerman, clanging through the building had not given him time to examine them. The girl had been like a long lovely wet fish strapped in the chair and Brunel was hung forward in the freezing water and heavily still. He had liked the girl very much and he felt sorry for her, dying like that in cold water, but he was not sorry about Brunel. It was a very good way for him to go. It amused him to think that any investigations would probably end with the conclusion that they had been up to some dangerous perversion, that Brunel had drowned the girl and

227

then himself. Certainly anything which might involve the name Keenor even being mentioned could be stopped at its source, quickly and quietly. He had successfully killed people before and the line between duty killings and private murders was almost impossible to distinguish. Yes, he was sure they were dead. He was not very worried about that, although he always had difficulty with all the details of such happenings. The next day he always felt quite different—sane. It was like sobering up.

Today, because of the seriousness of the occasion, Prudence was wearing a straight navy-blue skirt and a very white shirt-blouse. Keenor watched her go out on to the terrace and take instructions from Colonel Burroughs. Keenor watched Burroughs' eyes flick up to hers just once. Not that he was jealous. Anyone who reached Burroughs' rank and responsibility at forty deserved the best in life. Keenor, in seconds, emotionally adjusted himself to losing her to the higher echelon. It was a pity really because she was an efficient secretary and a first-class furgle.

Keenor went out and stood at the far end of the terrace. He sniffed the rheumaticky old air of the autumn day and regarded the lines of the forest, indistinct in the early afternoon light, gathered like a distant army. His jeep was in the courtyard. He walked to it and told the driver to take the mountain fork, the road up to the little castle where the two Russians, he knew, were waiting.

Half an hour before the first helicopter was due Keenor reached the flattened part of the forest track that ran up to the white castle. He walked down first to where the German security patrol was spread out along a crease in the rock, about half a mile from the place where he had instructed target practice on that early day of the operation. The men were young and strangers to the area, jittery as though they were in ambush. He guessed their nervousness was repeated all around the safety perimeter. He wished that he had been permitted to import two platoons of U.S. Army police. That would have been far better. For a while he grunted around in the patrol's position, stomach thrust out, truculent and grumbling like an obese hedgehog.

The respectful young German men were glad when he left them and, sniffing, went up the long steady incline to the table of land just in front of the little castle. He stood, with his back to the white walls, Traveski and Gorin examining the valley of his back from their perch on top amid the teeth of the turrets, and looked with an appreciative eye on the monochromed country around.

He realised that there were no birds sounding that day. That, of course, was because of the men. Birds left when men arrived in large numbers in a place like this. He remembered when he was a boy in a town a hundred miles from Memphis, where the people called him Chuckles, how he learned about nature. Up until that time he had hardly killed anything, only small things like beetles or mice. But then, this day, a man had told him about the herons always staying home on a Sunday.

All the week they would fly beautifully and fish and stalk about in the rivers and lakes of that region. He had seen them, standing taciturn on their skinny legs but he had never been able to get close enough to kill one. Then the man told him they lay low in their nests on Sundays not even going out to get food for their young because that was the day when the lakes and rivers had plenty of people around them and on them, in boats and fishing and swimming. So the herons stayed away until Monday.

Keenor had gone out on Sunday, immediately after morning service, and taken his gun, climbed a big, easy tree, and almost immediately surprised a heron on its nest, killing it with his first attempt. It was funny the drunken way it died, falling down through the tree, hitting and bouncing, and ending up hanging over a low branch, its head dangling down, lolling, just like a Saturday night boozer. There were no little birds in the nest that time, but he picked up the big sad bird joyfully in his twelve-year-old hands and carried it back to the town. It hung down, its legs broken like those of a dead spider, and all the boys and girls heard what Chuckles had done, and came to see it and play with it until it got too smelly for him to keep any longer, and he had to throw it in the river where, he thought, the fish would eat it.

Keenor turned from his thoughts of nature and puffed into the castle door, swinging it easily, and tramping up the stairs. On the journey he touched, gently as one touches a familiar, the fist of his revolver. Coming out on to the roof he saw Gorin sitting on a small canvas seat he had been thoughtful enough to bring for the wait, and Traveski lying on his stomach looking at the falling land through his field glasses.

Traveski turned over heavily, like a bullock turns. He sat up in the corner against the stone parapet.

'Are our young German friends guarding us well?' he asked, nodding towards the security patrol bunched half a mile away in the trees.

'Jittery,' grunted Keenor in a way that indicated that neither he nor the Russians could ever like Germans again, that they had this strong thing in common. 'Let's hope these guys don't start shooting at anything. If they do I hope it's at the next bastard German.'

The Russians laughed agreeably. Keenor began to talk

to them and he wished not for the first time that Gorin did not have such huge, brown, liquid eyes, so full of interest and fun. They made him feel uncomfortable. He feared that Gorin would reach out and stroke his hand at any moment and he was not prepared to deal with that. Not that Gorin was necessarily like that, in fact it was he who most wanted the fat women, and that sort of thing was probably unknown in Russia anyway, but his eyes just made it seem so.

Keenor said: 'Yessir, this is a good day for both our countries, friends. In the war I knew guys who had a lot of dealings with you guys and they said you were okay.' He abruptly became confiding, leaning forward towards them. 'Why, *do you know*, I knew one of those guys who met up with the Russians during the last part of the war. When the two armies met. Remember? They had their pictures in the newspapers and everything. Well, this guy told me that when he shook hands with *his* Commie he had never felt such a warm hand. There! How about that!'

'Perhaps,' suggested Gorin simply, 'it was a warm day, Mr. Keenor.'

Keenor's surprise at the observation was cut short by the low, clipped, chopping nose of a helicopter nosing across the tree line. It circled like a big dog looking for somewhere to sit.

'They're here,' breathed Keenor. 'And here are the other three. Right on time.' He made it sound like an advertising jingle. Gorin shook his head agreeably, produced an outsized pistol, and ordered. 'Sit on the floor, please. And put your hands on your head.'

A quivering began in Keenor's face and spread like a wild disease to his whole body. It was not fear so much as indignation. 'You bastards can't do this kind of thing,' he said inadequately, nevertheless sitting down and placing his big hands across his creamed hair school-boy fashion. 'You'll be killed, mashed up. Both of you.'

'It's a day for killing,' observed Traveski rolling over on to his stomach and bringing the snubby rifle and its pick-a-back telescope to his elbow.

'You *can't* kill the United States President,' objected Keenor seriously. 'You *can't*.'

'He will not be harmed,' said Gorin.

'Nor the British guy,' stuttered Keenor.

'He will remain untouched.'

'The French and the German?' he asked.

'We are not after them.'

'The Commie? Your own guy?'

'Shut him up,' said Traveski irritably without turning. 'And fix your carpenter's wedges in the door.'

As he said that Brunel, with twigs and leaves on him, appeared like some pale forest sprite at the short door leading from the stairs, gun in waiting for Keenor.

Keenor was astonished, despite his own crisis. His eyes swelled.

'Brunel,' he croaked. Then hopefully: 'Good boy. Shoot him, Brunel.' Gorin heard Brunel and in one movement swivelled and fired, the bullet sending a blast of stone fragments into Brunel's cheek. Reacting at once Brunel hit Gorin in the thigh with his first shot and Keenor's boot caught the Russian a fraction from that place almost immediately. Brunel touched his cheek and felt the damp of blood. But it was only a scratch.

In the valley the slashing noise of the helicopter rotors buried the sound of the shooting on the tower. Five parties of stooping men, who were the Big People and their immediate staff, came from the noisy aircraft, ducking under the din and the ribbed wind as they left them. Four of the rotors suddenly died and swung like harmless roundabouts but the one with a Russian pilot, delayed its switch off.

There were no preliminaries on the landing area. The parties moved purposefully towards the terrace as though they had been practising and drilling it for a long time.

As they reached the exposed terrace Traveski began firing from the roof of the castle.

For him it was unlucky that his first shot, fired with hard dedication and without even a glance behind him at the battle between Gorin, and Keenor and Brunel, co-incided with the first hurried bullet that Keenor put into his left shoulder. Traveski, aiming for the Russian leader on the terrace, hit the Russian premier's secretary in the leg with that rifle shot, jerked off-target by the force of his own wound. The man on the terrace screamed and fell flat on the ground and Traveski desperately tried to steady himself and fire another round, but Keenor's next bullet hit him square in the back, kicking blood and life out of him in a second. His head rested gently on the neck of the rifle and he did not feel it when Keenor kicked him in the ribs.

On the terrace Burroughs, with one sweep of his arms, like a schoolteacher protecting infants, had knocked the leaders of the world into the deep end of the empty swimming pool, down in the safe concrete hole. They crouched and cowered there while everyone else from the terrace fell flat or jumped in on top of them. The Russian secretary's leg was pumping blood over every-one on the floor of the pool and the politicians struggl-ing like eels in a heap were already arguing nastily among themselves. Burroughs ran at a crouch for a jeep in the hotel courtyard and tore up the crooked mountain road towards the small castle.

He alone seemed to sense from which direction the

shot had come. In their position half a mile from the tower the German security patrol were looking uncomfortably about them in a variety of directions, their officer mesmerised by the panic on the terrace below.

On the castle roof Keenor had given Traveski one more heavy kick and had turned away to walk immediately into Brunel's fist. The blow dropped the heavy American and Brunel with gigantic difficulty leaned over him, tugged him up again and threw him back once more on to the stony surface. The effort left Brunel himself staggering, sucking in air, and doing a quaint jig around the roof. Three men were lying there now, Traveski at one corner, Gorin somewhere near the middle and Keenor on his face three yards away.

Brunel, foolishly, let himself stagger a bit too near Keenor. The hairy hand flew out like a spider's paw and hooked about his ankle. It turned viciously and Brunel tipped over, face forwards, jagging all the senses left alive in his big, weakly body. He knew he would have to get up before Keenor did. He managed it by a fraction, being on his feet, head down, to meet Keenor's charge as he came at him. Keenor's temper had sold out on him, he was charging wildly now whereas a considered move would have put Brunel away for good. As he charged Brunel's head came up and struck him in the arch of his neck and chin. Brunel felt all the pipes and organs in Keenor's throat crunch together as he got the top of his fair head in there.

Keenor gurgled not much louder than a contented child. He fell on to his knees clutching his throat and Brunel who was giddy with the force of his own blow comically stepped back, tripped over Gorin, and eventually descended heavily on the dead Traveski. He tipped right over the Russian's cooling corpse and ended in an awkward sitting position against the stone battlements with Traveski's awful dead eye looking askance at him.

From below, and somewhere distant, Brunel could hear the shouts of the German security patrol and realised that they must be doubling up the slope. He could hear the faint vibration of a roughly-driven jeep too. They would all be there very soon. Keenor must be killed now or the chance would go and there would not be another.

Keenor was moving again, getting up from his oddly devout position and looking towards Brunel with knowing wickedness. Brunel did not have another blow or breath left in him. Keenor knew that. He began to crawl towards his gun which was lying on the stones. He was injured enough to have to take his time and Brunel began feeling about for Traveski's pistol. But it was not there. The rifle had jammed under his body and there was no getting that.

Keenor was greedily keeping his eyes on Brunel as though daring him to try to escape. Then Gorin moved, slowly like Keenor, and began to go on his hands and knees towards his own pistol which was lying five yards away. They were like angry snails, Gorin and Keenor, manoeuvring for battle. Brunel watched with hollow fascination. Keenor was going to get there first. He could tell that. Keenor was going to win.

Brunel inched himself along on his back, lying full out like a lazy sunbather, at first with the vague idea of trying to get to the door. He had no sap of strength left in his body and he could only shudder along like yet another creature. But he rolled a bit, painfully, and then Gorin's pistol was only an inch from his right toe. He stretched his leg for it. Both Keenor and Gorin, astonishingly stopped on their slow journeys, and stared like spectators at some sort of contest, to see if he would reach it. He did. Another weak shuffle on his bottom and the pistol was at his toe. He could hear the jeep finishing the last stretch to the flat surface to the castle door, and the running German voices too. Gorin looked at Brunel and Brunel looked at Gorin and then at Keenor.

Gorin, who thought he was about to kick the pistol out of his reach had a liquid look of crying disappointment in his fat eyes like a child who has suddenly seen a valued prize taken from it. Keenor, who guessed better, but still wasn't sure, gaped helplessly.

Deliberately, so that he would not miss, Brunel stuck out his toe and hit the pistol sending it slithering across the stonework right to the hand of Gorin. The Russian's wet eyes shone at the weapon and then at Brunel with gratitude but no understanding. Greedily his hand went out for the weapon and Keenor made a heaving effort to reach his. He was pawing, on his knees, when Gorin fired first. It was a huge explosion for a pistol. The force of the shot must have been tremendous because it hit Keenor in the lower chest and stood him upright, something his own strength had failed to do.

He seemed to hang, suspended on an invisible line, crucified in air, his arms struck out, his body straight, his knees bent and his toes on the ground. Gorin fired again and the shot kicked Keenor in the chest again. The first had been a hard but clean puncture, but this one, throwing him backwards sent blood squirting out through the front of his shirt.

Keenor did a bouncy, fairy-like, dance backwards and without undue fuss or sound tipped over the battlements. The trees were close on that side, brushing the castle, and he crashed down through the sleeping twigs and branches before hitting a fork junction and lodging there, bleeding and heavily dead. The blood ran down from his chest and made a pool which ran away into the roots of the tree.

Brunel lay still, wondering what the chances were of Gorin now turning on him.

But men were coming up the stairs now, their stone echoes clattering before them. Gorin threw his gun decisively away and sat, hands held high above head, with his pleading, worried eyes on the door.

Burroughs, followed by the officer of the German security patrol, jumped through the doorway on to the rooftop. They took in the surrendering Gorin and then turned on Brunel.

'Brunel!' exclaimed Burroughs.

'Bone,' breathed Brunel.

A quarter of a mile away Lestrange, in his position, had watched it all happening on the terrace and felt a bitter frustration that with shooting going on there had been no cause for him to pull a trigger. He wriggled and almost wept with the injustice of it, rough-handling his rifle like a drunk might rough-handle his wife. Then, like the answer to a killer's prayer, Lestrange saw something coming through the forest, something brown breaking cover and making for the maximum security area of the hotel terrace. The figure, a round runner in a ridiculous cowboy suit, rushed clear of the trees and fell down comically, picked himself up and panted on. He ran down the eighteenth fairway, shouting in German and waving his arms, and there was a cumbersome gun in a holster at his belt.

Lestrange heard the shouted German and recognised it as the appetising sauce to a promised meal. Here was not only a target, but a German target. He nodded as though giving himself an order, then smiled as he prepared to carry it out. He folded his rifle into his shoulder and at two hundred yards let the sight find the stout, rushing, shouting man. Lestrange pulled the trigger firmly, at a steady pressure, and gurgled with satisfaction as the man shot up into the air, his legs folded abruptly beneath him, like a Cossack dancer, and then fell heavily on his face about thirty yards short of the smooth grass of the final green.

There were anxious shouts coming from the German security patrol positioned near the Frenchman now, so he stood up and waved to them, calming his hands at them, so that they quietened down. Then, following the set instructions appertaining to any emergency, he returned to his position and squatted quietly to await further orders. It was getting late afternoon now and the man he had shot was as indistinct as a molehill in the middle of the course.

Ten minutes went by before a jeep, its lights cutting across the growing greyness, went out to the lying man. Brunel left the driver in the vehicle and walked weakly across to Otto on the ground. The old German was bleeding lustily from a wound in his neck. His cowboy shirt with its frills was soggy with his blood. He had half rolled on to his plump side and his Colt had slipped from its holster and was lying on the grass. He had just opened his eyes as Brunel reached him and knelt close to him.

'I cannot see very well, Brunel,' complained Otto.

'It's getting dark,' said Brunel. 'Why didn't you go back, as you promised?'

'The bus does not run today,' muttered Otto. 'It's a Wednesday in winter, you understand. Did they sign the treaty?'

Brunel hesitated. 'All signed and sealed,' he lied eventually. 'You're all one mob again now.'

'I'm glad,' said Otto giving a harsh cough that jerked the blood from the wound in a quicker jet. Brunel put his handkerchief there. Otto said: 'You understand, don't you. I was foolish to run. One of your guards shot me.'

He could not say much more. He managed three difficult words. 'Heil Hiter, Brunel,' he said softly.

'Yes,' nodded Brunel. 'Heil Hitler, Otto.' When his friend was dead he added tenderly: 'You old fool.'

16

Brunel saw the logs, laid in a lumpy line like baking bread, spread across the wide red fire, when he awoke at six in the morning. He felt better, thawed out; he could feel his body working again. There was a rough rug lying across him, to the armpits, and he was lying on a couch in the hotel lounge. Prudence was sitting, hunched like a blonde witch, near the fire. A cup of coffee, half drunk and then neglected, hung from her index finger, a tenth of an inch from spilling. She was wearing black trousers and a loose wool sweater.

She saw he was awake. 'I never thought I'd spend a whole night with a man and do nothing,' she said.

Brunel levered himself to the points of his elbows and looked at the remainder of the room. A dreary old standard lamp stood like a beggar in one corner and this apart from the fire, was the only light in the long place.

'Think how Florence Nightingale must have suffered,' he said eventually. 'All those men and all those nights.'

'Some of us are simply dedicated,' she answered in a dull way. 'How do you feel?'

'Warmer,' he said. Then he coughed. 'But I've got a cough. How are you, Prudence?'

'Very sad,' she said looking hard into the cup. 'Now that Keenor is dead. Shot.'

'I was there.'

'Yes, of course. Colonel Burroughs told me.'

'He's a Colonel is he?'

'Colonel Burroughs? Yes, that's what he is. Poor Keenor. You might not believe this, Brunel, but I think the strain was telling on him. I think he was going out of his mind.'

'No!' exclaimed Brunel. He coughed heavily again.

'He used to talk to me, you know, and tell me things that he told no one else. All about his life and his childhood. When he was a little boy, in some place in Tennessee, they used to call him Chuckles, you know.'

'It suited him,' agreed Brunel.

Prudence finally took the rest of the coffee. 'The whole thing was terrible,' she said eventually. 'They never signed the treaty, of course. They got the Big People out of here so quick you wouldn't have believed it. It could have been much worse, I suppose. At least the Russian leader went home on his own two feet. I was glad really. He looked a very nice man, you know. Very sexy in a way. He had those Russian lips, you know the ones I mean.'

'Like Russians?' suggested Burroughs coming into the firelight. 'How d'you feel, Brunel? You looked rough earlier.'

'Fine,' said Brunel. 'I'd like some coffee though, if the pot is on.'

'Will you get some, Pru?' asked Burroughs. 'Me as well.' He seemed purposefully calm. Prudence went out.

Brunel said: 'You *do* get around, don't you, Colonel. I mean, it shook me to see you. Last time we met you were called Bone, a mere lad at college. Do I have to call you "sir", sir?'

'I shouldn't bother,' said Burroughs without annoyance. 'You're not going to be in anybody's army for long. You'll be given a passport and the usual papers and a little money and out you'll go to the big wicked world.'

'That won't be as bad as the little wicked world,' said Brunel flexing his aches.

'You'll be put on the road pointing home. If ever you feel tempted to tell anyone about what went on here recently, then don't. I tell you this in all sincerity, friend, because I like you.'

'Keenor said he liked me too.'

'Good man gone there,' said Burroughs. 'Without him we'd have had a war on our hands this week. The second Russian, Gorin, who, by the way, has just had the hell of a nerve to ask for political asylum, which he will probably get, has told us what the plan was.'

Brunel said: 'What was it? Am I allowed to know?'

'They were members of a group in Moscow who wanted the Russian leader assassinated so that the treaty could be prevented and, at the same time, the blame put on someone else. Like the United States or Germany. In the Kremlin a new clique, who by now have certainly been dealt with, was ready to take over.'

Prudence returned through the shadows with the coffee. Her breasts looked swollen under the sweater. Burroughs took his coffee and turned to Brunel again. 'What the hell were you doing on the roof anyway? Keenor told me he had deployed you.'

Brunel took a hot mouthful of coffee and was then seized with a genuine fit of coughing. Then he said carefully: 'That's right. He had me up in those woods, the top ground, watching what happened on the roof of the castle.'

'You shot Gorin? It was your gun.'

'Yes, I shot him. But not hard enough. He got poor old Keenor.' Brunel hung his head.

'Poor old Keenor,' echoed Burroughs. 'Too good to lose.' He looked closely at Brunel. 'We've had a little collection for a wreath. He's going to be buried as a road accident. Would you like to put something in?'

Brunel hesitated. He remembered his loose change was at the bottom of the Fulsbad baths. 'I will,' he said. 'But I haven't got any change on me. Tomorrow. Is that all right?'

Burroughs said: 'Sure. The old German guy who got himself killed running up the fairway, he'll be buried in the same way. Road accident.'

'Same car?'

'Yes, Keenor was giving him a lift. What a crazy rig-out he was wearing. Did you see it?'

'Yes, I went over to him. It's a sort of cowboy suit some of the old boys in the town wear. They've got a cowboy club and they go hunting redskins in the woods. They've got them in Munich and in Paris and other places.'

'Sure, I heard about them,' nodded Burroughs. He kicked the end log of the row on the fire. It rolled over and showed its burned face. 'It was a balls-up today,' he said thoughtfully, 'and nobody, least of all me, says it was anything else. But the reaction from the governments seems to be that the best thing is to keep it all quiet. Nobody is even getting any blame, thank God. I guess they're glad that the security arrangements worked well enough to stop the assassination. Full marks to Keenor.'

'He was always one for full marks,' agreed Brunel.

'Sure was,' said Burroughs. 'Maybe they'll sign that treaty yet. Somewhere quiet and safe, like Fort Knox. At least nobody will be any the wiser about this. I think it was kept good and quiet, even the security force did not know exactly what was happening.'

'Say something leaks out,' suggested Brunel.

'We'll find that leak and *plug* it,' said Burroughs coolly. 'If it is necessary to find a story to put forward to the world at any time in the future then we can always say that the little fat guy in the cowboy suit was the would-be assassin. We could say he was nuts. And that he was dealt with before he could do any real damage.'

A great bitterness rose in Brunel's gullet. But he drank the rest of his coffee quickly and said: 'I knew him, you know.'

'I know,' replied Burroughs his voice a shade off a warning.

'He had a little cafe and a daughter,' said Brunel.

'I remember, though I'm trying not to. Understand?' said Burroughs. 'He will have to be the scapegoat, if we need a scapegoat.'

'Absolutely,' agreed Brunel dully. 'He looked like a villain, didn't he.'

'Yeah, I thought so too.'

Prudence, who had sat and watched and listened, got up and said: 'I'm going to bed.' She looked at Brunel. 'Are you staying, Brunel?'

Brunel said: 'If I can leave now I think I'll take a walk down to the town. It will be light soon.'

'You can have a jeep,' said Burroughs.

'No, I'll walk, thanks.'

'Stay at Ma Snellhort's place for a couple of days,' said Burroughs. 'You'll get a visitor with a parcel. After that you can take off. Okay?'

Brunel nodded. He shook hands with them both and said he would wait a while and drink some more coffee, by which time it would be light. Burroughs said, as an afterthought: 'Some funny things happened today, you know. The French people took Lestrange back with them for promotion on the spot. Something to do with the Ben Barka business. And—you'll not believe this—but the two British guys, Smith and Findlayson, had a fight in their room a couple of hours ago. One of my people heard them calling each other cowards and cheats! How about that! I guess they were drunk. See you, Brunel.'

Burroughs and Prudence went out. He was as tall as her. Brunel watched them go from the room and into the hotel lobby. '*Blokundtackel-unterhandlunder?*' he recited quietly to himself, but putting the question mark at the end.

In the lobby of the hotel in a dim wedge to one side, was a queue of old overcoats. They hunched on a row of pegs left there over many seasons by visiting golfers, most of whom would never return. Brunel had noticed them before and had idly thought, at the time, that it was possible that some ancient guest might still be imprisoned in them.

After drinking three more cups of coffee Brunel went to the coats and shuffled through them resurrecting small puffs of dust which squeezed up his nose and into his throat making him rattle with coughing. He found, eventually, a toffee-coloured coat, very long, patterned with a thick check of darker brown, and enhanced by an attached cape of the same material. It was the sort of garment that Christmas card coachmen wear. He shook it and disturbed great settlements of dust, which made him cough again, but decided it was sturdy and warm and was the thing he wanted.

The coat itself, as though shocked by the abrupt intrusion of a human body after so many vacant years, seemed to shiver like an old maid suddenly assaulted, as he put it on. It was so heavy with disuse that it felt like a thick, rough rug around him, and the cape bore down on his shoulders with the weight of a half-full sack. But he knew that once he had settled into it the coat would warm him from its hem at his instep to the grand pile of collar about his throat.

He went outside and a tongue of cold struck his face. The sky was sleepy, dawn grey, with ribbons of flaming orange where the sun was pushing up behind the far forest. It was about seven-thirty. Brunel began to walk down the road towards the town, the brown coat dragging around him like a monk's habit. There was a white light on top of the little castle far to his right and he guessed they were clearing up the blood and filling in the bullet holes, so that the tourists would never know. At half a mile he came upon two of Burroughs' men pushing brush and brambles into place at the spot where one of the security patrols had been sitting and waiting. Two men with a roller were on the distant grass rolling away the indentations left by the helicopters.

He went gliding on down the road, almost celestially, his feet hardly in view under the coat. Next he came to a clear place and saw a man with a spade cutting a square of turf from the fairway just below him. It was the place where Otto had bled and Brunel realised that they were removing the evidence. He had half an idea to ask the man if he could take the blood-marked turf away, but the digger was already chopping it into small squares with the sharp blade. He carefully lifted the replacement turf and put it into the square, giving it friendly pats to bed it home.

'Please leave the bloody Fulsbad golf course as you would expect to find it,' groaned Brunel to himself. He felt, at that blinding moment, as though he had seen the final despair of man, the death of the human heart, the small, eventual idiocy. He supposed that after the Bomb someone would be delegated to sweep up the ashes with a dustpan and brush. This is how they behaved, these men from offices, these little workers behind the Big People.

They wanted the treaties signed, so they shot people like Otto, a small funny man, and still they didn't get their treaty. Nothing would be left now, at Fulsbad, not even the piece of red on the earth, not a spent cartridge case, not a hole in a wall, nor a pen in an inkwell. People would go back to Fulsbad in the spring and play golf, and sit and sip on the terrace in the new sun, and never knew how near to marvellous history, or farce, or whatever it was, they were straying. One of them might even wonder what had happened to his overcoat.

The man on the fairway stood back to consider his work with all the grave concern of a sexton. He turned after that and scooped up the old broken turf and the pieces of Otto's blood, and carried them carefully away to some garden dump. Brunel walked on and felt the insect bite of a snowflake on his face. Another stung his nose and he could see them coming like a million moths through the trees, finding his open skin and embroidering the front of his big coat.

He left the outer ranks of the forest eventually and went down the slanted road and into the town. The snow was not thick and in quite small pieces. It ran about the pavements and the cobbles, trying to escape to some secure place for crouching until the reinforcements of the first big snowstorm would arrive. There were some people in the streets, moving on foot or on bicycles, and there were two tradesmen's carts drifting along to early lighted shop fronts.

There was a yellow light at Otto's cafe. Brunel could see it from the far end of the narrow street, through the cold trees. He could see someone moving and knew it was Hilde. Like a weary ghost, dragging the hems of his huge coat, he went up the street through the snow.

He was at the front of the cafe when she turned from her cups and saucers and saw him. Her face was oddly shrunken and paper white. She saw his coat and she started a small crying-laugh, the tears on her cheeks, the reluctant giggle on her lips.

'It looks very nice Brunel,' she whispered. 'Very warm.'

'It is,' he nodded. 'I had it made specially for the snow.'

They both stopped then, ten feet apart, each waiting for the other.

'Otto is dead, Hilde,' Brunel said at last.

She dropped her head. 'I know,' she said. 'The police came here. They told me. It was a car accident, Brunel?'

'They told you that, didn't they?'

'Yes. That is what they said.'

'Well that is how it was.'

She walked the few paces to him and folded her slim self into the icy surface of the coat, clutching at the old material with her bitter hands. 'Oh, Brunel,' she wept. 'I loved him so much.' He made to put his great flapping arms about her, then paused and shook the hanging snow away before he did so. She wiped her face roughly on his chest and looked up, pale cheeks with red blotches, and eyes very dark. 'I will get some coffee,' she said. 'It will warm you.'

She came back with it at once and, because they had never sat inside the cafe, they brushed the skin of snow from one of the outside tables and then from two chairs, and sat silently drinking the coffee. It went down inside Brunel like hot steel. It was very sweet and thick. He saw that she felt its benefit too. They finished without speaking. Then she said: 'Can we go for a walk? Just a short one.'

Brunel said he would go with her and she went within the cafe for a moment and returned with a crimson coat and hood. She wrapped herself in it and brought the hood up over her soft hair. They walked quietly through the snow now gathering in the streets, across the river bridge where there were already some footprints marked out, and then along the paths of the wide gardens in front of the Kurhaus. The trees that in summer gave such shade to the place, that cooled it with their thick fans of leaves, were already rimmed with the fresh snow. It was salted across the grass, lying folded in hollows, and fell to its quick death in the small flowing river.

Hilde touched the sleeve of his ridiculous coat with her glove, and then pushed her arm into the warmth of his. They went unhurriedly through the spreading white.

Without turning his head in the great hole of a collar, now sharp with a ring of wet snow, Brunel said: 'Do you still feel bad? After the baths, I mean?'

'I am recovered,' she said in her direct way. 'I left the hospital last night, about one hour before they told me about my father.'

'Keenor is dead too,' said Brunel. A dog walked by them sniffing an anxious snout at the strange ground.

'I am not sorry,' she said simply. 'I would find it very difficult not to be glad about that. Who killed him?'

'Car crash,' said Brunel.

'The same one?'

'Yes.'

They had walked to the extreme of the Kurhaus gardens, where in the summer the rhododendrons were massed, and they turned and followed their own footsteps already being filled by the snow that fell after them. She was inside her hood and he was crouched in his collar like a fox in its earth. She said: 'Brunel, I do not wish to know all the strange things that have been taking place in our town these weeks. But no one . . . no one did anything to my father, did they? Nothing to give him pain? I mean in the way they did to us?'

'No,' he said. 'No one hurt Otto. He died, that's all.'

Where the river leaned against the wall of the Snell-hort's hotel, he said: 'In a few days I'll be clearing out of here. I'll stay for your father's funeral and then I'll be going.'

'Where will you go?' she asked apparently unsurprised.

'Home, I suppose. To England. God knows where though. But I'll be going there, anyway.'

'No more a soldier?'

'No more. They won't miss me. I was never Field-Marshal material.'

Now they had gained the bridge, the place where their ways divided if he were going back to the hotel.

'I think,' she said, suddenly looking out from the hood, very straight. 'I think I will brighten up the cafe. Paint it and have a juke box put in there. Make it a place for the young people of Fulsbad.'

'Good idea,' he muttered. He kissed her lightly and she remained still. He was on his way then, and she had turned and was hurrying through the snow. He stepped towards the hotel and said: 'For the young people of Fulsbad . . . dancing . . . fun . . . head-smashing contests nightly.'

It snowed in short spasms for the next two days but it had stopped when they buried Otto. The grave, the earth box looking colder than the crystals on its lip, took him in wearing his cowboy suit with shiny boots. A few feet away, but afterwards, they put Keenor in the ground. Nobody in the United States could be traced who wanted his body back, so they buried him there near Otto.

Burroughs and some of the others, including Prudence, who looked bristling in black, turned up for the second funeral only. The local undertakers stood and wondered why the road accident was so special that they had received orders from the Fulsbad police, who had received them from some higher place, that neither body was to be viewed by anyone, nor treated, nor made to look nice in any way.

After Otto was buried Brunel walked away with Hilde's cold hand in his. As he went by the open hole awaiting Keenor he gave a sly push-kick at a large frozen stone lying on the side, knocking it into the grave. He hoped it would give Keenor a nasty, unbalanced Eternity.

He took Hilde back to the cafe where she served sad drinks and little hard cakes to the other funeral guests. The other members of the cowboy club were there, heavy with middle-age and stupidity, drinking and eating a little. In one corner, already, was a shining new juke box, unlit, but still bright, and Brunel wondered what the effect would be if he connected it and started it playing. It had been delivered with unexpected speed, Hilde had told him with embarrassment. She had made some inquiries merely to keep her mind occupied, contacting a firm in Stuttgart who, unfortunately, were so eager for business that they had carried the chrome monstrosity in just as her father's coffin was being borne out. It was not a good moment for her. But the decorators were not due for another week.

Brunel left the cafe and returned to the Snellhort's hotel. He had told Frau Snellhort that he was about to leave and since then she had been unable to face him without exploding with great gravy tears. When he had first told her she had stood shocked and then howled and threw her arms about him, hugging him with sorrow, and making her tureen-sized breasts bang against him in a frightening manner. Herr Snellhort had shaken his hand and turned away to thrust his face into his other palm. It was possible he might have been laughing, but Brunel did not think so.

He returned after the funeral and found a man waiting for him with the documents Burroughs had promised. There was a British passport containing a picture he could not recall being taken. All the entries were correct and there were customs stamps for Italy, Turkey, Iraq and Cyprus, none of which he had ever visited. There was also a National Insurance Card, stamped up to that week, a British Eagle Airways ticket from Stuttgart to London, and one hundred pounds in marks and sterling. The messenger left him these items and took away his uniform, his rifle, and revolver and all ammunition, oddments of other army property, and the key to the Moribund Documents office.

Fortunately the messenger was still at the hotel when Frau Snellhort came to Brunel, still running tears, and gave Brunel his bill for just under two years bed and board. Brunel told Frau Snellhort that he was sending it via the messenger to his superior officer who would pay it in full. He even added a ten per cent gratuity. The old lady rushed from the room holding her head in her apron. Brunel signed the bill and sent it to Burroughs.

He had few personal belongings. The suit he stood in was one he had bought at Burtons before he joined the army. His Waikiki shirt and his other chattels hardly occupied the space of a single hold-all. He decided to keep the toffee-coloured overcoat because he had to walk to the bus-stop and he had no other protection from the cold.

There was nothing now for him to do so he left. He embraced the Snellhorts both together in such a flurry of embarrassment that he kissed the old man instead of the old woman. At her request he gulped a final cup of coffee to keep any cobwebs away, and then went heavily out, the overcoat dragging him down with its bulk and the weight of the snow it had recently soaked up.

It was nearly a mile uphill to the place where the bus from the south crossed the Fulsbad road on its journey to Stuttgart. He plodded up through the covering of snow, making difficult going of it, pausing and turning to see how far the dear little town had fallen away beneath him. He could see the baths from half way up the hill and saw that the window of his office was open and some one was throwing big squares like boxes down into the street. They were taking the files away at last. He shrugged because he had no feelings about the moribund documents, although he would miss the afternoon naps with the cat. During the past weeks he had forgotten his anaemia and he suddenly wondered if it were any better.

A distance further up the hill and he could see the trees and the roofs of the short street in which Hilde's cafe stood. He counted the roofs along and decided which one was hers. The end of the street he could see clearly and as he looked at it for the last time a motor-cycle combination turned it and spluttered and snarled up the hill towards him.

There was no difficulty in distinguishing Gunter of the Panzers on the neck of the machine, nor in seeing Hilde hanging on to him on the pillion. Brunel sighed and stopped, putting his small bag on the snow and waiting for them to reach him. Gunter predictably skidded in the road slush sending up a fine bow-wave, and Hilde half fell, half jumped, from the motor-cycle.

'Hello, Gunter,' said Brunel defensively. 'How's the *kannon*?'

'It points East,' confirmed Gunter charitably.

'Why did you go away?' demanded Hilde angrily. She was wearing her cherry coat and hood. Her face was warm now, all the whiteness gone from it, and so tender he wanted to reach out and touch it.

'I told you I was going,' he said.

'Not today. You did not say *today*. I telephone the hotel for you and they told me. Why do you do this?'

'Oh, you know me, I just wander off as the fancy takes me.'

She stood, very young and lovely, close to him and she said softly: 'Please, Brunel, you must take me.'

'No,' he said firmly. 'No. No. No. You are fifteen. I am going to England.'

'I am too young for England? Next week I will be sixteen. I told you.'

'What about the cafe?' asked Brunel practically.

'I will give it to the young people. To Gunter here. He can make a youth club.'

'The Young Men's *Kannon* Assocation,' mused Brunel.

'You are *not* funny,' she snapped. 'Yet you always make jokes.' Then her voice dropped. 'Please, Brunel, I must come.'

'You cannot.'

'We will get two bicycles and explore the sea. Like you did alone ... Don't go without me, Brunel. I love you so really ...'

'Truly,' corrected Brunel. He bent and kissed her on the forehead, feeling himself shaking as he did so. His hands went out and he caught hers. 'You cannot come with me,' he said. 'I have nothing in England for myself yet. Go back and get the cafe painted and all that, and next summer I will visit you. I promise.'

She was weeping very seriously, the tears flopping from the round of her cheeks and into the pavement snow making small bullet holes.

'Your father would want you to do that,' added Brunel 'He would know what was right.'

'In the summer you will come?' she said, wiping her hand in a dirty trail across her eyes.

'In the summer. Now go back. Someone will be raiding the till.'

'I do not care,' she said.

'You must. Go now and I will be back. Cross my heart.'

'Cross your heart then,' she sniffed.

He did, making a cross in the snow on his big coat.

She stretched up and kissed him on the lips. He did not kiss her nor make any movement. She turned and sat on the pillion of the motor-bike. Gunter, who looked as though he had not understood said: 'You go home to England. Give love for me to people in Pant-coed Bricklayers Arms.'

'I'll go in there tonight,' promised Brunel. 'Cheerio.'

'Cheerio,' echoed Gunter stamping on the starter.

If Hilde said anything it was forced to nothing by the noise. As the machine turned in the slush, she looked at Brunel again and half raised a sad hand. Then she leaned forward against Gunter and cried down his back. They went away from Brunel down the snowy hill.

There was still half a mile to trudge. He went heavily, so lonely now she had gone, walking up the hill until it turned and ran around one elbow of the forest. He stopped and looked at the negroid trees, so hard in winter. Then he saw the file of forest rangers coming up a path running parallel with the road, puffing and snorting into their furs. Now the snow had stopped they were on their way to make their deer count in the forest.

They made a charming sight, moving like fairytale woodsmen against the black trees and the white snow. Brunel stopped and laid the bag down and waited for them to go by.

...'Guten Tag,' he observed to the leader.

The man nodded and went on.

'*Guten Tag*,' he tried with the man in the middle of the file.

The man grunted.

'*Guten Tag*,' he called to the forest ranger at the rear.

The man blew through his furs.

They went on their journey.

There was no doubt about it, Brunel thought, they were a miserable load of bastards.